Caffeine Nights Publishing

COMING, READY OR NOT

*The fourth novel in the
DS Hunter Kerr series.*

Michael Fowler

Fiction aimed at the heart
and the head...

Published by Caffeine Nights Publishing 2014

Published in Great Britain by Caffeine Nights Publishing

www.caffeine-nights.com

British Library Cataloguing in Publication Data.

A CIP catalogue record for this book is available from the British Library

ISBN: 978-1-907565-78-6

Cover design by

Mark (Wills) Williams

Everything else by

Default, Luck and Accident

COMING, READY OR NOT

MICHAEL FOWLER

Michael lives in the Dearne Valley area of South Yorkshire with his wife and two sons.

He served as a police officer for thirty-two years, both in uniform and in plain clothes, working in CID, Vice Squad and Drug Squad, and retired as an Inspector in charge of a busy CID Department in 2006.

Coming, Ready or Not is the fourth novel in the DS Hunter Kerr series.

Aside from writing, his other passion is painting, and as a professional artist he has numerous artistic accolades to his name. His work can be found in numerous galleries throughout the UK.

He is a member of the Crime Writers' Association.

He can be contacted via his website at www.mjfowler.co.uk

PROLOGUE

25th July 1986.
Harlyn Bay, Cornwall.

The noise jolted her awake. Startled, Helen Moore snapped open her eyes but she couldn't see a thing. A thick tar wall of darkness faced her. For a moment, the intensity of the blackness threw her and she scrambled together her thoughts. Then she remembered. She was surprised as to how dark it was inside their tent.

'Did you hear that?'

Beside her James jumped. 'What?'

Helen wrenched her eyes wider, trying to pierce the gloom. But it was pointless. It was pitch black dark and so she strained to listen, holding her breath.

She whispered, 'That noise?'

'Noise?'

In the distance a percussive crash of thunder fractured the silence. Helen's heart leapt.

'It's only thunder,' her husband said.

Somehow, she was pretty damn sure that the noise, which had disturbed her only a few seconds ago, hadn't been thunder, but it was now trapped in the depths of her sub-conscious and she couldn't drag it back. Through gritted teeth she sharply replied, 'That's thunder now, but I heard something else. I think I heard someone moving around outside.'

'It'll probably be a fox.'

She made an attempt at sitting up but her sleeping bag was wrapped so tightly around her that she slumped sideways. She shouldered the ground tarpaulin heavily and let out a moan. As she fought to prop herself up a second clap of thunder peeled in the distance.

After a couple of seconds of awkward shuffling she manoeuvred herself into a sitting position, anchoring herself by drawing up her knees. Holding her breath she listened.

Silence.

Suddenly feeling foolish, Helen shook her head. It must have been the storm, she told herself, and her half-asleep mind had been playing tricks with her thoughts.

And then the noise struck up again – a rustling sound close by.

Goosebumps prickled her flesh. She stiffened. It sounded as if something or someone was dragging their way through the grass.

'There,' she said. 'There it is again. Listen!'

This time she honed in on a soft shuffling sound. It sounded as if someone was padding around only a few yards from the tent's entrance.

'Did you hear that?'

With a hushed moan James said, 'I'll take a look. I'm telling you it'll just be a fox, or even a badger, something like that.'

She heard a zip unfasten and although she still couldn't pick anything out in the darkness she could visualise her husband pulling himself out of his sleeping bag.

James brushed past her and then she heard him zipper apart the entranceway. A silvery thread of moonlight washed in through the opening, and she caught his silhouette, on all fours, edging outside.

As the tent folds closed behind him, once again her vision was overcome by blackness and she turned an ear to the entrance. At that moment, despite being encased in her sleeping bag, she felt exposed. She leaned forwards, wrapped her hands around her legs and pulled her knees tightly towards her chest.

For a few seconds the only sounds she could hear were the swish of grass and James's soft curses. She had a vision of her husband scrambling animal-like amongst the damp undergrowth.

A sudden cry of 'Oi' made her jump. Helen tightened her grip on her knees. Scuffling broke out. Then, a desperate scream of 'No' pierced the night air.

An overwhelming sense of fear and dread enveloped her as she desperately fought to make sense of what was happening outside. A split second later she felt the ground reverberate – as if someone had fallen with a heavy bump nearby.

Helen's chest tightened. Her heart contracted and a sharp pain made her flinch. Then, her stomach turned making her feel sick and faint. She gasped and froze. She took a hold of herself. Instinct was telling her something was wrong. Dead wrong! Especially that something bad had happened to James and yet she still whimpered his name.

For a few seconds there was complete silence. She pulled her legs even tighter. Braced herself so tight that pins and needles sparked through her lower limbs.

Soft spoken words broke the peace. It sounded like someone was whispering numbers. Counting down.

Then a high-pitched tone hissed. 'Coming, ready or not!'

- ooOoo -

CHAPTER ONE

17th March 2009.
Sheffield.

In the Frog & Parrot, on Division Street, Leonna Lewis's 'Bleeding Love' boomed from a large set of speakers, piled high upon the staging area, reverberating into the room, tormenting Gemma Cooke's hearing. Tormenting her, because picking her way through the song, some of the lyrics were so adversely poignant, given what she had recently gone through, and in another time and another place she might have shed a tear. But, not right now. Tonight she was going to celebrate with her friends. Added to that, the large amount of vodka and coke she had drunk over the last few hours had numbed any feelings of sorrow.

She felt her mobile vibrate in her pocket; the noise had stifled its ringtone. She moved to retrieve it. For a few seconds she fumbled around, struggling to pull it out – the combination of the tightness of her jeans and her slouched position in her seat making it difficult. Finally she tugged it free. Flipping it open she saw that she had one new message, though it wasn't from anyone on her contact list. In fact, she didn't recognise the number. She pressed the OK button and the text flashed onto her screen. It took her only a few seconds to read the three lines of text but in that short space of time the drunken happiness she had been experiencing abandoned her, as her stomach turned-turtle and the bile rose in her throat.

An anxious voice opposite broke her free from her trance-like state.

'Gemma, what's the matter? You look like you've seen a ghost.'

Across the table, over a sea of alcoholic drinks, Gemma sought out her best friend Lauren. Catching her concerned look, in a loud, vitriolic tone, she snapped, 'Look what that bastard's just sent.'

She picked out a space amongst all the glasses and bottles, and set down her phone in the centre of the table, enabling all her friends who were hunched around to catch a glimpse. Depressing the OK button again she activated the back-lit screen.

'Im gonna slit ur throte an burn ur fuckin hous down bitch.'

ooOoo -

CHAPTER TWO

DAY ONE OF THE INVESTIGATION: 18th March 2009.
Barnwell.

The bedside phone rang, jerking Hunter Kerr out of a deep sleep. Beside him Beth moaned her disapproval and rolled over. It took him a couple of seconds to pull his thoughts together. The alarm hadn't gone off. It was still dark outside. That phone call could only mean one thing. A job. Bad news for some poor sod. He grabbed the handset and hoisted himself up.

He said softly, 'DS Kerr.'

He hung onto every soft Scottish syllable the woman uttered. Her voice was steady, almost soothing, despite the nature of the message she was relaying. He stored everything to memory and as she finished he let her know that he was on his way. Then he ended the call.

Fumbling around in the darkness he returned the handset, and as carefully as he could, so as not to disturb his wife further, he dragged himself out from beneath the duvet. The chill in the room caught him unawares and gave him goose pimples. Shivering uncontrollably he pulled himself into a stretch and set off for the bathroom.

Manvers Terrace looked every inch the crime scene by the time Detective Sergeant Hunter Kerr arrived. Halfway down the street a length of blue and white POLICE LINE DO NOT CROSS tape spanned the road, barring his way: fixed between two lampposts, it performed Mexican waves on a sharp early morning breeze.

He pulled his black Audi Quattro into the kerb, slotting it behind three liveried police vehicles, an ambulance, its strobe lights still whirling, and a CID car, all of which appeared to be in a state of abandonment rather than parked. For a few seconds he surveyed the street. The incident had already brought a cast of onlookers out from their homes to collect and gossip on the pavements. Some of them were in their dressing gowns. The majority however, had on jogging pants and T-shirts, or sweatshirts; well prepared for their long haul of gawking. Two uniformed officers, in high visibility coats, were doing their best to shepherd the separate groups into one assembly. Hunter scanned a few of the faces, wondering how many of them would willingly come forward as witnesses given the wickedness of the crime.

Killing the engine, he reached behind and snatched his outdoor coat from the rear seat and pushed open the door. Nudging an arm through one sleeve he stepped out onto the road and cast his steel blue eyes around the scene again. The view stretching out before him wrenched back distant memories. In his early years he had lived only two streets away, and this had been one of the neighbourhoods he had frequented, before his parents had moved to their present home. As happy childhood images tumbled around inside his head it suddenly dawned on him just how long ago that had been; he had last set foot in this terrace twenty-three years ago, when he had been thirteen years old, and although the general appearance of the two rows of red-brick Victorian houses remained very much the same, he identified a number of cosmetic changes which had given the place a much needed makeover. For one, the old concrete stanchion lamps had been replaced by modern metal ones. Recalling how the area had been one of gloom, especially during the winter months, he saw that the street was now bathed in a warm ambient light. Secondly, and more significantly, the view at the head of the two rows had changed dramatically. Where there had once been wasteland and an old dilapidated set of buildings, which had once been a brickworks company, there was now a carpet of well-maintained grass. Metal bollards at regular placed intervals prevented vehicle access to the area and through it snaked a footpath towards a newly constructed industrial estate, the perimeter of which had been artistically landscaped. And though the look of the place interfered with his nostalgic memories he had to admit that it looked better like this.

As he switched his gaze back to the onlookers, finally being corralled into one group, he wondered if any of them before him were those from his childhood years and if so would they remember him.

The chilly breeze picked up a notch, brushing his face, blowing away the memories and snapping his thoughts back to the moment. He zipped up his padded coat, tucked his chin into his collar, dipped his hands into his pockets and made towards the cordon. Another uniformed officer, highly visible in a fluorescent jacket, guarded the barrier. Hunter recognised him, though he couldn't recall his name, and so instead of saying something, gave him a nod of acknowledgement as he ducked beneath the tape to enter the outer cordon. As he passed by he saw the officer lift his clipboard and write upon it; Hunter knew that he'd been given the job of logging the comings and goings of everyone who visited the scene.

Straightening himself Hunter slid his left hand out of his pocket and glanced at his watch, mentally noting the time: 3:40 a.m. – thirty-five minutes earlier he had been tucked up in his warm bed, dead to the world.

Then up ahead he spotted the person who had dragged him out of his warm bed. Detective Superintendent Dawn Leggate was striding purposefully towards him. He couldn't help but notice that even at this time in the morning she cut quite a stylish figure in her knee-length camel coloured cashmere coat and calf length boots. As if she was on a night out. He fought back a smile. His new boss reminded him so much of his long-time working partner, DC Grace Marshall, who likewise never turned out anywhere without looking her very best – even to a gruesome murder scene.

Slugging his hands back into his coat pockets he picked up his heels. Striding to greet his Senior Investigating Officer he said, 'Morning, boss.'

In her silky Scottish burr she replied, 'Morning, Hunter, sorry to call you out. The night detective from District CID is here but this is one I think we should be involved in, it's a repeat domestic.'

Hunter immediately knew that his SIO was referring to the fact that the address where the murder had occurred was one

14

which had been repeatedly attended by the police as a result of reports, or complaints, relating to violence being perpetrated upon one or more of the occupants. He enquired, 'The victim?'

'I'm told it's a lady by the name of Gemma Cooke. Twenty-nine-year-old. Lives at number thirty-four.' She half turned and pointed towards the head of the street. 'Duncan Wroe from SOCO arrived five minutes ago. He's in there now.' Detective Superintendent Leggate spun on her heels, flicked her head at Hunter – a gesture for him to join her – and set off in the direction she had indicated.

Hunter fell in beside her. 'You said on the phone it was a stabbing.'

'Aye. Repeatedly with a kitchen knife by the look of things! The young lady's in a bit of a mess! I've only briefly viewed the body. Only got here myself ten minutes ago.'

'Suspects?'

'One line of enquiry – a former partner. The night detective is with a witness as we speak – a female neighbour. She made the three-nines call. She was woken up by the man banging and shouting at Gemma's back door. Did a runner before we got here.'

'Do we have his name and has he been circulated?'

'Guy by the name of Adam Fields. He's known to us, and he's on the system as living at this address, so I've asked communications to see if they can come up with any other addresses where he might be. And I've got patrol cars out scouting around the area as we speak. The neighbour saw him running off towards the industrial estate so I've requested a dog to carry out a search.'

Number 34 was two houses from the end of the terrace. Looking at the front of the house sparked another image inside his head. Old Ma Briggs used to live here. Fearsome woman! She'd once clipped his ear for kicking his ball against her kerb. That was a long time ago now. He shook the memory away. A murder victim now occupied this house and he zoned his thoughts back to the present.

To the left of the front door a narrow passage led to the rear, and Hunter and Dawn took it. They emerged into a small yard, its cracked concrete surface partially lit by a shaft of fluorescent light, pouring through the gap of the open kitchen door.

Hunter spotted slithers of broken glass, glistening back like diamonds from the ground. A tiny, bright yellow, plastic evidence marker, bearing a black letter 1, lay among the shards. Removing his latex gloves from his coat pocket, he caught Dawn's eyes and darted his gaze to the ground.

Returning an understanding look she nodded towards the debris. 'We believe her attacker kicked the door in. It was like this when uniform got here.'

Slipping on his protective gloves Hunter strode over the broken glass onto the threshold. Edging the damaged door inwards with his elbow, he caught the unpleasant whiff of a strong coppery odour, and knew instantly that he was going to be faced by an awful lot of blood. Swallowing, he took a deep breath and held it. Before him several SOCO metal footplates, laid to protect the scene, paved the way into the house. He stepped onto the nearest plate and craned his neck around the door to get his first glimpse inside. A frenzied scene met his eyes. He hadn't been wrong about the blood. The body seemed to swimming in a sea of it. A single, bloodied, smeared handprint scarred the white surface of an upright refrigerator, next to the corpse. Hunter's eyes lingered on it for several seconds. The solitary graphic image pricked his conscience, ramming home the horror and torment of what had gone on here. He knew that this single snapshot would remain locked inside his head, gnawing away at him until he caught the sick bastard who had done this.

There was certainly no doubt about how Gemma Cooke had been murdered. The kitchen knife was still embedded in the centre of her chest.

Scenes of Crime Supervisor Duncan Wroe, in a white protective over-suit, hunkered over her body. Raising bleary eyes to meet theirs he said, 'I wondered how long it was going to be before they called out the cavalry.'

'And a very good morning to you as well, Duncan,' Hunter returned. 'What've we got then? And don't tell me a dead body.' Despite the sarcastic retort Hunter was pleased it was

Duncan who had been turned out. It meant that nothing was going to be overlooked.

'I've only just started processing the scene. I don't know if you've managed to have a word with the CID guy yet but he's told me that the body's been disturbed since the incident. She wasn't found like this. Apparently uniform found her just behind the door still alive and when he got here a policewoman was frantically trying her best to save her. Paramedics got here pretty quick and took over. They worked on her for a good thirty minutes but unfortunately nothing could be done.'

Hunter could see that the result of those actions had added to the scene of carnage – tracks of smeared blood and bloodied footprints caked most of the floor space. In fact there was so much blood about that it was virtually impossible to determine the pattern of the floor's vinyl covering.

Duncan hovered a gloved hand over Gemma's chest. The short purple satin night-slip she was wearing was soaked in blood. 'And I'm not surprised. I've counted at least ten separate knife wounds. Some look pretty deep. She didn't stand a chance.'

'Do we know if she managed to say anything before she died?'

Duncan raised his head, hunched his shoulders and gave Hunter a no idea look.

'Do you know where this policewoman is?'

Again, he hunched his shoulders. 'No idea, but I hope someone's bagged up her clothes.'

Hunter knew what he was alluding to. The policewoman had been in direct contact with the victim providing opportunity for trace evidence of the perpetrator to be transferred – linking the offender to the crime. Therefore, for evidential purposes her clothing required removing and sealing inside evidence bags. He said, 'I'll chase that up, Duncan. Anyway looking at this lot you look as though you've got your work cut out.'

'Tell me about it.' He drew back his gaze and returned to his examination of the body.

From the doorway Dawn Leggate said, 'The pathologist is on her way and I've got communications to start ringing

17

around the call-out list. A forensic team should be joining us within the next hour. Do you need anything else, Duncan?'

Without looking up the SOCO Supervisor replied, 'We could do with a forensic tent to seal off this back door.'

'Already sorted that.'

'That's it for now then. Now if you'd give me a bit of space. My crime scene's mucked up enough as it is.'

With a smile Hunter said, 'I know when I'm not wanted, Duncan,' and he stepped back into the rear yard.

Dawn joined him. Resting a hand on his shoulder she said, 'Is there anyone from MIT you want turning out – Grace?'

'No, not Grace, I'm thinking about giving this one to Mike Sampson.'

Hunter watched his SIO's eyebrows knit together.

She said, 'Are you sure Mike's ready?'

'Absolutely. He's been back a good month now. All he's been doing is paperwork and I can tell he's itching to get his teeth into something. This will be right up his street – a domestic.'

She relaxed her frown, but still held Hunter's gaze. 'But a stabbing?'

He acknowledged the question she had raised with a solitary nod. He knew where she was coming from. He said, 'Believe me when I say that Mike's well over the attack. This is just what he needs. He's been chewing at my ear for the past week to give him the next job in.'

'Okay, your call, Hunter, but just keep a close eye on him.'

'Sure will.' He dug around in his coat pocket and pulled out his BlackBerry. Scrolling down his contacts he hit his team member's number. It rang for a good ten seconds and then he heard a tired voice respond with a drawn out 'Hello.'

'Good morning,' Hunter cheerfully exaggerated, 'This is your early morning call.' He paused for a brief second and then continued, 'Get your arse out of bed, Mister Sampson, you've got yourself a murder to deal with.' He gave him the address and then disconnected the call.

Dawn Leggate set off back down the narrow passageway, 'Now let's see if we can track down this night detective and see what we've got.'

18

While SIO Dawn Leggate, DC Mike Sampson and the night detective huddled together at the front of number 34, determining the high-priorities, as well as overseeing the work of the small forensics team and construction of a tent against the back door of the premises to act as a sterile barrier, Hunter trawled the street to track down the policewoman who had rendered first aid in her attempt to save the life of Gemma Cooke. He found her in a house opposite number 34 nursing a mug of tea. Two of her colleagues were alongside, together with the Paramedics who had attended. The elderly lady who owned the house appeared to have had opened up her home to provide refreshment for the emergency services.

Despite being invited in and offered a cup of tea, Hunter remained on the doorstep and gratefully declined the offer, stating that he needed to have a word with the policewoman.

The very young-looking, dark-haired girl engaged his gaze and returned a wan smile. Then she set down her cup on the kitchen work surface and followed Hunter out of the house. She fell in beside him as he walked back to his car.

In a calm reassuring voice Hunter asked her name.

'Nicki Wileman,' she replied and didn't stop there. In a voice that was brittle and nervous she added that she had only been in the job eighteen months. Hardly stopping to draw breath she told him her previous job was as a pool lifeguard, well versed and trained in first aid, and the use of CPR, but this was the first time in a real life-threatening situation she had used it. 'I'll never forget this,' she said, shaking her head.

As he neared his Audi, Hunter aimed his key fob and popped the locks. He went round to the front passenger side and opened up the door for the young policewoman. As she lowered herself into the seat he rested a hand on her shoulder and said, 'Nicki, I can say from experience that in this job there'll always be some things that stay with you, but those memories will fade over time and I can assure you that they'll make you a much stronger person.'

He closed her door and went round to his own side. He got in, pushed his seat back as far as it would go and stretched out his legs. 'As you were one of the first officers on scene I need to ask you a few questions regarding your actions, Nicki. Do you feel up to this?'

She glanced towards him. Her face was very pale. She gave a quick nod, then turned away and set her gaze out through the windscreen somewhere along the road in front.

Hunter took out a small notepad and pen from his inside jacket pocket. As he opened the pad he gathered his thoughts, for even though Nicki Wileman was a policewoman, trained and practised to recall every detail of an incident for evidential purposes, he still needed to treat her as a key witness. And his own detective training determined that he should only lead with open questions and then allow plenty of time for her to answer. He said, 'I know everything would have been happening very quickly because of the nature of the call but tell me everything you did and saw as you turned onto this street.'

She closed her eyes and pinched the bridge of her nose. 'We were the first car here.' She expanded her answer by adding that she was the passenger in the response car, which was being driven by her colleague, PC Kyle Stevens.

'Did you see anyone in the street?'

She seemed to think about the question for a few seconds and then answered, 'Only the neighbour. Gemma's next door neighbour. She was standing by the alleyway and told us it was her who'd made the three-nines call.'

'What else did she say?'

'That she'd been woken up by this shouting and banging noise, and had got up, and looked out of her front window, and seen Gemma's boyfriend, Adam, come running out from the alley and run off towards the industrial estate.'

'She's absolutely sure it was Adam?'

Nicki nodded. 'Well that's what she said to us. That's what we told DC Stapleton. He went round to talk to her. Have you spoken with him?'

Hunter told Nicki that the night-duty detective was currently with his boss going through everything he'd gathered from the neighbour.

'Had the neighbour been in Gemma's house before you got here?'

She shook her head. 'No, she said she'd been round the back, but she saw that the door had been bashed in. She said she'd called out Gemma's name, but when she hadn't answered back she'd got scared and come straight back to the front to wait for us.'

'What did you do then?'

'Me and Kyle when straight round to the back and that's when we found her – in the kitchen.'

'Gemma?'

'Yeah. She was lying next to the sink. There was blood everywhere and the knife was sticking out of her chest.'

'What did you do then?'

'I could hear her moaning. She was still alive and I went straight to her. You've seen how narrow the kitchen is haven't you. I couldn't get to her properly so I asked Kyle to give me a hand. We had to move her around a bit so I could get to her head, but there was nothing I could do.'

Hunter saw Nicki's eyes glass over.

She gulped. 'I couldn't do CPR or anything because of the knife in her chest, I raised her head to try and help her breathe, but then blood started gushing from her neck. I think her throat had been cut.' She paused and gulped again. 'Her throat had been cut. I just couldn't do anything. Just tried to make her as comfortable as best I could. Told her the ambulance was on its way and to hang on. The paramedics got here pretty quick but I think she was already gone when they worked on her. She died in my arms and I couldn't do anything about it.' With the back of her hand she dabbed away a tear. Her face had a pained look.

'Nobody could have done anything for her, Nicki. You did the best you could under the circumstances.' For a moment his thoughts drifted away. Nicki's last sentence had pricked his conscience. The image of Gemma's bloodied body scurried into his inner vision and he wondered what her final thoughts would have been. Had this brave young policewoman, sitting next to him, brought Gemma any comfort in her final dying moments or had she just succumbed to the inevitable.

He shook himself out of his reverie and morphed his thoughts back to the job in hand. 'Did she say anything before she died? Did she manage to say who'd done this to her?'

The policewoman shook her head. 'No she was beyond that.'

Hunter set his notepad down on top of the dashboard and turned to her. 'You've done great Nicki. Now we need to get it down in a statement while it's still fresh in your mind.'

It was after 6.00 a.m. before Hunter finished Nicki Wileman's statement. While she read what he had written, Hunter wound down his driver's window and rested his arm on the door panel. He caught the sound of the first twitterings of the dawn chorus and he noticed the darkness of the night sky was starting to break; a dull orange glow appeared above the rooftops of the industrial units in the distance.

After obtaining her signature he drove the young policewoman home and waited for her to change out of uniform, bagging her outer garments as exhibits, before leaving her to grab some sleep – though he guessed, from his own similar experiences, that would be a long time coming. Then he journeyed back to Barnwell Police station with the radio cranked up and the window open, the loud music and cool morning breeze refreshing his mind and body. As he locked up his car and ambled across the rear car park he met a couple of the uniformed members coming in for the day shift. He rode the sarcasm aimed at him as to his unusual early appearance and told them about the murder on Manvers Terrace. He knew that in less than an hour's time those officers would be taking over the roles of the uniformed team, currently maintaining the integrity of the scene, and would be pretty hacked off within a couple of hours; the routine ahead for them would be one of tediousness, occasionally exchanging pleasantries with the inhabitants, but in the main standing around watching crime-scene trained officers going about their job while waiting in anticipation to be relieved by the next duty team on.

Once inside he made straight for the ground floor men's washroom. Turning on the cold tap he supported his weary

22

body on rigid-straight arms, staring at his reflection in the mirror while waiting for the sink to fill. Slowly turning he saw that the whites of his eyes were starting to look bloodshot and dark stubble now framed his strong jaw line. He not only felt tired, he looked tired.

Splashing his face repeatedly with cold water, he re-checked himself in the mirror, buttoned up the collar of his shirt, set the knot of his tie straight and left the washroom feeling slightly better. He climbed the stairway up to the first floor. The Major Investigation Team office was empty; no one had arrived yet and all around peace reigned: within the hour he knew all that would change; the office would be buzzing with excited chatter as the team geared up at the prospect of handling a new case.

Pausing before his desk, he picked up his empty mug, switched on his computer, and made his way across the room to where the kettle, and tea and coffee making facilities were. Giving the kettle a quick shake, to check there was enough water in it he set it back down, clicked it on, dropped a tea bag into his cup, spooned in some sugar, and then as the water bubbled away he roamed his eyes around the room. The incident board, which took up a large proportion of the front of the room was at present in a clean state, though he knew by the end of that day that would have also changed; a penned opening chronicle relating to the murder of Gemma Cooke, together with the beginnings of a timeline sequence of events would have been initialised upon it. His thoughts drifted back to the murder scene and he began to tick off inside his head what had already been done. The click of the kettle, turning itself off, broke into his preoccupation. He made his tea and carried it back to his desk.

Entering his password into his desktop computer he directed the cursor straight to the District's 24-hour incident log icon and opened it up. Scanning the list he selected the emergency call to 34 Manvers Terrace. The event, currently running to five pages, had already been tagged by Communications for the attention of the morning Command Team, across at District Headquarters and for the Chief Constable's daily log. He began to scroll his way down through the text, noting the time of the initial call, double-checking it was the neighbour who had called it in, and then focussed on what action had already been done. So far as he could see it was a by-the-book incident with all bases covered. And he could see that from the scene a manhunt was being orchestrated to capture the chief suspect Adam Fields. As he hit the print button to get a hard copy the office doors burst open making him jump. His working partner, DC Grace Marshall, appeared in the doorway looking flustered. Her hair, normally a bundle of tight corkscrew curls, was damp and clinging to her face and she was devoid of her usual make-up.

'God, what a rush,' she exclaimed, dropping her leather jacket onto her desk opposite. 'Left David to see to the girls. Haven't even had time to do my hair.'

Hunter stared across at her and fixed her gaze. 'Well we can't let a little murder get in the way of that now can we.'

She screwed her eyes to narrow slits and offered him back an exaggerated scowl. 'Mister sarcastic. You know what I mean.' She snatched away her eyes, opened up the shoulder bag she was carrying and began rummaging around inside. 'You been here long?' Before Hunter had time to answer she brought out a small make-up kit, eyeliner, and lipstick, from the bottom of her designer leather bag, and scuttled back towards the doors she had entered by without giving him a second glance. Over her shoulder she called, 'Bring me up to speed in a couple of mins. I'm just gonna put on my warpaint.' And, on that note Grace left the office.

Quarter of an hour later his partner had returned, her blonde highlighted, dark hair, fashioned into its normal bunch of tight curls, and her tawny face stylishly made up with a light dusting of foundation. A hint of eye shadow framed her burnt umber eyes. She dropped her make-up back into her bag. 'There,' she said taking a deep breath, looking across her desk and fixing Hunter with a smile, 'Normal service resumed and ready to face whatever the day throws at me now.' She picked up her cup next to her computer, 'I'll just make myself a coffee.' She pointed her cup towards him, 'Want another?'

While Grace made them both a hot drink Hunter brought her up to date. As he finished, DC Tony Bullars, together with

Civilian Investigator Barry Newstead, sauntered through the door. As per usual Tony looked dapper. This morning he was dressed in a two-piece charcoal grey suit, while Barry displayed his typical dishevelled look; a checked jacket, years out of fashion, trousers creased, rather than pressed, and the cream shirt he had on was at straining point because of his pot belly.

Barry offered a curt nod as he dropped down into his chair before his cluttered desk. 'You look shit, Hunter. Out on the piss last night?'

Hunter rode the sarcasm without a hint of expression. 'No I wasn't on the piss last night, I, being a dedicated detective – unlike some of us – have been at a murder scene most of the night.'

Barry returned a wry smile, 'Well for your sake, and looking at the state of you, I'm hoping you've solved it, so that you can get yourself off and get some shut-eye.'

Hunter shook his head, 'Do you know, Barry, sometimes you leave me speechless.'

Wrenching his big arms out of his jacket sleeves Barry returned, 'Give us the run-down then, Sergeant.'

'For what you've just said, Barry – No. You can wait for the gaffer to come back to do morning briefing.'

Barry reached behind and tossed his coat over the back of his chair. Calmly he said, 'You're always a grumpy bugger when you're tired.'

It was almost 9.00 a.m. before morning briefing got underway. Led by Detective Superintendent Dawn Leggate, she brought the room to attention by slapping a hand flat against the large dry-wipe incident board. 'Morning everyone, we'll get things started, shall we.'

Dawn reached across the front of the board, stopping her hand at the first of four photographs stuck upon it. She tapped a finger over a portrait pose colour photograph of a very pretty, cheery faced, young woman, with shoulder length, honey-blonde hair.

'This is our victim, twenty-nine-year-old Gemma Cooke, a mobile beauty therapist,' she opened. 'At two eleven a.m., this

25

morning, Valerie Bryce, Gemma's next door neighbour, at number thirty-six, made a three-nines call to the police, to the effect that a man was banging and shouting at Gemma's back door and that she had heard glass break. She told the operator in Communications that she thought it was Gemma's boyfriend and that we should get there quick because he was violent. The operator asked Valerie to stay on the line and describe what she could see and hear, and at two thirteen a.m. she told the operator that Gemma's boyfriend had just come running out from the alleyway at the side of the house and was haring off towards the industrial estate.' Her eyes scanned the room. 'Valerie is absolutely certain it was Gemma's boyfriend she saw running away from the address. She's been interviewed and we have a statement from her confirming this. She's told us that for the past twelve months Adam Fields has been living with Gemma at this address. She's also told us that a couple of weeks ago he confronted her in the street and called her an interfering old slag and threatened to "do" her if she didn't keep her nose out of his business. Apparently she has called us on a couple of occasions recently, after hearing Gemma shouting and screaming through the walls of the house. She also told us that she's seen Gemma in the back garden, when she's been hanging out her washing, with her arms all bruised. With regards those calls I've requested all tagged incidents to this address as well as copies of tapes of the phone calls.' She returned her eyes back to the incident board, manoeuvring her hand away from Gemma's portrait photograph to where a timeline had been drawn up, timed and dated at various points in black dry-wipe pen. 'Back to this morning's call, PCs Stevens and Wileman, who were in the Response Car, were dispatched to thirty-four Manvers Terrace, arriving at two nineteen a.m. They found Gemma lying in a pool of blood, with a knife sticking in her chest.' She drew her hand away and pointed out two crime scene photographs beside Gemma's portrait pose. Her crumpled and bloody corpse had been captured from two opposing angles. 'The officers state that Gemma was still alive and requested back-up and an ambulance. A Paramedic had already been dispatched and arrived five minutes after the police but he says

26

that when he got there Gemma was dead. The Pathologist who attended, our good friend Lizzie McCormack, has examined Gemma's body at the scene and so far has found fourteen separate stab wounds, eight of them defensive wounds to her hands and arms. Her preliminary findings are that there were two wounds which could have caused death. One is an elongated cut across her throat and the other is a deep stab wound to her chest. As I say this is only her preliminary finding. She will be carrying out a full post-mortem at eleven a.m. this morning.' She returned her gaze back to her team of detectives. 'Motive! Well at the moment it looks like revenge. And the chief suspect is her boyfriend, stroke partner, thirty-two-year-old, Adam Fields.' She banged a hand over the fourth photo affixed upon the board. This one was a head and shoulders police mugshot of a white male, clean shaven and sporting a shaven head. Solid shoulders and trapezius, which curved up and almost touched each side of his jaw, completed the appearance of a man who regularly trained with weights. 'This is one very nasty bully. He has previous for violence, especially against women. Six years ago he did an eighteen month stretch in Armley for wounding a previous girlfriend. He glassed her during an argument in the pub.' She paused, roaming her eyes around the room. After a few seconds, pulling back her gaze, she continued, 'With regards Gemma, there are seven tagged incidents for thirty-four Manvers Terrace, all relating to domestic violence. Four days ago, Adam was arrested on suspicion of assault upon Gemma, and all I know at the moment, from our system, is that he was given police bail to his parents' address. Uniform have been to that address this morning and carried out a thorough search. He wasn't there and his parents have told us that they haven't seen him since the day of his arrest. Apparently he never stayed there like he should have done. He told them he was going to stay at a friend's house, but he didn't say which friend.' She pulled away her hand and swept her eyes around the room again. 'I have drawn up a list of priorities but the main focus of the day is the capture of this ugly-looking heap of shite. And as an incentive, I have a bottle of Scotland's finest which I will donate to the one who locks him up before the day is out.'

By 8.00 p.m. Hunter was battling with tiredness. His head was thumping and he was sapped of energy. Sitting at his desk, cupped hands supporting his head, Hunter watched through eyelids that felt as if they were loaded with lead, as Dawn Leggate gave the evening debrief. He knew that she'd been going as long as he and was amazed at how fresh she still looked as she addressed the squad.

The day had been frantic. The team hadn't drawn breath while pulling out all the stops to locate Adam Fields, but they had failed in their task. Now the SIO was reeling off a long list of actions which she wanted prioritising for the following day.

Hunter tried to retain and store her words but he was struggling. His brain was as exhausted as his body. He made a few notes, to aid his memory, but when he checked them the words were disjointed. As the SIO called it a day Hunter picked up the notes and dropped them in his in tray. He couldn't even be bothered to tidy up his desk before he left.

Driving home, he had both driver and passenger window open and willed himself to stay awake. As he pulled into his drive he noticed his home was in darkness. Then he remembered the earlier text his wife, Beth, had sent. She was taking Jonathan and Daniel to the cinema that evening. She had signed it off with a couple of kisses, which had given him reassurance that she wasn't mad with him for breaking his promise to be with them.

Selfishly, Hunter heaved a grateful sigh. Though he deeply loved their company, right now all he wanted was peace and his own space.

He entered the house, switched on the hall light, keyed in the alarm code to deactivate it and trudged through to the kitchen. In the fridge he found a plate of cold spaghetti bolognese, cling-filmed. Microwave ready. He ignored it. He was even too tired to eat. Instead he picked a bottle of beer from the top shelf, screwed off the top and took a long gulp. It had an instant refreshing effect. He closed his eyes trying to reflect on the long day. The only thing flashing behind his eyelids was that image of the bloodied handprint upon the fridge door. He snapped open his eyes, stared at the bottle of beer for a few seconds and once more fixed it to his lips. He downed it in one and then dropped the empty bottle into the re-cycling bin. Leaving the kitchen he lazily climbed the stairs, needing the banister to haul up his muscle-weary body. In the bedroom he stripped off, draping his suit over the back of the chair by the dressing table and dropped the rest of his clothes into the wash basket. Then he made for the bathroom and climbed into the shower. He stayed longer than normal, leaning his head back, letting the warm jets of water play over his face. Drying himself vigorously he wrapped the towel around his waist and padded to the bedroom. He dropped backwards onto his inviting bed and laid back his head. The soft duvet and pillow moulded around him. For a few seconds he dragged his eyes around the ceiling. Slowly he found that his focus was blurring.

I'll just close them for a few minutes, until Beth and the boys get back.

He never heard them come in.

- ooOoo -

CHAPTER THREE

Day Two: 19th March.

Hunter's bedside alarm woke him with a jolt. For a couple of seconds his mind was in a state of confusion and then he heard a soft moan beside him and everything came back. He turned over and snuggled into Beth. She had her back towards him and he looped an arm over her, dragging her closer and he nestled his head into the nape of her neck. Her skin and hair smelt of fresh strawberries. He breathed in the perfumed aroma and then pressed his lips into her soft skin and kissed her.

'Sorry about last night.'

'Busy day?' she mumbled back.

'Hmmm. Tell you about it tonight.' He kissed her again, rolled away, flicked aside the duvet and sat up on the edge of the bed. He checked the bedside clock. It was just after 6.30 a.m. He launched himself out onto the carpet and stretched. As his fingers clawed their way up towards the ceiling a jolt of fresh energy surged through him like high-voltage electricity re-energising last night's drained body. Stepping into the shower his head was switching into work mode, thinking about the tasks which lay ahead.

'Can I have everyone's attention?' Detective Superintendent Leggate's voice boomed across the MIT office.

Hunter snapped up his head. He had been so absorbed in sorting out the paperwork littering his desk from the previous day's activities that he hadn't noticed his SIO come into the room. She was standing in front of the incident board, hands clasped before her, almost prayer-like. This morning, her ginger, auburn tinted hair had been swept into a chignon updo, the fringe sweeping across her forehead, partially covering her right eye.

'We have a lot to get through today,' she said. 'Last night more addresses were turned over for Adam Fields, but unfortunately we got no joy. We have now exhausted those enquiries and he has been widely circulated. An intelligence package has been put together for his arrest, and I want you, Mark' – she unclasped her hands and pointed towards DS Mark Gamble – 'and your team to focus on capturing him.' She withdrew her finger and swept the room with her gaze. 'But I want you all to make yourself familiar with the contents of that package before you leave the office today. The arrest of Adam Fields is our key priority.' Dawn Leggate laboured over her last sentence and stared into the room for a few seconds. Then she continued. 'Now to our victim, Gemma Cooke. We know that her address was tagged because of domestic violence and we also know that her boyfriend – Mr Fields – was arrested for assaulting her five days ago and released on bail. The full circumstances of all those incidents are in a file with the Public Protection Unit. I spoke with the DI who runs that last night and he's going to arrange for that to be made available for us this morning.' She fixed Hunter with her hazel eyes. 'I want you, Hunter, and Grace, to pick that file up and have a chat with the officer who dealt with Fields. See if you can glean anything different to what we have on our system, especially as to where he might be holed up.'

Hunter acknowledged with a nod.

'And now I want to bring in Mike who spent all day at the scene yesterday with forensics. He's going to run through what they've turned up.'

DC Mike Sampson scraped back his chair, used his desk to lever himself up and made his way to the front of the MIT room.

Hunter eyed him carefully. The ghost-like vision of Mike lying unconscious, on life-support, flashed inside Hunter's head generating a sudden feeling of anxiety. *It could have just as easily been me.* Taking a sharp breath he held it. Then he chased away his thoughts and followed Mike's progress to the front of the room. He couldn't help but admire how quickly Mike had recovered from the life-threatening attack three months earlier; Mike had been stabbed during a stake-out to catch a killer on the last case. The murderer had got away but Hunter had tracked him down several days later and cornered him. He had used the knife again in an attempt to evade capture. On this occasion the killer had not been so fortunate and Hunter had exacted his own brand of justice during his arrest. The man was currently in prison awaiting trial.

Continuing to note Mike's confident strut Hunter realised he had made the right decision to give him last night's job. Mike was ready. And it wasn't just mentally, he thought to himself as he monitored him closely. Mike's whole physical appearance had morphed during his period of rehabilitation. Three months earlier he had been considerably overweight, and now, although still on the beefy side, he was a shadow of his former self. His mode of dress had changed as well – no more ill-fitting suits. Today he was wearing a dark grey, two-piece suit, which looked new, and beneath that a white shirt, tucked neatly into his waistband, fronted with a deep red tie, which Hunter noted he could now knot at the collar. Mike had also grown his hair longer and he sported a goatee beard, but whereas three months ago his hair had been dark, now it was peppered liberally with grey. Nevertheless, Hunter had to admit, as he watched Mike preparing himself for his speech, that he looked a picture, both of health and of sartorial elegance.

Mike Sampson picked up a hand remote device from a table by the side of the dry wipe incident board and smoothed a hand down the front of his tie as he faced his colleagues.

'I've had much of the footage, which SOCO and Forensics took yesterday, put together for a presentation. I know how you lot struggle with the intellectual technical jargon,' he smiled.

He certainly hadn't lost his sense of humour, Hunter told himself.

Mike aimed the remote up towards the ceiling where a projector hung. Immediately a colour image of the front of 34 Manvers Terrace flashed onto the incident board. More pictures flashed onto the board, the alleyway at the side of the front door followed by the rear of the premises with its open kitchen door. Close-up shots of the broken lock and smashed glass panel quickly replaced the opening sequence of images.

'We can see that the rear door has definitely been forced. Several shoe prints have been lifted from the panels indicating it had been kicked in.' He paused a few seconds and then introduced a wide shot of the kitchen. Gemma's corpse dominated the picture, surrounded by blood. Its earlier crimson colour was now dirty brown. 'The post-mortem has revealed a catalogue of injuries, both old and new, on Gemma's body. Two of those were equally severe enough to have caused her death. The first was a six-inch long cut to her throat and the second was a penetrating stab wound to her chest. The knife was still embedded in her chest when uniform and paramedics got there.' Gripping the remote even tighter in his right hand Mike tapped the open palm of his left. 'Gemma had other stab wounds – two to the right side of her thigh and one to the stomach. She had defence wounds to both hands and arms. In fact, one of those injuries severed the tendons of her right hand. It looks as if she attempted to grab the knife away from her attacker.'

That last sentence jarred Hunter's concentration. The bloodied handprint upon the fridge door momentarily flashed inside his head again and an involuntary shudder ran down his spine.

Mike continued, 'She also had bruising to her face. The pathologist has determined that three of the bruises were old ones and puts them in the region of being approximately one week old. Those are more than likely the injuries she received when she reported the assault carried out by Adam Fields. I've requested those photos she had taken when she reported the assault for comparison. There is a fresh bruise to her left cheek, just below her eye. That more than likely happened during last night's attack. The blow fractured her cheekbone.' He aimed the remote back at the projector and the image slowly zoomed in on Gemma's body. Mike halted its progress at a close-up of the knife embedded in the centre of her chest. 'This is a steak knife, similar in make to other knives she has around the kitchen. Duncan Wroe has recovered several good prints from its handle, so we're hopeful they're those of the perpetrator and not Gemma's.' Mike expanded the focus of the picture back to the original shot. 'I just want to show you a couple more things. The first is this.' He half-turned to the board behind him and with the remote made a circle motion around a pizza box resting on the kitchen work surface. Then he flicked the remote back to the projector and the image changed to a shot of a lounge. A grey and black L-shaped corner sofa took up most of the right hand side of the room. In the centre of the picture was a chrome and glass topped coffee table, and in the top left hand corner of the shot was a large flat screen TV with DVD player. The picture zoomed in again homing in on two wine glasses on the coffee table. A residue of red juice was visible in the bottom of both vessels. The image remained on the screen for a good twenty seconds and then it was replaced by one of a bedroom. A white antique frame double bed took up most of the screen. The duvet had been thrown aside, cascading over the side of the mattress onto the floor. The picture zoomed in again and its progress halted on a small section of carpet by the right hand side of the bed. Here there was a discarded torn condom packet. 'All these indicate that Gemma had a visitor last night. Most of the pizza was eaten, an empty bottle of wine was in the kitchen bin and I don't need to enlighten anyone regarding the empty condom packet. We haven't found the condom. We think it might have been flushed down the loo. What we do have however is lots of trace evidence. Prints on the glasses, and on the bottle and what look like semen stains on the bottom sheet of the bedding.'

'Thank you for that, Mike,' interjected Dawn Leggate. 'And that gives us one reason as to why Adam Fields should turn up in the early hours of yesterday morning shouting the odds before kicking the back door in. And it gives us a motive for Gemma's murder.' She paused and her eyes scanned the room. 'But that, ladies and gents, is speculation and we don't do speculation, do we. We do facts. And those facts Mike has just shown you, are what we will be working on over the next few days. As he's just said we do have forensics which will match someone to the scene. Someone was with Gemma last night and it wasn't Adam Fields. Another immediate priority is to find out who that person was.'

The Public Protection Unit was based on the first floor of District Headquarters. It took up one end of the police building. Just after 10.00 a.m. Hunter and Grace entered the long oblong office.

Hunter immediately noted how light and airy and warm the room was. He wasn't surprised when he noted that almost three quarters of the room was fitted with large double-glazed windows. Looking around, he thought that it was a far cry from their own dismal office back at Barnwell. Most of the time there they had to have the fluorescents on to get sufficient light into the room. He also took in the layout of the room, quickly head-counting the cluster of desks and determined that the squad was about the same strength in officer numbers as MIT.

This morning only four of the desks were occupied. The detectives, two males and two females, were hunkered over their paperwork. Almost simultaneously they looked in their direction as they entered.

One of the male officers nearest to them, a tall slim man with light brown spiked and gelled hair, pushed back his chair and stepped out from behind his desk.

He enquired, 'DS Kerr and DC Marshall?'

Hunter let the door close, strode towards him and shook his hand. He tried to make eye-contact, but the detective shied his gaze away.

The PPU detective said, 'DC Tom Hagan. I dealt with Gemma's domestic.' He pulled two chairs out from beneath desks nearby and positioned them by the side of his own desk and with an open hand offered them both a seat.

Dropping back down into his chair he said, 'My DI has filled me in this morning. You want to see Gemma's case file?'

Hunter thought he sensed a strain in Tom Hagan's voice. It was barely noticeable, but it was there. He wondered if he was always like this because he usually expected this type of behaviour to come from a suspect.

35

The officer continued, 'By the way have you caught Fields yet? He's a real nasty piece of work you know.'

'He certainly made a mess of Gemma,' Grace responded.

Hunter added, 'There's a team out looking for him this morning. We're hoping you might be able to help us?'

'Help you?' Tom Hagan quickly replied.

The quickness of his retort took Hunter aback. He tried to catch his gaze once more, but the detective seemed to be looking through him rather than at him. He said, 'Yeah, you interviewed him. When the decision was made to bail him did he mention any addresses other than his parents' one?'

The detective returned a surprised look. 'Oh, I see what you're getting at. I thought you were insinuating that I knew him.'

Hunter squeezed his forehead tight as he fixed his look. 'No, I wasn't insinuating anything. I just wondered if he might have given an indication of where he might go when you told him that he couldn't go back to Manvers Terrace.' Hunter relaxed his look.

The detective shook his head. 'No. After I'd told him that Gemma didn't want him back, and that we were going to bail him, he asked if he could make a phone call to his dad, and although I only heard one side of the conversation, it seemed to me as if his dad had agreed to him going there and so that's where he was bailed to.'

'Fine. Now what about the actual case? The assault on Gemma?'

Tom Hagan dropped his head. A blue folder lay in front of him. He flipped back the front cover to reveal the contents; a small bundle of typed A4 documents. 'What do you need to know?' Then he offered, 'I was at school with Gemma you know?'

'Oh, that's interesting, you can give us something as to her background then?'

'Background. What do you mean?'

There it was again. Hunter sensed a hesitance in the detective's questioning intonation. He stored it and responded with, 'Yeah, background, seeing you were at school with her. Just her early stuff, you know, what she was like, etcetera.

You know the drill. We'll be seeing her parents and her friends, but you can give us a more balanced perspective, seeing as you weren't close to her.'

'Oh, yes of course.'

'So what was she like? Did you know her well?'

'I spent my last three years in the same class. It's thirteen, fourteen years ago now, but some people you just never forget do you?'

'She left that kind of impression.'

'Definitely, she was a real stunner, everyone fancied her. Well every hot bloodied male from thirteen onwards anyway. Still a stunner now.' He hesitated after his last sentence and then added, 'Well, she was.'

Hunter remembered the before and after photos he had seen of Gemma Cooke on the incident board. He zipped his mouth and nodded.

'She was very popular. Had a wide circle of friends from what I remember. Could be a bit wild at times and also very forward when it came to lads. From what I remember she never went out with anyone her own age. All the guys she went with were at least in the year above. In fact for a short time, when she was fourteen, I remember that she was knocking off the head boy. I think she was seeing him for a good few months even after he left. And there were rumours that she was having it off with the games master. She seemed to be sucking up to him at every opportunity.'

'Oh yes.' Grace intervened.

The detective threw her a glance and then chuckled. 'Don't read anything into what I just said. It wasn't more than a schoolgirl crush. And she wasn't the only one at the time. He was in his late twenties and had an army of drooling teenage girls following him around like lapdogs. Looking back he must have had a very strong resolve about him.'

'How do you know it was just a schoolgirl crush?'

The detective's cheeks flushed. He cleared his throat. 'Well, I'm a bit embarrassed about this, but I'm afraid I asked her when I took her statement last week.'

Grace smiled. Shaking her head she said, 'You guys, I don't know.'

'Anything else?'

'To be honest once she left school that was it. For a few years her name cropped up, only if I bumped into anyone from my old school, but it was just that. I know more about her now following the recent events. We did some catching up while I took her statement.'

Grace said, 'She worked as a mobile beauty therapist, didn't she?'

'Yeah, and from what she told me it seems as though it was nice little earner for her. She told me that she made a shed-load of money doing weddings – brides, bridesmaids, mums and the like. The house on Manvers Terrace was almost paid for.'

'So how did she let a shit-hole like Adam Fields creep into her life?'

The detective shrugged his shoulders. 'You know how some people have this knack of attracting the wrong type of person? Well that was Gemma. She had another boyfriend before him who knocked her about, you know. She told me that when I interviewed her. She never reported him to us and she dumped him two years ago.' He shook his head. 'Nothing should surprise you in this job, but you do find yourself questioning yourself about life, don't you. I mean she was extremely pretty, had a good job, bringing in a good income, and with her own home, nicely furnished and yet her choice of men was appalling.'

Hunter dipped back into the conversation. 'So who's this other guy, then? Is it someone else we should be looking at?'

'No, he died last summer. Fell from a hotel balcony while on holiday in Ibiza. Drunk. After she'd told me about him I remembered that I'd seen it on the local news and in the papers at the time.' Tom tugged at his shirt collar. 'No, Adam Fields is the only person you need to be looking at for this.'

'Do you know Adam Fields, then? Have you come across him before?'

'No to both questions, though of course I know a lot more about him now since the assault. Bit of a nut-jack according to Gemma. One minute he could be fine and the next as high as a kite. Apparently would snap over the least little thing. She said that he went to the gym most days, that he was absolutely obsessed with bodybuilding. He started turning nasty with her about six months ago.'

'Drugs?'

'Steroids. She told me that he started taking them about nine months ago. Used to inject in his leg. You've seen him, haven't you?'

'Only his mugshot on the board.'

'Well, he's the size of a barndoor, I can tell you. I took some back-up when I lifted him and thankfully he didn't kick off.'

Grace enquired, 'I thought he glassed a previous girlfriend?'

Tom Hagan nodded. 'I don't know all the circumstances but he has got a wounding conviction. Did eighteen months in Armley.'

'Well, it seems to me that he was a nut-jack before he started taking steroids.'

'Maybe you're right.'

'There's no maybe about it.' Grace responded sharply.

Hunter glanced sideways at his partner. The antecedents of Adam Fields' violence towards women had struck a raw nerve. He interjected, 'What were the circumstances of Gemma's complaint?'

'Well, six days ago they were both in the pub together and she went to the toilets. On the way back she happened to bump into this guy she knew – a boyfriend of a client. She said they had a bit of a general chit-chat, which lasted about ten minutes and then she returned to Adam and a group of friends they were out drinking with. She said that everything was fine between them until they got home and them he just went mental. Apparently started accusing her of ignoring him because she fancied the guy she'd been talking with. She told him not to be stupid and he slapped her across the face. Because of some earlier incidents when he'd threatened her she told him she'd had enough, and that she wanted him to leave and that's when he kicked off. Punched her in the face and blacked her eye. She kicked him in the balls and managed to get out of the house. Ran to the next door neighbour's house and called the police, but by the time they'd got there Fields had left. Gemma went to hospital for treatment and then stayed with a mate overnight. The next day she came in with her mum and made her statement. I arrested him at the gym he goes to later that afternoon. He admitted they had rowed but he said the reason for Gemma's bruising was because she'd been drunk and tripped and fallen against the coffee table. I couldn't budge him from that without the medical evidence so on CPS advice I bailed him to his parents' address.'

'What about the other incidents.'

'There were two previous calls from Gemma herself, and they were for threats and not assaults. He was warned by the officers who attended as to his future conduct. And there were three calls from the next door neighbour because of their arguing, but on each occasion Gemma refused to make an official complaint.' Tom Hagan tapped the paperwork, 'The logs for each of the incidents are in the file and as I said earlier I have summarised them.' He closed the folder, picked it up and proffered it across the desk.

Grace took it out of his hand. 'Thanks for this, we'll be in touch.'

In the secure car park compound of Divisional Headquarters, Hunter started the car but didn't immediately set off. He sat in the driver's seat, listening to the engine tick over, staring out through the windscreen, drumming his fingers upon the steering wheel.

'Did you sense anything about Tom Hagan?' Hunter asked Grace, his gaze still focussed on the set of blue garage doors in front of him. A large white sign in bold black letters read 'Overspill exhibits store.' It revived the bad memories again of the last case. The team had stored everything here from that investigation.

'What do you mean – sensed anything?'

Grace's quick-fire question snatched his thoughts back, 'I don't know exactly. It was early on in our conversation. Did you think he was a bit reticent with some of his answers?'

Out of the corner of his left eye he caught his partner shaking her head. 'I think you'd be a bit reticent if you were in his shoes, Hunter. Think about it. He's just dealt with a domestic, in which the complainant has been murdered, and there were five previous domestic incidents logged to the address as well. The IPCC is going to be crawling all over this one, checking to see if everything was done according to the national policy. I think I'd be a little nervous as well.'

'Yeah, I suppose you're right.' Hunter engaged gear and reversed out of the parking spot. But as he made towards the barrier exit he wasn't convinced by what Grace had just said. There had been something about the detective's demeanour which had disturbed him, and the first thing he was going to do when he got back in the office was to go thoroughly through the file that Tom Hagan had handed over.

Hunter grabbed a sandwich for lunch and then spent the afternoon wading through Gemma Cooke's case file. He made his desk a jumble as he separated documents and made copious notes. He learned that Gemma had begun her relationship with Adam Fields eighteen months previously when they had met in a bar. Three months into the relationship he had moved in with her. Her first contact with the police to report a domestic incident was in September of last year, after they had both been out drinking in Barnwell town centre, and upon their return home he had begun shouting and swearing at her for no apparent reason. This had been repeated a month later, and on both occasions the police had attended and warned him as to his conduct. On the latter occasion they had made the decision to escort him from the house, taking him to his parents' home, where he had slept off his drunkenness. In January and February of this year, Gemma's neighbour, Valerie Bryce, the lady who had called in the previous night's stabbing, had telephoned the police after hearing Gemma's cries, and Adam Fields' aggressive behaviour, through the adjoining walls of their houses. She also reported that she had seen bruising to the upper regions of Gemma's arms. On all those occasions Gemma had refused to make any official complaint. Hunter noted that the compulsory Multi Agency Risk Identification Form had been completed for each three incidents and the PPU Sergeant had made the assessment – 'standard' risk level. As he took a break from reading, to make a cup of tea, he pondered over the judgement and re-visited the sequence of events inside his head. As he dunked the teabag he came to the conclusion that given these circumstances he would have made the same call.

Upon returning to his desk he picked up the report containing the details of the attack upon Gemma five days earlier. The events of that incident were more comprehensively recorded and he slowly went through the narrative. He noted the following: on the night of the assault, Gemma and Adam had visited a number of town centre bars and the pair had come home in a drunken state. She reported that she had gone to bed and quickly fallen asleep but had been woken up by him standing over the bed accusing her of having an affair with a man she had chatted with earlier that evening. She had got out of bed and told him to leave and he had started packing a bag. While in the middle of this, without warning, he turned on her, grabbed hold of her jaw and pinned her against the bedroom wall, banging her head. He had slapped her face and then punched her on the cheek. She had retaliated by kneeing him in the groin, making him release his grasp. She had then fled down the stairs, making her escape to the next door neighbour's house, where she had called the police. By the time uniform officers had arrived Adam Fields had bolted. Everything else was as Detective Tom Hagan had explained; Fields was arrested the next day at the gym he used, and when interviewed had put Gemma's injuries down to a drunken fall – she had banged her face against the coffee table. As there were no independent witnesses Adam Fields had been bailed pending a medical examination of Gemma's injuries.

As Hunter pushed the papers to one side and rubbed the tension away from his temples, he let out a deep sigh. The report showed that the actions of every officer involved had been carried out to the letter. It seemed his suspicions of any irregularities by Detective Tom Hagan were unfounded and yet something was still nagging deep in the depths of his consciousness.

- ooOoo -

CHAPTER FOUR

Day Three: 20th March.

'Heads up everyone, latest intel is that Adam Fields has acquired a gun,' Detective Superintendent Dawn Leggate announced as she walked to the front of the room. 'A man from the gym Adam uses, came forward late yesterday afternoon with this information.' She halted in front of the incident board and swept her fringe to one side. 'He hasn't seen the gun but he's given us the name of the guy who's supplied it. So this raises the status of his arrest and therefore later this morning I've a briefing with the Tactical Support Unit. We have two new addresses to turn over and I am involving the Firearms Team in those searches. In the meantime, I am suspending our involvement in tracing him and I want everyone to make sure they have their protective vests with them at all times.' Slowly she searched out the faces of her team. 'I want no one taking any unnecessary risks.' She waited a few seconds while her words sunk in and then continued, 'Right, now to the business of the day.' She tapped the incident board. Her manicured nails clicked on the hard surface. More details had been added to Gemma's profile, and the timeline sequence had been extended and new witnesses added.

'Okay, this is what we learned yesterday.' She began by divulging the information Hunter and Grace had acquired from PPU about the previous domestic related incidents. 'We've also spoken with, and got statements from, two girlfriends she was with on the evening of the seventeenth – St Patrick's Day – hours before her murder. Apparently a group of them caught the ten past seven train to Sheffield and visited a number of pubs and bars on Division Street. They told us that a few hours into the evening, somewhere around ten p.m., Gemma got a threatening text message to the effect that her throat was going to be cut and her house burned down. She showed everyone the message. Although it came from an unlisted number they were all of the opinion, and I include Gemma in this, that it was Adam Fields who'd sent it. The two friends say that this affected the rest of Gemma's evening. Her mood changed. And in the last bar they visited they say that she had a row with a guy who tried to chat her up. A couple of the girls got involved and dragged Gemma away because they thought she was going to hit him. Just before midnight she told everyone that she had a stinking headache and was going to get a taxi home. One of the friends offered to share the taxi but she told them all to carry on and then left alone. Given this information some new priorities have been generated.' Hands extended, she pressed one forefinger against the other. 'I want the pubs and bars she went to visited to see if there is any CCTV evidence and I want it seized.' She moved onto her middle finger. 'And we know that some of Division Street is covered by our own cameras, so I want the footage of that area during the relevant times. With regards her mobile, we've recovered that and it's on its way to the techies this morning to see if we can trace the number that text came from.' She folded her hands. 'One final thing before we all disappear. The Family Liaison Officer will hopefully be getting a statement today from Gemma's parents. Until now they've been too upset. And we'll be seeing the rest of her friends she was out drinking with on the evening before she was killed. I'm also generating some new actions relevant to Gemma's lifestyle, especially relating to her job. As well as her phone I want her diary checked. I want her clients' partners and husbands all checking against the Intel database.'

Within the room chairs began scraping back as members of the MIT team pushed themselves away from their desks to begin the day's work. Dawn Leggate clapped her hands and brought their attention back. 'I want to reiterate to everyone about Adam Fields. Until I've briefed Firearms, any actions to arrest him are on hold.'

Driving back from Sheffield, Hunter's BlackBerry, seated in the hands-free mounting bracket on the centre console, rang. He glanced at the screen, saw Barry Newstead's name listed and with a nod of his head indicated for Grace to take the call.

She hit the receive button. 'Hi Barry, it's Grace, Hunter's driving.'

'Where are you?' There was an exited intonation in Barry's voice.

'We're on the Parkway, just coming towards the Rotherham turn-off. We've been to get the CCTV footage of Division Street.'

'How long will it take you to get back?'

'Thirty minutes. Something like that.'

'Can you meet me in the car park at the back of the marketplace?'

With a sideways glance, Hunter met his partner's gaze. They exchanged puzzled looks.

Hunter piped up, 'What for, Barry?'

'I don't want to say too much over the air. It's about our prime suspect.'

As the call ended Hunter changed gear, floored the accelerator and swung the car into the outside lane.

They made it back to Barnwell in a little over twenty minutes. Hunter screeched into the car park at the rear of the marketplace and rocked to a halt. Today wasn't a market day so the car park was relatively quiet and they quickly spotted one of the office pool cars tucked into a bay at the top of the large public parking area. Hunter eased off the brake and coasted to where Barry had parked.

Easing open the door and then using it as support Barry tugged himself out from the driver's seat and piled into the back of Hunter's car. Beads of perspiration had formed between his hairline and brow. With a slash of his fingers he sliced them away.

'What's with the cloak and dagger stuff?' Hunter said, half turning in his seat and glancing over his shoulder.

'A snout of mine gave me a bell half an hour ago about Adam Fields. Asked me if I could meet him.'

'Have you told the gaffer?'

'She's out, doing her briefing with the Firearms Team. Her phone went straight to voicemail. Anyway it's only meeting a snout. I don't know yet what he's gonna tell me. All he said on the phone is that Fieldsy had rung him last night and asked him if he had a reasonably priced car, which was roadworthy.'

Hunter screwed up his forehead and offered Barry a scrutinising look.

'My snout runs a small garage out of a lock-up next to the canal. Does up old bangers and knocks them out cheap. He's heard that he's on the run for murder and doesn't want to get involved so asked me if I was interested in setting something up to catch him. Told him we might be and so he asked me if I could meet him in the pub at lunchtime.' Barry shuffled his weight and slipped one leg out through the open rear door. Planting it firmly on the ground he heaved himself out of the car. He called back, 'Anyway it gives us an excuse for having a pub lunch.'

Leaving their unmarked vehicles in the car park they traipsed down the hill towards Barnwell's main shopping centre. Barry made up the rear and Hunter and Grace had to keep slowing for him to catch up. As they neared the pedestrian crossing, opposite the pub, where Barry had arranged to meet his informant, Hunter gave him a sideways glance. He noticed several bands of sweat trickling down one side of Barry's face, collecting along his jaw line, and caught him snatching at air, breathing heavily. He studied his old colleague carefully. It was the first time Hunter had taken note of how out of shape Barry had become. Whereas he had always seen him as a big heavily made man, he had also seen him as one who had always been able to carry that weight comfortably and still be active. In fact in the past that bulk had been to his advantage. Back in Hunter's early CID days, he had seen Barry use his big powerful fists on more than one occasion to mete out his own brand of justice. But then, that had been sixteen years ago. Now, he knew that Barry had not long had his fifty-sixth birthday and giving him a second look it seemed as if that extra weight was now telling on his health.

The beeping and flashing green man dragged Hunter's thoughts back. He stored his contemplations, about speaking with Barry about his well-being, until later, when they were alone and he changed focus. Switching brainwork he knew how important it was to capture the fugitive Adam Fields. Then they could put this investigation to bed. Rubbing his hands together vigorously in anticipation of a good outcome with this informant he stepped onto the pedestrian crossing and aimed for the pub.

The Horseshoe was a large Victorian double-fronted building on High Street. It had always been a pub, and one which had always been a hive of activity, especially on market days. Two years previously it had been taken over by one of the decent pub chains and been completely refurbished. It now served guest beers and good meals at a reasonable price and therefore was a popular place for those who worked locally. When Barry had told him where they were meeting his informant, Hunter had to agree it was as good a place as any to meet; occasionally in the past he had walked into a pub to meet with an informant and he might as well have had a placard hung around his neck advertising he was from CID. At least in this place he knew they would be absorbed amongst the crowd of local white-collar workers.

Hunter pushed open the glass-panelled door and let Grace and Barry through first. The pub was busy and noisy. Hunter eyed the clientele. It was as he thought – the majority of punters here were on lunch break from their place of work. Then he switched his gaze, following Barry's eyes as he strafed the interior.

Suddenly Barry nudged Hunter's arm and said, 'He's over there,' and broke away to his right.

Ten yards away, seated behind a table, cradling a pint glass, which contained the dregs of a beer, was a man in blue overalls. He looked to be in his late fifties with close-cropped, grey-almost-white, hair. As they approached Hunter spotted an immediate change to the man's expression. His face took on an agitated look. Releasing his glass, the man half-raised himself and leaned forward across the table. As they landed within earshot he rasped, 'Barry, he's here. Adam Fields. He turned up ten minutes ago. I couldn't ring you.' Barry's informant switched his gaze, glaring out over their shoulders to a place somewhere behind them. 'He's just gone to the toilet,' he nodded sharply, still staring beyond them.

47

Hunter spun on his heels, fixing his eyes upon a woodgrain door signposted as leading towards the ladies and gents toilets. He grabbed hold of Barry's coat sleeve. 'Back me up,' he ordered and set off swiftly across the carpeted floor. He called back over his shoulder, 'Grace, call it in.'

The first door Hunter shouldered took them into a tiled corridor. Behind him, he could hear Barry scurrying to catch up. Hunter spied that the gents was through a second door to the right. As he reached it he slowed his pace, took in a deep breath and palmed it open slowly. Immediately, to his left, were three hand basins and above them, fixed to the wall, was a bank of mirrors. In their reflection he saw man-mountain Adam Fields. He was standing in front of a urinal and he appeared to be in the middle of taking a piss. Apart from Fields the room was empty. Balling and squeezing his right hand into a tight fist, Hunter rocked back on his heels, took in another deep breath and launched himself through the door.

Swinging his arm back beyond his waist and putting all of his weight behind it he arced it forwards. Adam Fields didn't have time to react. The targeted punch thumped into the region over his right kidney, felling him at his knees and propelling him forwards, causing his groin to collide with the porcelain urinal. He let out a deep agonising cry. In another swift movement Hunter lashed in his right foot and swept Fields' feet from beneath him. The momentum sent him sideways, crashing his head against another urinal. He was unconscious even before his face collided with the tiled floor. As Adam Fields hit the deck Hunter caught a flash of something fly out from the rear waistband of Fields' jeans and heard the distinct rattle of metal ring against porcelain. Quickly diverting his eyes he sought out the cause of the clattering sound.

From behind him Barry appeared, gasping and clawing for air. Red-faced he pointed to an object resting against tiled skirting. 'Fucking hell!'

It immediately dawned on Hunter what Barry was pointing at; the metallic, satin finished object was a handgun. He thought its shape resembled that of a Glock semi-automatic. Spinning his blue eyes away from the shooter he settled them

48

on his prisoner's prostrate figure. Blood was frothing from his mouth and nose.

Barry rested his arms on his hips, dropped his head onto his chest and filled his cheeks. Exhaling loudly, he said, 'I can't fucking believe you've just done that.'

'Neither can I.'

'Remind me never to back you up again. I'm getting too old for this lark.' Shaking his head, Barry added, 'Do you know, you're fucking crazier than I used to be. I mean I took chances, but never with an armed man.'

Hunter's eyes rested back on the gun. He could feel the rush of adrenalin bolting through him, but this wasn't a roller-coaster surge of adrenalin. This one made him shake. Suddenly he felt sick.

Detective Superintendent Dawn Leggate leaned halfway across her desk, supporting herself on her hands. Her face was thrust forwards and it had a thunderous look.

'What were my last words this morning?' She spat out in her thick Scottish accent.

At a safe distance, on the opposite side of the desk, Hunter stood before his SIO, back straight, hands down by his side. He'd already had his ears bullied with a tirade of vitriolic expletives for the past two minutes and he was wishing this to end.

'You made me look a right twat in front of the Firearms Commander.'

'Sorry, boss.'

'Sorry – sorry. Is that all you've got to say for yourself.'

'But it was a replica.'

'I don't give a flying fuck whether the gun was a replica or not. You disobeyed an order.' She pushed herself back in her chair. 'And don't you dare try to pull the wool over my eyes with that answer, DS Kerr. You couldn't have known when you tackled him that the gun wasn't real. You didn't just put yourself in danger. You put a colleague's life at risk as well.'

Hunter offered her his best contrite look. He just wanted to be out of here. 'It won't happen again, boss.'

She speared a finger towards him. 'It had better not, because I'll tell you here and now you'll be off the team. Savvy? I want players not mavericks. I want people who can take orders. Do I make myself clear?'

Hunter nodded.

She took a deep breath. 'Now get out of my office before I change my mind.'

Hunter turned towards the door. As he opened it and stepped out onto the corridor his SIO called to him, 'And you can make amends by doing your job and getting Adam Fields to cough.'

Hunter entered the office, faced flushed with embarrassment and smarting from his rollicking. He could feel all eyes on him as he sauntered towards his desk. As he sank down in his chair he aimed a glance across his desk to where his partner sat.

Raising her eyebrows, Grace offered back an 'are you okay' look.

Tight-lipped, leaning across, he said in a hushed tone, 'It's a long time since I've had a bollocking like that.'

Grace shrugged her shoulders, 'Are you surprised. If that gun had been real and given a different scenario you might not be here now.'

Dejectedly, he returned, 'Yeah, okay.'

'And then I'd have been looking for a new partner. And I've only just got used to working with the crap one I've got.'

Hunter watched Grace's mouth curl up at the corners. He exchanged grins.

Grace picked up a file in front of her and flung it across their desks to Hunter. 'Come on, Sergeant, stop feeling sorry for yourself. We've got a murder to solve.'

Hunter and Grace checked in with the Custody Sergeant before they went into interrogation. They were informed that Adam Fields had been examined thoroughly by a doctor and had been given a clean bill of health. His only injuries were a chipped tooth, and severe bruising to his face, especially around his nose and eyes. They also learned that he had opted for the duty solicitor and was currently engaged in a privileged briefing session in an interview room.

Hunter always found himself getting wound up at this stage. This was where he knew the law prevailed but in his eyes Justice failed.

Hunter cursed beneath his breath, for he could visualise what was going on behind the closed interview room door right now. The solicitor would be explaining in detail exactly what evidence they had against him and would be advising Fields on what precise answers he should give to the easy questions and that when things got difficult to merely state 'no comment'; it was the rules of the Police and Criminal Evidence Act, brought in to protect the Human Rights of the prisoner. In effect it prevented the police springing any surprises upon the suspect during interrogation. Hunter had done enough interviews throughout his career to know that villains were already well-schooled enough in the art of mendacity and it was his view that the last thing the guilty should be given was the protective cloak of any government legislation to help them evade prosecution.

The sudden opening of the interview room door brought Hunter back from his ruminations. He caught Grace's eyes, flicked his head sideways and set off down the corridor. As he swept into the uncomfortably warm room he was greeted by a strong smell of stale urine. He knew where it was coming from. Adam Fields had been in the midst of taking a piss when Hunter had steamed into him and he had wet his trousers. The pungent stench had nowhere to go in the small room. Hunter crinkled up his nose and looked across the table. His eyes were met by a basilisk stare from Adam Fields, who was pointing at his own face.

'Are you the fucker who did this?'

Hunter saw that he was sporting two black eyes and his nose was red and swollen. Splashes of dried blood caked the front of a grey designer T-shirt. He fought back the urge to smirk.

'If I hadn't done what I did, you and I might not be having this conversation. I saved you from getting shot, didn't I?'

'It was a fucking replica.'

'A gun is a gun to a police firearm's officer. In my book you got off quite lightly.'

Adam Fields gave a snort of derision and then winced as the pain registered in his nose. Pushing his muscle-bound frame back in his seat he folded his arms in a gesture of defiance.

Hunter placed Gemma Cooke's case file on the desk and seated himself opposite Fields and his solicitor.

Grace took up the spare chair, next to the tape recorder. Removing a pack of blank evidence cassette tapes from her pocket, she tore away the plastic film securing them and slotted the two tapes into the machine.

Unfastening the cuffs of his shirt, Hunter slowly rolled back the white cotton to reveal his own muscular forearms, and then rested them over the blue evidence folder, entwining his fingers.

He opened, 'You've already been briefed by your solicitor?' He looked across and caught the nod offered by Adam Fields' legal representative. He had met this solicitor during other previous encounters with prisoners and knew that he wasn't one who would continually interrupt proceedings so long as he stuck to the procedures. That eased Hunter's tension. He unlocked his fingers and flipped open Gemma Cooke's file.

Grace switched on the recording machine. A loud buzz resonated for a few seconds and then stopped, throwing the room into silence.

Hunter fractured that stillness by clearing his throat and introducing himself and Grace and followed that up by voicing the customary preamble to taped recorded interviews. He ended his opening sentence by reminding the prisoner that he was still under caution.

Adam Fields' pumped up arms were still clamped firmly to his chest.

With a forefinger, Hunter slipped out a written statement from amongst the paperwork and then locked eyes with Fields.

'Adam, I first want to talk to you about your relationship with Gemma Cooke.'

'What about it?'

'Well, would you consider that you and she were an item?'

'We were till that nosy cow of a neighbour and you lot stuck your oar in.'

'That neighbour and the police, and using your phrase, stuck their oar in, because you assaulted Gemma.'

'That's what you say. I've already been questioned about that and given my statement. Gemma fell down when she was pissed.' His mouth creased into an unctuous smile.'

Hunter eyed him for a few seconds. If truth be known he wanted to reach across the table and wipe that supercilious smirk off Adam Fields' face with the back of his hand and he could feel his fingers wrestling one another as he fought to keep control of his emotions. He took a deep breath and said, 'The medical evidence we've now got would say different, but I don't want to dwell on that for now, Adam. That's for later when you go to court. I want to talk with you about other matters. Would I be right in saying that a week ago, following an incident involving your girlfriend Gemma Cooke, you were ordered not to go back to thirty-four Manvers Terrace.'

'You know I was. It was your lot who said I couldn't go back there after you'd nicked me.'

'Just to confirm then, Adam, you were arrested by us for assaulting your girlfriend Gemma Cooke, and then given bail to your parents' address, and as part of the conditions of your bail were told not to go near her, or contact her. Am I right?'

'You never gave me a chance. You're all the fucking same.'

'I'll take that as a yes, shall I?'

'Take it whichever way you want.'

Slowing the pace of his questioning Hunter said, 'The next two questions I'm going to ask you Adam, I want you to think very hard about the answers you give me.' Hunter stared out his prisoner. 'Did you contact Gemma after you were bailed?'

He shook his head, 'No.'

'I'm going to ask you that question again Adam?'

'The answer will still be the same. Are you fucking thick?'

'Well, that is interesting because I have a statement here which contradicts what you've just said. And that statement is from a close friend of yours. It relates to an incident on the night of the seventeenth of this month when Gemma got a threatening text from a mobile. We've traced that number to the person who gave us this statement.' Hunter paused and stabbed a finger at the handwritten document in front of him. 'He tells us that on that night he was out with you and several mates drinking in town. And that in one of the pubs you asked him if you could borrow his phone, which you used to send a text and then joked with everyone you were with, and I quote, "that'll shit the bitch up, making a statement against me." Do you remember that, Adam?'

Fields' face coloured up. He eased forward, dropping his elbows on the desk. Jutting out his chin, he said, 'No comment.'

'Well, I'm entitled to infer that you did if you won't give me a proper answer. Anyway I'll leave that awkward question for now and move on a bit.' Hunter fingered out another statement from the folder. 'As I've already said we know that on the night of St Patrick's Day, you were out drinking in and around town and that you went in various pubs. We know that because we've now spoken with every one of those mates you were out with and they've all given statements. Just as a matter of interest can you remember which pub you finished up in?'

'Course I can remember. The Horseshoe. Where you did this to me this dinner time.' He unclamped his arms and pointed to his face again. 'I'm suing you, you know? You're not getting away with this.'

Unfazed, Hunter asked, 'And what time did you leave?'

He dropped his hand. Cockily he replied, 'Don't know. Midnightish I suppose. I'd had a skinful.'

'And did you go straight home?'

'Course, I was pissed.'

'When I say go straight home, I mean to the address where you had been bailed, because thirty-four Manvers Terrace was out of bounds for you, wasn't it?'

'I went to a mate's house.'

'Where was that address?'

'Just a mate's. That's all I want to say. I don't want to get him into any trouble. I know I should have been at my mum and dad's.'

'Okay, does this mate live in Barnwell?'

54

'Yeah, course he does.'

'Humour me, Adam, just give me a rough area where that is, if you don't want to tell us the exact address at this moment.'

Adam Fields looked sideways at his solicitor. They exchanged glances and the solicitor nodded his head. Fields returned his look to Hunter. 'The Wood Estate, that's all I'm going to say.'

'Okay, fine. And by my calculations the Wood Estate is roughly a mile away from Manvers Terrace. Would you agree?'

'Yeah.'

'And in the opposite direction to the last pub you were in?'

'Yeah. I know where the Wood Estate is, dumb shit.'

'So you had no reason then to be anywhere near Manvers Terrace in the early hours of the eighteenth?' Hunter caught a flinch in Adam Fields' face.

Fields blinked his look away and snapped back, 'No. I went straight to my mates.'

Teasingly, Hunter slid forward Valerie Bryce's witness statement. 'Then how come we have a statement from Gemma's next door neighbour, to the effect that she was woken at just after ten past two in the early hours of the morning of the eighteenth, by a man shouting the odds and banging on Gemma's back door. She recognised that voice as yours, Adam and so dialled nine-nine-nine. Then she heard glass breaking and a loud banging noise, and a few minutes later saw you running past her window in the direction of the industrial estate.'

Adam Fields flung himself back in the seat. 'No comment.'

'This is not some stranger who witnessed this, Adam. This is Gemma's next door neighbour. Someone who knows you. She recognised you.'

He jerked forward again, smacked a hand hard down on the desk and arrowed a finger at Hunter. He spat out, 'I know where this is leading. This is another one of your stitch-ups.'

Hunter slid his hands quickly away and eased himself back in his seat to put some space between himself and his prisoner. Slipping his hands beneath the table he balled them into fists. He gave back the impression that he was relaxed. In reality he was alert and prepared. Taking a deep breath he responded, 'That statement is from an independent witness. Nothing to do with the police and she has no need to lie. She saw you, Adam in the early hours of the eighteenth and called the police. Officers who attended found Gemma's back door had been kicked in and she'd been stabbed, less than ten minutes after you'd been seen running from the rear of her house.' He watched Fields closely for a few seconds, letting his words sink in, then added, 'Shall I tell you what I think, Adam? I think you're a man who can't accept rejection, and I think this was an act of revenge by a violent bully who couldn't also accept that the relationship was over.'

He banged his hand on the table again. 'You're all in this together. You're covering up for your own.'

That retort threw Hunter's thoughts. Recovering quickly he said, 'I'm not with you, Adam. What do you mean by those last comments?'

'You fucking do know. This is one big cover-up. Well I'll tell you this now, you're not pinning this on me.' Beads of sweat trickled down the sides of his face. 'Jesus, this is fucking murder we're talking about.'

'Yes it is murder, Adam, and if you don't make yourself any clearer about your comments, or give us an explanation, then how can we help you?'

Adam Fields looked to his solicitor again. His face had almost a pleading look about it.

The solicitor said, 'Can I have another word with my client?'

Outside the interview room Hunter and Grace stood at the far end of the corridor, out of earshot from the conversation that was going on in the room between the duty solicitor and prisoner. They exchanged glances from time to time but neither of them said anything.

Hunter was wrestling with his thoughts; going back through the interview inside his head, dissecting Adam Fields' last set of comments. None of it seemed to make any sense.

After ten minutes of waiting the solicitor opened the interview room door, hooked his head around and informed them 'that his client wished to make a statement.'

Hunter and Grace returned and began the interrogation process as before; preparing a fresh set of blank tapes for recording and switching on the machine.

Hunter opened things up by reminding Adam Fields he was still under caution. He continued, 'Adam, you've spoken with your solicitor and I think you want to tell us about the night of the seventeenth of March, going into the early hours of the eighteenth. Am I right?'

'Yeah.'

'In your own words then, go ahead.'

There was a nervous inflection in his voice, which took a few minutes to subside but once he had worked through his awkwardness, in a clear voice, Adam Fields narrated his story. He began by admitting he had lost his temper with Gemma on several occasions over the past six months and that a week ago he had punched her in the face during an argument, which he had instigated, because he suspected her of having an affair. Without encouragement he also admitted using his friends mobile to send the threatening text on the evening of the seventeenth. He said he had done it because he'd heard rumours that she was seeing someone. And he also wanted to scare her for 'grassing him up to the cops.' He went on to say that after that he had carried on drinking, ending the night in The Horseshoe, where they had a lock-in and didn't leave until about one thirty a.m. On his way back to his friend's flat, on the Wood Estate, he had received a phone call from someone he knew on Manvers Terrace. That person told him that he had just seen Gemma on the street with another man and had seen the pair going into her house. Fields said, 'I was fucking furious. I asked him if he knew who it was, but he didn't so I asked him to describe the bastard to me, and I swear it, the guy he was describing fitted that CID guy who nicked me down to a tee.'

Hunter interposed, 'DC Tom Hagan?'

'That's him.' He licked his lips. 'I thought, the bastard. He persuades Gemma to make a statement against me, nicks me and then moves in on her himself. I wanted to fucking deck him, so went straight round there.'

'And what happened next?'

'When I got there the kitchen light was on. You lot had taken my keys off me so I started braying on the back door. Shouting to Gemma to get that bastard out of her bed right now. I was gonna sort him. When she didn't answer I just got madder and madder and started booting the door in. That's when I found her like that. Stabbed.'

'Gemma?'

'Yeah. On the kitchen floor. To be honest I knew something had happened the instant I pushed open the door. There was blood everywhere. Scared the fuck out of me, I can tell you. That's when I legged it.'

'So you're telling me that when you'd kicked in Gemma's kitchen door, you found her on the floor and she'd already been stabbed.'

'Yeah, straight up. I swear on my mum's life. I didn't do it. I'm telling you it must have been that guy she went home with. The one that I thought was that detective who'd nicked me.'

'And that's why in the first interview you went on about being stitched up and insinuating that we were covering up.'

He nodded vigorously, 'Yeah, his description fitted that CID guy.'

For the next twenty minutes Hunter cross-questioned Adam Fields on everything he had told them, but he remained firm to his story. Unable to glean anything new Hunter drew the interrogation to a halt and returned him back to the Custody Sergeant, where the decision was agreed to detain him while they consulted with the local CPS.

As they sauntered down the corridor, back to the MIT office, Grace turned to Hunter. Her face masked with a veil of concern.

'You said you thought there was something funny about Tom Hagan didn't you?'

Hunter tightened his mouth, 'I did, though I hope to God, Grace, it's not what I'm thinking.'

- ooOoo -

CHAPTER FIVE

Day Four: 21st March.

Hunter awoke with a woolly head. He had hardly slept. He had tossed-and-turned most of the night, wrestling with his thoughts, repeatedly mulling over the interview with Adam Fields, attempting to analyse the content of what had been said. He had tried to tell himself that Fields was in fact a very convincing liar, and that his story about how he had found Gemma dying in the kitchen, after he had kicked in the back door, was completely false. And yet somehow Hunter's experience was telling him the way he had poured out his confession, that what he was saying was the truth. So no matter how many times he had scrutinised the conversation he had still come back to the same conclusion, DC Tom Hagan was somehow involved. And he knew that he wasn't alone in his cogitations. He had seen the strained faces of the team, at the previous evening's briefing, when he had revealed the facts of his and Grace's interrogation.

As he vigorously showered he told himself that he had enough on his plate without worrying about DC Tom Hagan. That problem was Detective Superintendent Leggate's and not his. He had other priorities to focus on that morning. Prior to leaving work last night, on the directions of CPS, he had charged Adam Fields with assault occasioning actual bodily harm upon Gemma, threatening behaviour towards her, possession of an imitation firearm and also with breaking the conditions of his bail. CPS had requested the convening of a special court later that morning; Fields was being put before Magistrates with an application for a remand in custody, and it was his and Grace's job to put together the remand file. He knew that the first few hours of the day were going to be full-on and that he would need to be totally focussed.

Following his shower he dried off in the bedroom. Glancing at the bedside clock he realised he had plenty of time before the morning's briefing and so donned his training top and jogging bottoms instead of his suit; a steady run into work would freshen his head as well as his body, he told himself.

After a quick breakfast of toast and tea he left home by the rear conservatory, yomped down the garden, and stepped through the bottom gate, entering the fields of the old racecourse, which bordered his property. Before him a landscape of winter-ravaged barren fields stretched out all across the Dearne Valley. He shuddered. Immediately to his right were the remains of the mile home straight of the old racecourse, once the training ground for the Earl of Fitzwilliam's horses. This morning, with a sky full of uniform grey clouds, the countryside was monochromatically stark. And it was cold, though the air was still.

Just the right conditions for running, thought Hunter, as he pulled up the hood of his training top. Slotting the micro headphones of his iPod into his ears he switched his track selector to shuffle. As the first chords of Guns n' Roses rendition of 'Live and Let Die,' reverberated against his eardrums, he stepped onto the home straight, and with a smart burst began his run into work.

For the second time that morning Hunter showered and changed. Leaving the station's ground floor changing room feeling revitalised, he bounded up the rear stairwell and entered the MIT office in a better mindset than the one he had woken up with an hour earlier. Now, he was ready to face the day.

Mike Sampson was the sole occupant of the office. He was writing up the incident board.

Making his way across the room to make a hot drink he commented, 'You're in early.'

Over his shoulder, light-heartedly, he answered, 'No thanks to you, Hunter.'

'What do you mean by that, Mike?'

'Four days ago you called me out in the middle of the night telling me you'd got an easy domestic murder for me. Do you remember saying that?'

Hunter knew where this conversation was going given what they had learned yesterday. He switched on the kettle.

'Well this is a right monkey you've handed me.'

Shuffling two cups together he responded, 'You've only yourself to blame, Mike. You were the one who kept pestering. And now I've given you a simple job to get your teeth into all I get back in return is a moan. Some people are just never grateful.' With a smirk, he dropped two tea bags into empty mugs.

'Simple job!' Mike offered him a single finger salute. 'Swivel on that Detective Sergeant.'

Hunter returned a quick grin, then straightened his face. 'Anyway on a serious note, while there's only us two in the office, how are you bearing up?'

Mike stopped writing. 'I'm good, Hunter, thanks.' He lightly brushed the right hand side of his abdomen. 'The scars are getting less noticeable every day and it's done wonders for helping me to lose weight. I can recommend to anyone, who's wanting to lose a few pounds, not to bother with Weight Watchers, instead they should consider getting themselves stabbed by a psychopath.' He flashed a smile and returned to his work.

His colleague had definitely not lost any of his humour, mused Hunter, as he poured hot water into the cups.

'It would be fair to say that we all now know the sensitive nature of this investigation. What Adam Fields suggested in interview yesterday has thrown everything up in the air.' Detective Superintendent Leggate addressed the room. 'But we mustn't be distracted by this. We have to put the sensitive issues to one side. It is not our job to investigate those. We have a murder to detect. And on that front we have a mountain of actions to plough through and we have forensic evidence from the scene still waiting to be examined.' She tapped one set of fingers against the other. 'On the actions front, we still have to speak with Gemma's parents. They were still too upset yesterday. Also, I'm told that last night Adam Fields gave up the name of the person he has been staying with during these past few days, and also the name of the person on Manvers Terrace, who witnessed Gemma, and the unidentified man, going into her home in the early hours of the eighteenth. Those actions will be followed up straight after briefing.' She continued tapping her fingers. 'We need to know how she got home. We know that she told her friends that she was getting a taxi when she left the pub. Did she get one or did she get a lift from our mystery man. If she did get a taxi, we've got CCTV all around the location she was drinking so I want that checked today. We also know she got a pizza from somewhere. There's a couple of places on the High Street where she could have got that. I want them visiting. See if anyone remembers her.' She stopped tapping and interlinked her fingers. 'On the forensics front let me remind everyone that SOCO have lifted fingerprints from the knife which was used to kill Gemma. We've got prints on the pizza box, on the bottle of wine and two glasses, and we've got semen stains on the bed linen. And we've also got fibres. Lots of them. Given the circumstances Headquarters have allocated the funding to get those fast-tracked. And so, until we are absolutely sure, one hundred per cent, that the mystery man is DC Hagan, and evidence points towards him, then we go nowhere near him and we certainly do not say anything about this outside of this room.' She raked the room with her eyes. 'Do I make myself clear?'

An arrangement of nodding heads answered her question.

It was mid-morning before DCs Mike Sampson and Carol Ragen – the appointed Family Liaison Officer – got to Gemma's parents' place. Stuart and Margaret Cooke lived in a three-bedroom, detached, Edwardian house, next to the church rectory, in the older part of Barnwell. A picturesque section of the Dearne navigation canal flowed past the bottom of their garden.

Mike had already phoned ahead, and spoken with Mr Cooke, to check if it was okay for them to come and chat some more about Gemma. He'd already had two interview sessions with Stuart and gained much about Gemma's early life. What was missing were the more recent events in her personal circumstances, especially with regards her activities in the days prior to her murder, and, as he got out of the car, he double-checked his folder of documents, ensuring everything was in the right order and that his checklist of questions was to hand. He wanted to make this visit as short and as painless as possible: Mrs Cooke had taken the news of her daughter's death very badly; upon the communiqué being delivered Margaret had collapsed and had been rushed to hospital with a suspected heart attack. She'd only been released two days ago after being given the all clear following tests.

The detectives had only just closed the entrance gate behind them and started their walk up the path when the front door opened sharply.

Stuart Cooke stepped out through the wide doorway and in an excited voice said, 'The local news has just been on. It says that you've arrested a man.'

Mike inwardly cursed. *How on earth had they got hold of that?* He had promised right from the outset of the investigation that he would be the first to inform them should there be a significant occurrence in the enquiry. He sighed inwardly in exasperation. Throwing up his hand in a halt signal he said, 'Can we just go inside, Mr Cooke?'

The detectives were let in and guided through a wooden panelled hallway into a high-ceilinged lounge. The room they entered was warm and bright. Huge bay windows let in an abundance of natural light.

Margaret Cooke was sat on the sofa wringing a handkerchief around in her hands. She looked weary. 'Have you caught Gemma's killer? Is it Adam?' Her voice begged. She started to rise and Carol Ragen indicated with her hand that she needn't do so. Margaret sank back into the cushions.

Mike responded, 'Is it alright if we just sit down a minute?'

'Yes of course, sorry.' Mr Cooke pointed out two easy chairs positioned either side of a dark wood surround fireplace and then dropped down beside his wife. 'She's feeling a lot better now. The doctor gave her something to sleep last night,' he said and clasped a hand around one of hers. She met her husband's gaze with a sideways glance and gave him a wan smile.

Mike made himself comfortable in one of the armchairs and then leaned forward, see-sawing his gaze between Mr and Mrs Cooke. 'Firstly, I'd like to apologise. I said I'd be the one to break any news to you, but it seems as though the media has somehow got hold of the information. I can confirm that we've arrested a man. The news is absolutely right, but we don't know yet if it's Gemma's killer. He's not admitted to her murder.'

'And is it Adam?' asked Stuart Cooke.

'Yes, it is Adam who we've locked up, and he is going to court this afternoon. We're requesting he be remanded in custody. But as I've said, he's not admitted to killing Gemma. We've got him for other things as well, which I'm afraid I can't discuss at this moment in time.'

'I always knew he was a wrong 'un. Soon as I clamped eyes on him. We told Gemma – didn't we love?' Stuart connected with his wife's grief-ridden look. 'More than once. Our Gemma could never pick a gud 'un. Ever since a teenager. I mean look at that last one, before Adam, who died, falling off that balcony abroad when he was pissed up. He used her like a punchbag. I know she could be a bit mouthy at times, but no man should hit a woman, should they?'

'No they shouldn't, Mr Cooke. And yes, we do know that the previous boyfriend used to beat her. We've learned such a lot since your daughter's death,' interjected Carol.

Mike nodded sympathetically. 'What I will say to you both is that as soon as we have something positive to tell you about Gemma's murder, you will be the first to know.' Pushing himself back he rested his folder on his knee and opened it. 'Now if I can just ask you a few more questions so I can bring everything up to date.' Mike glanced at the notes he had made from his previous conversations with Mr Cooke. The team now knew that she had been an only child and that she'd had a good, untroubled childhood. At school she had shown great promise, but between the ages of fifteen and nineteen she had 'gone off the rails,' as Stuart Cooke had put it, and been a great disappointment. During one of the very first interviews, tears had welled in Mr Cooke's eyes as, with great consternation, he had detailed how he and his wife had regularly had to deal with Gemma coming home drunk, sometimes having to physically restrain her because she'd threatened to assault them both. It had also troubled him when he found she was associating with lads a lot older than herself.

He had tried to stop her going out of the house by locking her in her room, but she had climbed out of the window and shinned down the drainpipe. But in the next breath Mike had watched Mr Cooke's face light up as spoke fondly of how at the age of twenty she had transformed her life. He'd said that she had come home one day, not long after her twentieth birthday, and 'out of the blue' announced she had got herself a job in a hairdressers' and was enrolling in college. Since then she had qualified as a beauty therapist, and five years ago had decided to go it alone and set herself up in business as a mobile beauty therapist. And was making a very good living for herself, he had proudly announced. He had finished his tale by telling Mike that 'Gemma had a good head and good common-sense when it came to business but rotten sense when it came to picking men.'

Dipping a hand inside his jacket Mike withdrew his pen and tested it on the top line of a sheet of foolscap. 'If I tell you that we've now tracked down all of Gemma's friends that she regularly associated with and built up a pretty good picture of her life to date, what I need from you is just to fill in the gaps regarding what you know about Adam Fields and of your daughter's movements in the week leading up to her death.'

Stuart and Margaret Cooke exchanged looks.

'When did your daughter and Adam Fields first get together?'

Margaret Cooke released her hand from her husband's and began wringing her handkerchief. She said, 'It was roughly a couple of months after she split up with Jamie – James Blaney. He's the one who fell off the balcony on holiday last summer. They'd already been split up a good while when that happened. She was already in a steady relationship with Adam when he died. In fact Adam had moved in with her.'

'Do you know how they met?'

'Gemma told me she knew Adam from before. I think they used to bump into one another when she went round town with her mates. She brought him round here before he moved in, but I couldn't take to him. There was something about him I didn't like. You've seen him haven't you? All brawn. He was too fond of himself for my liking. Used to act like he was

God's gift. I tried to warn Gemma but she wouldn't listen and now look where it's got us.' She released a sound which was the start of a sob and then caught herself.

'Well as I say, Mrs Cooke, we don't know for sure yet whether Adam is involved in Gemma's death, we've still got a lot of enquiries to do.' Mike scribbled down a few key words of what Margaret had just said. He would expand on them later when he formulated her statement. He asked, 'Did Gemma ever mention to you if Adam had hit her or not?'

Mrs Cooke exchanged looks with her husband for a few seconds and then returned her gaze. 'Gemma wouldn't tell us anything like that. We didn't find out that Jamie had beat her until well after they'd split up.' She paused and looked up towards the ceiling momentarily. Returning her look with glassed-over eyes she continued, 'I could tell though that something wasn't right between her and Adam.'

'What makes you say that, Margaret?'

'Oh, I could read our Gemma like a book. She was such a bubbly outgoing person normally, but these last couple of months she's not been herself. I asked her more than once if things were all right between them and she just kept telling me "not to fret" and then changed the subject.'

'Do you happen to know if she was seeing anyone else?'

'Our Gemma?'

Mike nodded.

'Not that I know of. Why has somebody said she was?'

He made a note. 'It's just a line we're following up.'

She looked to her husband again. He shook his head. Margaret responded, 'Our Gemma kept things close to her chest, but I don't think she'd have been so down as she was if she'd been seeing someone. I know what our Gemma's like when she starts a new relationship.'

'Okay, Mrs Cooke, just one more question and then we'll leave you in peace. You've already said Gemma was a bit down, but had you noticed anything out of the ordinary about her recently. Something she might have said, or reacted to, while you had been chatting with her? It might just be her manner, or the way she's done something that was different to her day-to-day routine.'

Margaret shook her head. 'No, nothing like that at all. Just a bit down that's all.'

Suddenly her demeanour changed, Mike spotted it. 'Is there something, Margaret?'

'Well there is something unusual, but it's not about anything Gemma has said or done, it's relating to what she was wearing.'

'Wearing?'

'Yeah, you know when she was found. When we went to identify Gemma, the officer there handed over Gemma's personal effects. One of the things he handed over was a silver locket which I knew wasn't hers. I quizzed him about it. He said it must be hers because it was around her neck when they found her. But I definitely know it didn't belong to Gemma. And the initials inside prove it.'

Mike's eyebrows knitted together, 'Initials?'

'Yeah, when I got the locket home I had a closer look at it, just in case I'd got it wrong. It's quite an old one you see and I was trying to remember if anyone in the family had bought it her when she was younger. I knew in my own mind that nobody had, but I wanted to make sure, for myself. When I opened it I knew it wasn't Gemma's. They weren't Gemma's initials inside.'

Mike threw his colleague a puzzled look before returning his gaze to Mrs Cooke. 'Margaret, can you show us the locket?'

She pushed herself out of the sofa and padded towards a set of drawers, in the alcove to the right of the fireplace. She opened the top drawer, dipped a hand inside and after a few seconds withdrew a clenched fist. She reached out to Mike and sprung open her hand.

'Have a look inside it.'

With thumb and forefinger Mike delicately lifted a silver coloured chain and heart shaped locket from Margaret Cooke's palm. The face of the locket had a leafed flower engraved upon it. It looked like a daisy. It took him thirty seconds of messing with the clasp before he prised it open. He surveyed the inside.

'See what I mean.'

Mike was about to shake his head. At first he hadn't clicked on to what Margaret Cooke was alluding to. Then the light bulb lit up in his head. He said 'JC.'

'Yes, JC. Our Gemma's name begins with a G, not a J.'

'Then who does this locket belong to?'

Mrs Cooke shook her shoulders. 'Search me.'

- ooOoo -

CHAPTER SIX

Day Five: 22nd March.

In the gloom of the MIT room silence reigned. A sea of detectives' faces were glued to the 42 inch plasma TV screen at the front of the room. They were watching the dying seconds of two minutes worth of CCTV footage, which had already played out. Many looked on with horror. Some shook their heads.

Detective Superintendent Leggate freeze-framed the last section. The picture was clear and sharp. It depicted a man holding open the rear door of a black taxi cab. Gemma Cooke was about to climb into the back. She tapped a finger over the man's image.

'You all see the same as me. Conclusive evidence I think you'll agree. And unless he has a twin brother there's no doubt who this is getting into the taxi with Gemma, at Barker's Pool, just after midnight on the eighteenth. Added to that, is the statement we have from the man who lives opposite Gemma, providing the description of the man who was seen going into the house with Gemma, at roughly quarter to one that morning. Finally, we have the forensics' evidence. That came back late yesterday. The prints on the pizza box in the kitchen, on one of the wine glasses in the lounge and on the handle of the knife used to kill Gemma all belong to DC Tom Hagan.' She deliberated over her words as she released the officer's name. 'I have no doubt once we get his DNA that it'll match up with the semen stains on the bedding.' She clicked the DVD remote's stop button and the image cleared. The screen turned blue. 'Lights on, please.'

Someone at the back switched on the fluorescents. Within a couple of seconds the room was awash with a bright white light.

Everyone blinked to adjust their sight.

Tightening her eyes, SIO Dawn Leggate continued, 'This has cast a very dark shadow over this enquiry. DC Hagan is now the prime suspect in the murder of Gemma Cooke. I have already informed the Chief Constable and Professional Standards. I've also spoken with his DI this morning. She informs me that DC Hagan is day off today, but he's not at his home, is not answering his mobile and she doesn't know where he is. But, he is due in at nine tomorrow and so she's bringing him across here the minute he gets in.' Dawn Leggate still held the remote in her hand. She sought out Hunter with it. 'As you and Grace have already spoken with DC Hagan I'm handing you two the task of interviewing him.'

SIO Dawn Leggate ended briefing by determining that everyone should clear up what current work they had on and finish the day early. She told the team that she wanted them fresh for the new week ahead, and so, the remains of the day fell away with detectives spending their time reviewing and consolidating the priorities and actions they had already been allocated.

Individually Hunter and Grace worked on their evidence journals, formulating their notes on their interview with Adam Fields. He had been put before court and had been remanded to Armley jail, where he would remain pending a trial date. After lunch they went back over Gemma Cooke's case file, to prepare themselves for their interview with DC Tom Hagan. By late afternoon they had pulled together crime scene photographs and the key witness statements and were in a state of readiness for the following day.

On his way home, Hunter stopped off at the supermarket and bought a decent bottle of red wine. The past few days had been manic and he wanted nothing more than to spend that evening with Beth winding down after they had put Jonathan and Daniel to bed. Times like this were precious and he wanted to make the most of it, he said to himself as he climbed back into his car.

- ooOoo -

CHAPTER SEVEN

Day Six: 23rd March.

Hunter and Grace stood in the Custody Suite waiting area. An uncomfortable silence prevailed and was only broken by the odd discordant sound erupting from one of the cells down the corridor. It sounded like one of the overnight drunks was still in high spirits.

Opposite the reception desk, one leg hooked across the other, Hunter leaned back against the wall, bracing himself with his shoulders. Waiting.

Glancing at the clock on the wall opposite it dawned on him that he and Grace had been here for almost half an hour. During that wait, he had attempted to exchange looks with the three members of staff working behind the desk, but they had snatched away their eyes the moment they had met his gaze.

He felt isolated.

Feeling the need for support he glanced down to where his partner was sitting on one of the secured metal seats that were there for the use of prisoners who were waiting to be booked in. She was hunched forward, elbows resting on her knees, eyes fixed forwards. She reminded him of someone who was waiting to see the dentist.

What they were in fact waiting for was the consultation to finish between DC Tom Hagan and the Federation appointed solicitor so that they could begin their interview; since the booking in procedure the pair had been locked in conference.

Tut-tutting to himself he lifted his eyes to the ceiling. Given that the suspect they were about to interview was a fellow detective he tried to focus on his line of questioning but his thinking was a shambles. He couldn't even remember the first question he had written in his pre-interview notes only three quarters of an hour ago. He dragged back his gaze and flipped open his case notes. As he started to read his script the interview room door swung inwards, startling Hunter. Tom Hagan's solicitor appeared in the doorway.

'DS Kerr, DC Marshall, my client is ready.'

Hunter sprang himself forwards at the same time as Grace pushed herself up from her seat. They exchanged knowing looks. It was time.

Hunter snapped shut his file, collected his messy thoughts and marched into the room.

What faced him took him by surprise. He had expected to be met by someone who looked as though they were prepared to do battle, yet the display on DC Tom Hagan's face was anything but. He was ashen-faced and wore a mask of defeat. He slouched in his chair, elbows on desk, hands supporting his head.

His solicitor took the chair next to his client. Making himself comfortable he announced, 'Detectives, Mr Hagan has made it clear to me that he realises the seriousness of his predicament and wishes to fully cooperate. He has prepared a statement.'

Hunter dropped the folder onto the table and took his place opposite Tom Hagan. 'That's good but I would still like to ask him a number of questions.'

Tom Hagan never even conferred with his solicitor. He met Hunter's eyes and nodded.

Grace switched on the tape recording machine and administered the introduction and caution.

Hunter opened his folder. His pre-interview notes took centre stage. He checked the first few sentences he had written, but before he even had begun to speak DC Hagan said,

'It's not what you think.'

Hunter glanced up and offered a questioning look.

'I didn't kill Gemma. I hadn't anything to do with her death. She was alive when I left.'

'Then why didn't you say anything to us the other day when we came for Gemma's case file. You must have known your prints and DNA were all over her place.'

'Course I did. You just hope against hope don't you, cos the whole situation was a friggin' mess. I knew I was in a heap of shit.'

'Enlighten me.'

'You know the story of how I came to meet up with her again after all this time.'

'Do I?'

'Yes, from the complaint that was made. You have to believe me when I say this. When it came across my desk and I was asked to follow it up, I spotted her name, and wondered if it was the same Gemma Cooke from school, and of course when I went out to see her, it was.'

'So what happened?'

'Nothing happened, like you think it did. I did my job. Sure we caught up, but genuinely I did my job. I gave Gemma my card, like we always do for follow up contact, and then I arrested Adam, and afterwards I phoned her up and gave her an update. While I was chatting with her she happened to mention she was going out with her mates into Sheffield for a night out celebrating St Patrick's Day. She said she needed to just chill out after everything that had gone off. I told her that was a coincidence because me and a couple of the CID lads were having a night out that same night in Sheffield, but that we were going to go to the casino after a couple of drinks.' He sought out Hunter's eyes and locked gazes. 'You can check this out. I didn't arrange it. It was a CID thing and they asked a couple of us in the office if we wanted to join them. It's a regular thing.'

'Okay, so you and a few of the CID lads went into Sheffield on St Patrick's night. What happened there?'

'Well, we started in that old pub opposite Sheffield railway station. Stayed there about an hour and then went to a few real ale pubs around Kelham Island and then we made our way up to Division Street. That's when we bumped into Gemma and her mates. It wasn't planned I can assure you. They were in the Frog & Parrot, I think it's called and they'd had quite a few by the looks of them. We got in a round of drinks and I went across and chatted with Gemma for a while.'

Hunter interrupted, 'What about?'

'Mostly about our schooldays, what we'd done with ourselves and of course the circumstances of how we'd met up again. You know, her domestic I'd just dealt with. That was it.' He see-sawed his eyes between Hunter and Grace. 'Honest.

73

There was nothing in it. I didn't chat her up. Nothing like that at all. I spent about twenty minutes with her. I finished my beer and then me and the lads went on to the next pub and left her and her friends to it. As I say it was planned that we'd do a few pubs and then go off to the casino.'

'But that never happened?'

'Well you know that, because I ended up at Gemma's, didn't I? But that's also not how you think either.'

'Tell me how it was.'

'Well, me and the lads did a few more pubs, and were about to jump in a taxi to go to the casino, when Gemma rang my mobile. She said she'd had enough. That she wasn't in the mood and so she'd left her mates in the pub and decided to call it a day. She said she thought she was being followed. She sounded really panicky on the phone. I asked her if it was Adam, and she said, she didn't think so, but she wasn't sure. I asked her where she was and she said near the City Hall. I was only round the corner from there, and so I told her to hang on and I'd shoot round. I left the pub and found Gemma by the front steps of the City Hall. She was in a bit of a state. And I don't mean drunk. In fact she appeared to be pretty much sober.' He lifted his head off his hands and pushed himself back in the seat. 'She then told me that she thought Adam had texted her early on, threatening to slit her throat, and burn her house down, and that she didn't know if it was him, or a mate of his, who was following her. She said whoever it was had kept dodging out of sight so she hadn't been able to see them. I had a good look round but I couldn't see anyone so I told her I'd see her into a taxi. And that's what I intended doing. Except when I got her a taxi she asked me if I'd come home with her and just see that everything was okay when she got there.' He paused a second and again sought out Hunter and Grace's faces. 'I guess that's when I should have said no, but I didn't, did I? Like an idiot I got in with her. On the way back, she said she was starving and asked me if I fancied sharing a pizza with her. We were getting on all right and I thought there was no harm in it and so we got the taxi driver to drop us off on High Street. The pizza place was still open, so I grabbed one and then we walked back to her place. Her house is only

74

ten minutes from there, when you cut through the backs. When we got to her place she opened up a bottle of wine, while I divvied up the pizza and she poured out two glasses. I guess you know what happened then.'

'You went to bed and had sex?'

Downheartedly he answered, 'Yes. We had sex.' Then his eyes lifted. 'But that was it. Once the moment had gone I felt awful. I know I shouldn't have done it. I said to her afterwards that we shouldn't have done that. She told me not to apologise. There was no harm done, she said. We were both adults. I told her that I couldn't stay and so I had a quick wash, told her I'd catch up with her later and then left. She let me out by the back door and I cut through the back streets home.'

'Did anyone see you leave?'

'No, not that I know of. To be honest I really was feeling shitty over what had just happened. And you know my circumstances. I didn't want anybody seeing me there. That's why I used the back streets.'

'When you say circumstances, what do you mean by that?'

He sighed, 'That I'm married. Six years, this year. She's going to find out, isn't she?'

Hunter shrugged his shoulders. Resolutely he replied, 'You don't need me to answer that question, do you, Tom? I think you know the answer yourself. This is a murder investigation.'

He hunched his shoulders, 'This is going to crucify her. We've not had a good couple of months together. Things have been a bit strained of late. We've just had a baby – a little girl – three weeks ago.' He shook his head, 'How can I have been so chuffing stupid?'

'Let me pull you back here, Tom. You're telling us that when you left Gemma she was alive. Am I right?'

He looked aghast. 'Course I am, for Christ's sake. She was alive. She saw me out of the back door. I just said I'd be in touch. That was it.'

'And you never argued.'

'No, why should we? I hold my hands up I went to bed with her when I know I shouldn't have done. I'm not proud of what I did, but that's how it was. What else? Why should I harm her?'

'I don't know. Maybe she wanted more from you, after you'd had sex together. Maybe she asked you to leave your wife.'

He shook his head vigorously. 'No. Although I'm guessing she probably knew I was married she never asked me. It wasn't like that. Jesus, you've got to believe me. It happened exactly like I've just told you. Gemma was fine about everything. In fact she gave me a peck on the cheek and said something like "if I ever needed her company again to give her a ring." Honestly that's exactly how it was. I'm telling you, when I left her she was alive.'

'Okay, Tom, what time did you leave?'

He thought about the question for a few seconds. 'It would've been roughly about quarter to two. I say that because I can remember looking at my watch after we'd done it and it was just before half one. Like I've said, I got up had a quick wash, got dressed and then left. So at the most that was quarter of an hour.'

'And what time did you get home?'

'I guess it's roughly twenty minutes to my house from Gemma's, and I wasn't strolling. I put in a bit of a jog so it could have been quicker.'

'Will your wife be able to corroborate this?'

Shaking his head he sighed, 'As I said earlier, things have been strained between us. Baby blues and all that – I don't know. She's at her sister's. She felt she needed a break, so she's been there for the last couple of days.' He took a deep breath and exhaled slowly, 'This is not going to help things with our relationship, is it?'

No more than you deserve, because instead of being at the casino with your mates you were getting your end-away with a vulnerable witness, Hunter thought to himself.

DC Hagan's face changed and took on a worried look. 'What a fucking mess, and all because of a one-night stand. Shit.'

Least of your troubles, mate. Hunter then asked, 'Just going back a bit, Tom. You said you divvied up the pizza. What did you mean?'

His forehead creased into a frown, 'I cut it in half. Well not just in half, into three slices each, but neither of us finished it. We left it on the side in the kitchen. I think there were a couple of pieces left.'

'What did you cut it with?'

'A knife. I asked Gemma if she'd got a pizza slicer, but she hadn't.'

'Where did the knife come from?'

Tom Hagan's brow creased, 'Kitchen drawer, I think. To be honest I didn't see. Why?'

Hunter didn't respond. He simply bunched his shoulders. *That's the answer I would have given if I had stabbed someone to death with a kitchen knife.* He quickly tumbled this interview, and everything else he knew from previous briefings, around in his head. He lowered his eyes, pretending to read his notes as he gathered his thoughts. He recalled how the neighbour, Valerie Bryce had made the three-nines phone call to the police, telling the operator that Adam Fields was shouting and banging on Gemma's back door, at just after ten past two on the morning of the 18th March. If what Tom Hagan had just told them was the truth, this meant that the time-gap between Tom leaving number 34 Manvers Terrace, and Adam Fields arriving at the address, and discovering Gemma's body was approximately twenty-five minutes. Not a tight window, but neither a large one for them to focus on. He was just about to go back over Tom's story when he recalled what Mike Sampson had introduced at this morning's briefing. He asked, 'When you last saw Gemma, what was she wearing?'

Tom Hagan's eyebrows knitted together. For a brief moment his eyes blanked. A few seconds later he answered. 'A nightie.' He pursed his mouth and momentarily gazed up to the ceiling, obviously thinking about the answer he had just given. Then his eyes returned and he nodded. 'Yes, a short satin one – purple – and a matching kimono-type dressing gown. When I came out of the bathroom she was waiting for me on the landing. She had on the nightie and was wrapping the dressing gown around her. She said she'd see me out. Why?'

'Anything else?'

Momentarily, he screwed up his face.

Hunter examined his face. Tom Hagan's eyes were wide open but they weren't focused anywhere. There was an eerie silence for a good ten seconds and then he captured Hunter's look. He shook his head, 'No, just her nightie and dressing gown. I don't think she had any slippers on or anything like that. I think she was barefooted when she let me out of the back door. She said she was gonna go straight back to bed, cos she was going to be knackered otherwise. She had a busy day ahead of her.'

'Did you notice any jewellery she had on?'

'Jewellery? Jewellery as in rings, bracelets?' He seemed to think about the question again for a few seconds and then returned, 'No. I remember she'd a watch on earlier, but she took that off before we went upstairs.' He raised a finger. 'Yeah, she took it off when we were kissing cos the strap caught in the back of my hair.'

'What about a necklace?'

He screwed up his forehead. 'Necklace? No, she didn't have a necklace on. Just a watch.'

Hunter and Grace grilled Tom Hagan for another hour, but they couldn't shift him from his story. Following consultation with CPS, he was granted and given police bail. Two officers from the Professional Standards department had been waiting for the PPU Detective, and the moment he had stepped out of the interview room they had confronted him. They had served him with a 'discipline notice' and had duly suspended him from his duties.

It was well into the afternoon by the time Hunter and Grace had finished fingerprinting and photographing Tom Hagan and furnished him with the appropriate release documents.

Hunter returned to his desk feeling low and his head was mashed. He had to get out of the office to unpick everything and make some sense of it all. He made the excuse to Grace that he was just nipping out for something to eat and then jumped into one of the MIT cars and drove out of the station yard at speed with no direction in mind. By the time he had gathered his thinking he was near to Manvers Terrace. He took a detour to the murder scene.

Most of the street had been re-opened to the residents, though a line of blue and white tape secured the immediate area around number 34 and a Community Support Officer was standing guard to prevent trespass of the inner cordon. Hunter pulled into the side of the road, killed the engine and stared out through the windscreen. By Gemma's front door Hunter couldn't help but note the line of colourful floral tributes decorating the footpath.

Obviously very well thought of.

For several seconds his thoughts drifted. He tried to focus on the interview with Tom Hagan but being here interfered with his concentration. His thoughts were spiralling around and he found himself reflecting on his childhood and early teenage years rather than that morning's work. He set his sights beyond the crime scene tape and rested it on the grassed area at the head of the street. He had shared some good times here in the early 1980s; playing football. That piece of grass, back then, had been rough wasteland that backed onto derelict Brickworks. There was no sign of it now. He and his mates had used part of the broken perimeter wall as one of the goals; chalks marks outlined goalposts. While at this end jumpers or coats signified the other goals. He'd been Kevin Keegan, midfield dynamo. Other members of their imaginary England Squad had been taken up by his best friends, Tony Mitchell, Rob Jenkinson and the McCarthy brothers – Danny and David. He tumbled their young, cheery-faced images, around in his head and as their faces hazed away he wondered what they were all doing with their lives now. He caught himself and dragged back his thoughts. He switched focus, delivering his gaze upon number 34. What he had previously believed, about Gemma Cooke's murder being 'domestic' related, was turning out to be nothing as straightforward. Something else was puzzling him as well. It had to do with that necklace they had found on Gemma's body.

- ooOoo –

CHAPTER EIGHT

Day Seven: 24th March.

Pulling his Audi into the car park of Barnwell Police Station, Hunter ratcheted down the music of Blondie, while simultaneously scanning the rear yard for a parking place. Spotting an available space, between two marked patrol cars, he freewheeled into it and switched off the engine. In buoyant mood he nudged open his door and took in a deep breath. He filled his lungs, catching the morning freshness. Birdsong was the only sound around him. He listened to the exalted exchanges between the different species and pondered for a moment, staring skywards. As he caught a glimpse of the sun breaking through a thin veil of light grey clouds, he mused it was one of those days where he'd rather be out painting than being cooped up in a stuffy office. He shook himself out his reflections. One day, he told himself, and that's all I'm going to do. Every day, come rain or shine.

But today, Detective Sergeant Kerr, you have a killer to catch.

Locking up the car he marched off across the car park, singing the chorus of 'Dreaming' inside his head. As he neared the rear door a smile played across his mouth; as a teenager he'd lusted after Debbie Harry; pouting images of her had adorned his bedroom walls. He caught himself again. He was in a contemplative mood this morning and he needed to get his head clicked into the right gear. Dismissing the thoughts of his adolescent years, he punched in the code to the security lock and entered the rear of the building. Two uniformed officers were by the back stairwell, putting on their protective vests. Hunter bid them 'Good morning,' as he took the stairs.

Neither of them replied.

Hunter slowed his pace and with a surprised look glanced over his shoulder. He was just in time to catch their backs as they were leaving the building. Shrugging his shoulders at their lack of response, speculating that they were rushing off to a call, and therefore focussed upon that, he continued on up the stairwell. At the top he caught the sound of a raised voice back along the corridor. It was Detective Superintendent Leggate in her office. She sounded angry. Swear words littered her tirade. He slowed his pace and tried to determine if he could pick out anyone else's voice. He couldn't. He smiled to himself. She was either tearing someone off a strip in her office, who dare not reply, or she was on the phone. Suddenly, he remembered his own rollicking from her four days earlier. He held that thought as he entered the department.

Grace was at her desk. She snapped up her head and wide-eyed zoned in on him.

Hunter flicked back his head, 'Someone's coppin' an earful this morning from Ma'am,' he started, and quickly halted his voice when he saw Grace nodding frantically in his direction. She was staring beyond him and giving him a sign which said 'shut the door.' He set the door to and held on to the handle. Knitting his eyebrows, in a low voice, he asked, 'What's up?'

'Have you not heard?'

'Heard what?'

'Tom Hagan's attempted suicide.'

'What?'

'Yeah, took an overdose. Last night. His brother found him. Apparently he popped round to see if he was alright after Tom told him about what had gone off, and that his wife's found out and now she wants a divorce.'

Hunter dropped down onto his chair. 'Shit.'

'Exactly.'

'Is he okay.'

'As far as I know, but as you can guess, the proverbial's hit the fan.'

He flicked his head backwards towards the door. 'And is some flack coming our way.'

Grace shrugged her shoulders. 'The Super popped her head in just before you arrived. She said she wants to see us both the minute you got in.'

Hunter scooted his chair out from beneath his desk. 'Well if what I've just heard is a sample of her temper I suggest we put a book down the back of our trousers before we go in.'

Pushing himself up he added, 'Do you know, a few minutes ago I was in such a good mood as well.'

Detective Superintendent Dawn Leggate was slamming down the phone as Hunter and Grace stepped into her office. The door was open but Hunter rapped politely on the panel.

She lifted her head, offered a wan smile, beckoned them in and pointed out two chairs, next to the wall, for them to take.

She set her sight on Hunter. 'You've heard about DC Hagan?'

Hunter nodded, 'Grace has just filled me in.'

'Professional Standards have rung me. They want to talk to you both.' She ping-ponged her eyes between the detectives. 'Today.' She diverted her gaze to the phone. 'I told them we're up to our necks in a murder enquiry, but they insisted it had to be today.' She huffed, 'Apparently Tom Hagan's DS is questioning our tactics. Thinks we could have made a better job of it.' She threw up our hands. 'As though it's our fault that his wife left him and caused him to take an overdose.' She shook her head. Her face was unusually flushed. 'I've just finished with the supercilious prick on the phone. Given him a piece of my mind. I told him that what happened to DC Hagan is down to DC Hagan and not my officers. If he'd have kept his cock in his pants then he wouldn't be in this predicament, and that if he'd have done his job properly as his supervisor, then his DC might not be looking at a charge of misconduct.' She took a deep breath and sighed. 'I guess he'll want to make a complaint about me now, as well.' She flattened her palms upon her desk and fanned out her fingers. She glanced at them for a few seconds and then returned her gaze to Hunter and Grace. With a resolute smile, she said, 'Hey-ho, never mind. These things are sent to test us. Now let's make sure all our bases our covered before Professional Standards get here.'

Hunter and Grace missed morning briefing. Detective Superintendent Leggate had given them the use of her office to confer notes and double-check documentation before 'The rubber-heeled Squad,' as all officers referred to them, arrived. Hunter already knew that the evidence, to justify the bringing in and interviewing of Tom Hagan, was good, yet nevertheless he and Grace went back over it, scrutinising their witness statements and forensic exhibits, and even checking that every report, certificate and legal instrument was correctly filled in. Hunter knew from experience that there was no room for error when under scrutiny by the 'Discipline and Complaints Team,' as they were normally called.

By 9.30 a.m. they had sifted through everything and talked over the likely format of their forthcoming interview. As they ended their scrum-down they met each other's eyes and swapped tight-lipped smiles; despite their nervousness it was a reassuring look they exchanged.

A half an hour later they were called down to the Custody Suite.

They were to be interviewed separately. Hunter was first in.

Across the table in the soundproofed interview room Hunter faced two smartly suited detectives, who introduced themselves as Detective Superintendent Chambers and Detective Inspector Wilson. Even though he knew he had nothing to fear he could feel himself starting to sweat, and as the DI went through the preamble of informing him that 'he wasn't under arrest and that he could leave the interview at any time throughout the proceedings,' he felt a knot tighten in his stomach.

For forty minutes Hunter was questioned, though surprisingly he felt that the nature of it was more informal than formal, and there were times when he found himself waiting for that sucker punch question. It never came. Although the two Senior Officers scrutinised the evidence of Adam Fields, and his friend on Manvers Terrace, who had placed Tom Hagan at Gemma Cooke's house, most of the probing centred upon what his personal observations had been of the DC. Especially: 'was there any time, either while he was interviewing him, or during his time in custody, did he express, or show any signs that he was going to commit himself harm.'

Unflinchingly, staring both Senior Officers in the face, Hunter answered, 'No.'

After that the questioning was brought to a close. He was served with the customary 'Regulation 9,' notice of disciplinary proceedings and allowed to leave.

He left the room drained. Mentally and physically he was exhausted. As he trudged up the stairs back to the department he could feel a headache coming on.

Hunter walked into an empty office. He checked his watch. Lunchtime. He didn't feel hungry. In fact, his guts were churning. And he didn't feel like doing any work. Straightening his desk, he scribbled out two notes. He slid one across to where Grace sat, telling her he'd ring her later to see how it had gone. The second note he dropped onto DI Scaife's blotter informing him that he was taking some time off. Then he left.

- ooOoo -

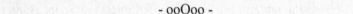

CHAPTER NINE

Day Eight: 25th March.

The minute Hunter got in he brought himself up to date by checking the incident board. There were no new revelations. Grace arrived ten minutes later looking slightly the worse for wear. Hunter guessed, that like he, she had slept very little. He offered her a smile and made them both a hot drink.

Placing a mug of steaming coffee before her, he said, 'Sorry about not ringing you last night. I had a few hours with Beth and the lads and then went to bed early. I had a stinking migraine.'

'Don't worry, Hunter I didn't feel too good myself. I shared a bottle of wine with Dave, let off some steam about the crap day I'd had and then hit the sack early myself.'

He sipped his tea. 'Anyway how did it go?'

Grace gave him a blow-by-blow account of her interview with Professional Standards. He quickly learned that hers had followed an almost identical line of questioning.

Between them, as they finished their drinks, they came to the conclusion that Professional Standards had merely been covering their 'own backs;' that their quick response would enable them to make 'all the right noises' when The Independent Police Complaints Commission came calling.

Their brief conversation had made them both feel better.

The day's briefing was led by Detective Superintendent Leggate. She told the MIT team that nothing fresh had come in overnight to move the enquiry forward. She did update them on DC Tom Hagan's condition. She informed everyone that there was no lasting damage and that he had been released from hospital. She finished by saying, 'Despite what's happened Tom Hagan is still a suspect.'

Beside her on the sofa, Linane Brazier's mobile rang, making her jump and breaking her concentration. She threw aside the magazine she had been reading and scooped up her phone. The number that flashed up on screen was on her contacts list. She knew who this was, and glancing across the room, to where the clock was hung on the wall, she noted that her caller was two hours overdue.

Hitting the answer key she answered brightly, 'Hi.'

On the other end of the line, in broken English, her friend and working partner Elisabeth Bertolutti said, 'Linane, I'm so sorry, you wouldn't believe what happened to me today. I've only just got in. I'll tell you about it later.'

Unable to stop the pitch rising in her voice Linane asked, 'Do you have it with you?'

In similarly excited fashion Elisabeth answered, 'Yes, yes, I'm just unwrapping it now. Turn on your laptop, I'll show it you.'

Trapping her mobile between her ear and shoulder, Linane hoisted herself off the sofa and rushed across to where her laptop sat on the breakfast bar. As she booted up her computer she listened to Elisabeth's child-like voice ecstatically announce, 'You'll be so pleased when you see it. It's far better than the photograph. It's worth every penny.'

Eyes glued to the screen, anxiously tapping her French manicured nails upon the dark granite surface, Linane mentally willed the computer to go faster through its start-up process. She had been waiting all day for this. Ever since Elisabeth's phone call that morning to say she'd bought the piece. After what seemed an eternity, but in reality was less than a minute, Linane's screen appeared and she clicked open her web-cam browser. Quickly typing in her Skype account number and password, she brought up her contacts and saw that Elisabeth was already waiting on-line. She hung the cursor over her name and double-clicked again. A split-second later Elisabeth's head and shoulders appeared on screen. A beaming smile lit up her face. In the background she recognised part of the lounge of the cottage they rented up north in Yorkshire.

Talking to the web-cam image Linane said, 'Show me then,'

Her friend's head and shoulders ducked away a second as she reached off-screen. Then, re-positioning herself back into view she held before her an oil painting. 'Ta-dah,' she exulted.

Linane's eyes roamed every which way around the canvas. She was captivated by the mastery of the brushwork. She had to agree with her partner's sentiments, even though her only view of it was through a computer screen, it certainly looked to be worth every penny of their investment. Cleaned up, she thought, this will make a handsome profit.

Unexpectedly, the painting dropped at one corner and she caught sight of her friends head, partially turned, looking back over her shoulder.

'Just a minute, Linane, there's someone at the door.'

She watched Elisabeth set the painting to one side, push herself away from the desk, rise from the antique Captain's chair and step towards the front door.

Linane pressed her face towards the screen. Elisabeth's image had become grainy in the distance. At that moment a strange sensation overtook her. It started as a tingling feeling in the base of her spine, which quickly shot up into her head and buzzed her ears; it felt as if she had been hooked up to a low voltage generator and it made her shudder. For a brief moment the room spun, and then everything seemed to close in on her and slow down, and she could feel all her senses heighten. She smelt things she hadn't smelt before, and one of those smells was fear – her own fear. It made her call out, 'Elisabeth, put the security chain on.'

Her warning came too late.

Before her eyes the door of their cottage swung sharply inwards, clattering hard against the wall. There was a resounding crack as the metal handle smashed against the plasterwork.

It made Linane jump.

A split-second later Elisabeth flew backwards into the room, arms flailing, trying to stop herself from hitting the dark wood sideboard, set against the far wall of their lounge. She barrelled into it with such force that it scattered two Rockingham Pottery 'blue ware' plates, they had recently bought from an antiques fair. One of them broke before it hit the floor. The replica Tiffany lamp went next, toppling over the side, its cord saving it from hitting the deck.

In through the open door followed a tall, dark-clad intruder. In a flash, that raider was clawing at Elisabeth's throat, pressing her hard against the sideboard, lifting her off her feet.

Linane froze, eyes transfixed to her laptop, watching in horror as the dark invader launched Elisabeth over the back of sofa, dumping her to the floor. She saw the intruder vault after her friend, landing on top.

A strident, pain-filled, shriek exploded from Elisabeth's mouth, jarring Linane's ears.

In the eerie half-light, cast by the swinging table-lamp, Linane saw something glint. She realised what it was. Her heart raced. Simultaneously bile leapt up from her stomach and into her throat. It stung and gagged her, stopping her screaming out another warning.

The monster had a knife.

Linane's stomach muscles tensed as she witnessed the first thrust. The action was repeated; again and again. And in a few seconds she lost count of the number of times she saw the knife plunge into Elisabeth's torso. She was amazed that her friend didn't cry out. All Linane could hear was the sucking sound of the blade being yanked out after each fresh stabbing.

The attack stopped almost as quickly as it had started. And it was at that stage that Linane came to her senses. Although her insides were churning and she felt faint she knew had to do something. She snatched her eyes away from her screen and searched out her mobile. It was only a few yards away. As she was about to reach out and grab it, at the periphery of her vision a sharp movement caught her attention. She snapped her eyes back upon the screen. The dark-clad killer was standing in the centre of the lounge, slowly roaming his head around. She thought she heard him chanting numbers, counting them backwards. He stopped when he spotted their computer. And that's when she caught a proper view of Elisabeth's murderer; until now his features had been in shadow. Her legs wobbled and she had to grab hold of the granite work surface to stop herself from collapsing. Into view came the most hideously masked face she had ever seen.

She slunk back sharply, knocking aside her phone.

The masked-killer stepped forwards and leaned in, pressing his face closer, taking up the whole of the screen.

Once more Linane froze, her hand covering her mouth. She couldn't say a word. Not even issue a cry.

Without warning a muffled voice boomed 'Boo!' out through the speakers.

Elisabeth's heart leapt against her chest.

Then in deep gravelly tones the mask said, 'Coming, ready or not.'

It was at that stage she let out a piercing scream.

By the end of the afternoon Hunter still had his head buried in his hands. Except for the occasional stroll across the room to make a hot drink he had been desk-bound for most of the day, sifting back over evidence and reading through statements. He had even tediously listened back through the tape recordings of the interviews with Adam Fields and DC Tom Hagan to check he hadn't missed anything. As he chewed another lump of plastic off his decimated Biro top his thoughts became distracted. The last case the team had worked on had been complicated by the fact that former detectives had been involved in a very complex web of deceit. Now, in this latest investigation, there was the distinct possibility that one of their own might be a murderer. And, although Tom Hagan had given them a timeframe of when he had left Gemma's house and returned to his own home, it could not be corroborated. Therefore, he had no alibi. Things were not boding well for the PPU Detective. He knuckle-rubbed his temples and lifted his head, setting his eyes across the desk where his partner Grace also had her head buried in her hands, eyes drilling her own paperwork.

He was about to suggest they take a break and grab something to eat when the office doors clattered open. Hunter whipped round his head catching sight of Tony Bullars storming into the room. At mid-chest he was thrusting out his mobile.

Catching his breath he blurted, 'My girlfriend's on the phone. She says her friend's just been stabbed! Uniform are on their way to her cottage. We need to go.' He swallowed hard.

Hunter sprung himself out of his chair. 'Bully, slow down, you're not making sense. What are you on about?'

He took several deep breaths. 'My girlfriend Linane has just phoned me. She's staying down in Richmond. She says that her friend, who she shares a cottage with in Street, has just been stabbed. She was Skyping her and saw it happen.' He aimed a finger at his mobile. 'She's rung me a few minutes ago. It's only just happened. I've contacted Communications and they're sending the response car. We need to get over there.'

Hunter threw his gaze back to Grace. Her eyes were wide open, engaging his and she was already pushing herself up from her desk. He grabbed his jacket from the back of his chair and snatched up the car keys.

Within minutes of screeching away from the rear compound Hunter was swinging the unmarked police car onto the main arterial road, which connected onto the Dearne Valley Parkway bypass – the fastest route to the tiny hamlet of Street. There were still the last dregs of rush hour traffic on the road, but that didn't deter or slow his driving, and many of his jockeying manoeuvres left behind a wake of cars breaking sharply, their drivers blasting their horns, and some making rude hand gestures, as he sped past. At Elsecar he pulled off the main road and continued driving at breakneck speed along the stretches of country lanes towards the tiny hamlet of Street.

In the back of the car Grace had turned up her personal radio, and as Hunter slickly switched up and down gears, and swung in and out of lighter traffic on the B roads, he strained his ears to monitor the update from the response car. Over the airwaves he heard other police call signs coming onto the net. More officers were responding to the call, coming from different directions, but all heading towards Tony Bullars' girlfriend's cottage.

In the front seat, eyes glued ahead, Tony fidgeted anxiously.

Approaching the outskirts of Wentworth, only five minutes from their destination, they heard the call they were dreading; the response car operator radioed in, 'We've got a female body. We need some back-up.'

Careering off the main traffic route onto Street Lane Hunter saw that three marked police cars had already beaten them there. The last car in had been angled to block off the narrow road; nothing was getting in or out. Hunter pulled the MIT car sharply across to the right, mounting the grass verge beside a dry stone wall and yanked on the handbrake.

Street Lane consisted of a dozen or so stone cottages, and Hunter could see that most of the activity was centred upon the end cottage some twenty yards ahead. A uniformed officer had already secured one end of blue and white crime scene tape to a telegraph pole and was quickly unwinding it across the road.

Tony Bullars was leaping out of the passenger side door even before Hunter had turned off the engine. Grace wasn't far behind.

Pushing open his door, Hunter watched the pair sprint across to the uniformed response car driver who was waiting for them by the gate, an anxious look on his face. For a brief moment Hunter cast his gaze across the roof of the car and surveyed the manic scene unfolding before him. He already knew from the radio traffic that there was going to be a dead body awaiting him and he began clicking his investigative brain into gear. Going to the boot of the car he took out a white protective oversuit and quickly slipped it on. Taking out two more for his colleagues he closed the hatchback and stepped onto the road. He hadn't gone more than half-a-dozen paces when his phone rang. He prised it out of his pocket and viewed the screen. It was Detective Superintendent Leggate. Slowing his pace he fielded the call while crossing the carriageway. She'd only just picked up the incident she told him, and in response he gave her what sketchy details he had from the conversation with Tony Bullars.

'I'll be in there in a couple of minutes, boss. I'll ring you back the second I know exactly what we've got,' he promised and ended the call.

Stepping through the garden gate his thoughts became distracted by the sound of sirens wailing in the distance; more police were arriving. He quickly re-engaged his brain. He needed to start directing things, but first he had to get inside the cottage and see what he was dealing with. Snapping on a pair of latex gloves he slipped around the side of the stone cottage to where he saw Grace and Tony standing by an open door. Tony had one foot on the threshold and was poking his head in through the gap. He pulled back as Hunter approached. His features were grim.

'It is Linane's friend,' he nodded. 'And she's in a mess.'

Hunter passed each of them a Tyvek forensic suit and edged past into the cottage. The first thing he noted was that there had been no forced entry. He halted one foot inside the doorway and peered inside the room. The low-ceilinged lounge was gloomy. There was light being cast, but it was coming from a decorated glass canopied table lamp, which was hanging at an odd angle, low down, almost touching the top of the skirting, and so the glow wasn't having much effect. It looked to have fallen from a nearby mahogany sideboard. Slowly roaming his eyes around the crime scene he clocked pieces of broken crockery littering the floor; all the signs of a struggle. Then his gaze settled on the body. Tony's comment had been spot-on. She was in a mess. Judging by the puddle of blood encircling her it looked as though she had met a tormented death. It hadn't even started to coagulate; she hadn't been dead long. Thinking about what needed to be done, especially to preserve the scene, he was about to issue instructions to his two colleagues when he caught sight of the bloodied T-shirt on the deceased. In that instant his stomach emptied and a fog clouded his vision. The room was suddenly stuffy. It seemed as though the walls were closing in and the floor was rising up towards him. Then the room started spinning and his legs felt unsteady, as if they were going to buckle beneath him. He put out a hand and supported himself on the sideboard. He needed to get out. He closed his eyes to shut out the image and swallowed hard. A few seconds later he snapped them open. He gawped again at the corpse, checking that his vision hadn't been deceived. It hadn't. Stumbling backwards out of the cottage and onto the path he took in a deep breath. A rush of blood pounded in his brain.

After all this time.

He pitched a hand into his trouser pocket and tugged out his mobile. Then he made for the gate. In the background he could hear his name being called, but his concentration was elsewhere. He needed to make a phone call. Urgently.

Barry Newstead turned up twenty-five minutes after Hunter had made his call. He had brought with him Detective Superintendent Dawn Leggate. By their arrival Hunter had composed himself and had got his brain back into gear. He had directed Grace to start the house-to-house and she was currently marshalling four uniformed officers into a group to begin that task. Hunter knew that it was an assignment which shouldn't take them long, given the small number of dwellings which made up the hamlet. Tony Bullars had a harder undertaking. Hunter had given him the job of carrying out an immediate search of the surroundings, firstly, for the weapon, to determine if it had been discarded, and secondly, for the killer. On that last charge it was a very long shot, he knew, especially given the fact that Street was surrounded by open countryside, but he wasn't going to be responsible for any embarrassing outcomes if he was orchestrating the initial actions at a crime scene he told Tony, who had returned a questioning frown.

Hunter qualified his instructions by adding, 'Just set up a perimeter, Tony. Hundred yards or so, for now. Just to make sure he's not hiding in the bottom of any hedgerow.'

He watched Tony stride away and then switched his attention to Dawn Leggate and Barry Newstead who were tramping towards him.

The SIO was pulling on her top coat. 'Barry says you've got something that we need to see?'

Hunter alternated his gaze between the pair, before settling his eyes upon Barry. 'I wanted you to see this, Barry, before I go any further.' He half turned and nodded towards the cottage. 'Just have a look at the body and tell me my eyes are not deceiving me.' He turned back and spotted his boss's eyebrows knitting tightly together. He said to her. 'I'll explain everything in a couple of secs after Barry's had a quick look inside.'

Hunter waited by the gate. He followed the path Barry took until he disappeared around the side of the cottage. For the best part of two minutes he waited in silence, conscious of his SIO beside him; she was impatiently tapping one foot and her leather sole gave off a sharp resounding clip.

Then Barry re-appeared.

Hunter scrutinised his face. His colleague's mouth was pursed tight. Hunter, back rigid, said, 'It's her T-shirt, isn't it?'

'It certainly appears to be similar, from what I remember. It's such a long time ago now, Hunter.'

'I know, Barry, but I'm telling you that's her T-shirt.'

'Will someone please enlighten me?' demanded Dawn Leggate.

Hunter dragged his eyes away from Barry and met his boss's searching hazel eyes. 'In nineteen eighty-eight my then girlfriend Polly Hayes was murdered. She was sixteen. Barry here was involved in that enquiry. When her mother last saw her on the morning of the day she was killed, she had on a Bon Jovi T-shirt. That body in there has on Polly's T-shirt.'

Dawn Leggate's forehead creased into a frown and her eyes narrowed. 'Hunter, just because the deceased in there has a T-shirt with the same band name on it as the one your girlfriend was wearing, doesn't mean it's the same one.'

A flashback jumped inside Hunter's inner vision; Polly bouncing towards him, arms outstretched, sashaying around, showing off her new T-shirt. As quickly as her wraith-like image appeared she was gone again.

He replied, 'Oh, but it is, boss. Hers was unique. You see, we both went to see Bon Jovi at 'The Monsters of Rock festival'. at Donnington Park She bought one of their T-shirts and waited backstage for him to sign it. When she got back home she embroidered over his signature so she wouldn't lose it when it was washed. That T-shirt on that woman's body in there has Jon Bon Jovi's embroidered signature on it – in exactly the same place as Polly's.'

Hunter watched the Detective Superintendent search out Barry's face.

Barry returned a nod. 'From what I remember, about how it was described, it certainly seems to be the same one, guv,' he said solemnly. ' Her mother definitely said she had it on when she left the house to walk the dog and we had a sighting from an old bloke who passed her approximately half an hour before the time when we believe she was killed and she had it on then. When she was found she was wrapped in a green cloak. Underneath it she just had on her bra. The Bon Jovi T-shirt was nowhere in sight. A thorough search was made but we never found it. And, regarding the cloak, we checked with her family and friends, and none of them had ever seen it before and we never managed to suss out how she came by it. It was a real mystery and we never bottomed it. 'He shot a sideways glance to Hunter, 'We even checked to see if she had another boyfriend.' He shook his head, 'No joy on that front as well.'

Tightly lipped, Hunter said, 'How on earth is that woman in there connected to Polly's murder?'

- ooOoo -

CHAPTER TEN

Day Nine: 26th March.

Hunter rested his head against the driver's side window and stared out across the road. He set his sights on the Task Force Search Team who had arrived minutes earlier in two vans. He watched them as they disembarked and scoped their surroundings. The two fragmented teams formed into a loose circle and casually chatted amongst themselves while donning their black overalls. Hunter knew that in another ten minutes these officers would be scouring the garden and perimeter of the cottage, searching for evidence.

Inside the cottage that search had already started; he had watched the forensic team go in there three-quarters of an hour earlier.

Also, since his arrival, a white forensic tent had been erected against the side door and an inner cordon had been put in place.

Hunter yawned and then he shivered. He was tired and he was cold. It had been well after midnight before he had got home. He had undressed in the dark, tossed all his clothing over the back of the dressing table chair and virtually collapsed into bed. Tired though he was he hadn't immediately dropped off. For the best part of an hour he had tossed and turned, re-running the unresolved event inside his head. As if his mind wasn't shredded enough with the Tom Hagan affair, the finding of Elisabeth Bertolutti's body dressed in Polly's T-shirt had well and truly messed him up. When his brain had finally shut down it hadn't been for long. He'd awoken several times during the night in the midst of a dream. The same dream. A young, strikingly pretty, blonde-haired girl was running towards him through a field of tall wheat, but never getting any closer. She'd call out his name and then disappear from sight. Polly. On each occasion, upon awakening, he'd wished away her image and then rolled over and cuddled Beth. Holding her tightly, he'd eventually dropped off nursing a feeling of guilt. At 6.30 a.m. he had been awoken by the unrelenting trill of the bedside alarm. He'd had to force himself out of bed and take a cooler than normal shower to invigorate his body. Though that effect had only lasted as long as his drive into work and he had struggled to get through morning briefing. He had only managed it by shaking himself awake each time his eyelids had closed for a blink.

It had been an extended one to take into account both murders; they hadn't managed to yet find a venue to house the latest investigation. That had been raised as the day's highest priority. On that footing Detective Superintendent Leggate had told the team that she'd already discussed the issue with the Force Crime Manager, and as well as getting a room to house the new enquiry she was also bringing in an SIO to manage it. She had also requested additional resources to staff the investigation, but for the time being she had directed Hunter, Grace and Tony Bullars to oversee the Street Lane murder until those arrived.

Hunter's task for the day was to liaise with the Crime Scene Manager and Forensics, and gather and catalogue any exhibits, while Grace and Tony had been instructed to collect Tony's girlfriend from the flat she had been staying at in Richmond upon Thames and bring her back to South Yorkshire. Detective Superintendent Leggate had told the team that Linane Brazier had already been visited and questioned by detectives from the Metropolitan police the previous evening, but she wanted Grace to do a more in-depth video recorded interview at one of the Force's Victim/Witness Suites. She ended the morning session by informing everyone that because of the staff shortage she would be overseeing the post-mortem of Elisabeth Bertolutti, which had been arranged for 10.00 a.m. that morning.

As he gazed out through the side window, he was pre-occupied with his thoughts. Polly's undetected murder, twenty-one years ago, had initially been the reason why he had joined this job. It had also been the reason why he had been so determined to join the ranks of CID – to enable him to be actively involved in local murder enquiries, as well as have access to behind-the-scenes information about other murders throughout the country to check if any had similarities to Polly's killing. There had been a couple of close ones, which he had actively monitored, but then they had caught the killer and the perpetrator hadn't admitted responsibility for her death. He now knew, that finally, after all these years, he had his first solid link to her slaying, and though that link was unable to give him anything concrete by way of testimony, there was the opportunity to get fresh forensic evidence. This was the breakthrough he had been looking for. It was also his chance to get closure. Not only for him, but for Lynda and Peter – Polly's mum and dad – who he had shared his grief with in the early years following her death. He was not going to let this slip away, he told himself. He owed it to Polly and he owed it to her parents.

Rousing himself from his feeling of ennui he snatched up his clipboard from the passenger seat and pushed open the driver's door. An icy blast of wind buffeted his face, and though it momentarily stung it also had the much desired effect of freshening him up. He slung his legs out of the car and braced himself against the weather. He was ready to begin his day's work.

Hunter knew that he wouldn't be allowed inside the cottage until Forensics had processed the scene and so he spent most of that morning anxiously pacing up and down the narrow tarmac lane of Street, each hour checking in with the supervisors of the house-to-house team and search team. Neither of them brought him any good news and by midday he had resolved that he was in for the long haul and returned to his car where he had a ham and cheese sandwich waiting for him in the glovebox. He had just taken his second bite when his phone rang. It was Detective Superintendent Leggate. Swallowing hard he hit the answer button.

'Anything, Hunter?' she enquired.

He gave her his negative update.

Then she said, 'Okay, no problem, there's not much happening this way either. I've just got back from the PM. Something of significant interest has cropped up during it, which I know you'll want to hear. I'll fill you in on the findings later at briefing. I've also spoken with Grace and Tony and it's going to be late afternoon before they get back up here. They're going to take Linane straight to the interview suite at Maltby, so I'm not expecting to hear anything from them until evening briefing. And that's another thing, Hunter, briefing is back here.' He caught a noticeable pause, which lasted a couple of seconds. Then she said, 'I've decided against us having an incident room at District. Feelings are apparently running high in CID and PPU there, over Tom Hagan, so I'm giving the place a wide berth. It's not that I think officers there would sabotage our enquiry, but it's sensitive as you know, and I wouldn't want anything leaking out which would compromise it, so I'm looking for us to go somewhere else. We might even have to run it from a neighbouring District.' With that she told him not to rush back and that briefing was at 7.00 p.m.; she was going to do two separate briefings again.

Before he had time to ask questions she ended the call. For a good ten seconds he stared at his mobile screen, ruminating on the call. He wondered what of significance had been uncovered at the post-mortem.

Staring at the phone isn't going to give you any answers.

He dumped his mobile on the passenger seat and finished his sandwich.

Chewing the last mouthful, he spotted that the Search Team were about to take their lunch break. He decided to go for a stroll.

Beyond the end cottage, where Elisabeth Bertolutti had been murdered, the stretch of tarmac along Street Lane ended and became a dirt track. He had been told by officers, who had sealed off the road the previous evening that this track wound its way past open fields, through an avenue of trees, and half-a-mile ahead merged into a winding B road back towards Barnwell. He had also learned that the track was mainly used by horse-riders, walkers and cyclists as the only vehicles equipped to negotiate it were motor cycles or four-by-fours. As he approached and clapped eyes on the deep water-filled ruts, he realised why.

Avoiding the worst of the sludge, he plodded along the track for a few hundred yards. To his right he noticed a large pond encircled by trees. There was a hand painted sign, just beyond the track-side hedge, denoting that the waters were for 'private fishing only.' Beyond that he had a view all the way to Rotherham. Here he came to a standstill and half-turned. He stepped up onto a grass verge, beside which a low dry stone wall meandered. It gave him another view across open fields. He did a three-hundred-and-sixty degree turn, quickly exploring his surroundings. He couldn't help but think that this was going to be a tough one. This was perfect killing ground – nothing but miles of open countryside for a killer to disappear in. If there was nothing forthcoming from the house-to house enquiry then he doubted very much if they would find anyone out here who had witnessed anything. He just prayed that Forensics would find something. His thoughts were suddenly disturbed by the sound of raucous squawking not too far away. To his right, up on the hillside, above a line of trees, he clocked a clamour of rooks scatter into the skyline. Something's disturbed them, he mused.

He stood, tucked away, amongst the trees, looking down over the fields, the focus of his prying eyes centred upon the end cottage on Street Lane – the scene of his latest triumph. He had arrived there five minutes earlier, just in time to watch the team of dark-suited police officers filing out through the garden gate. He now watched them making their way back to their marked van parked opposite the cottage. He checked his watch and guessed they were breaking for lunch. He also noticed the white forensic tent, which had been put up by the side door – the door 'that bitch had opened up to him.' He rubbed his gloved hands together vigorously. Boy, had he taught her a lesson. He couldn't believe his luck when he had spotted her in the service station on the M1 yesterday afternoon. He'd bumped into her, on his way to the toilets, but he could tell from the brief glance she had returned that she hadn't recognised him. That was when he had decided he wouldn't get another opportunity as good as this. He knew that he might be taking a real chance following her home, but then, he told himself, that was what life was all about – taking chances. And he had gotten away with it. Again.

He slipped off a glove and dipped his right hand inside his camouflage jacket pocket, stopping when his fingers found what he was searching out. He fondled the coarse material. An electrifying buzz surged through him. The mask was his greatest weapon of fear. Every time.

Hunter stood by the boundary wall of the garden and spent an hour watching Task Force Officers continuing their fingertip search of the garden. By 2.00 p.m. they had reached the perimeter hedgerow and had not found anything of significance. He was bored, though he tried not to show it, offering an encouraging smile, whenever he caught the eye of one of the officers. It was all he could do. He felt helpless and he guessed they were as frustrated as he. Rolling back his cuff he checked his watch, making a mental note of the time, while wondering if anything material was happening back at the incident room. It was then he spotted Crime Scene Manager, Duncan Wroe, emerging from the forensic tent by the side door. Hunter shook down his cuff and tramped towards him.

Anxiously, he asked, 'Anything?'

Duncan slipped down his face mask. As was usual he was sporting several days' growth of facial hair. He wiggled a hand in front of Hunter. 'Not sure. We've lifted a few sets of prints, but we've also got some glove marks around the entry door and jamb. Where the body was, we've got a definite shoe print and a few other partials of the same tread dotted around the room. Looks like her killer stepped in her blood. The tread looks as though it might be from a trainer, or something similar. It's good enough to run through the system.'

'Is that positive?'

'It's a start.'

'Good.'

'I thought you might say that.' Duncan paused. His face took on a questioning look. 'They've mentioned to me that the victim, possibly, was wearing a T-shirt which belonged to a girlfriend of yours who was murdered?'

'Not possibly, Duncan – definitely. When she was last seen she had on this Bon Jovi T-shirt, from a concert we went to. She got it signed, and then embroidered the signature so it wouldn't disappear. When they found Polly's body she had this cloak thing wrapped around her and no sign of that T-shirt. No one knew what had happened to it.'

'Until you found this victim.'

Hunter nodded. 'I know it's definitely Polly's T-shirt she's got on. It's not something you forget.'

Duncan pursed his mouth, gave him a look of understanding and then said, 'And so you're working on the assumption that this victim here...' He flicked his head back towards the cottage '...maybe, had something to do with your girlfriend's murder.'

Hunter shrugged his shoulders. 'I'm trying to keep an open mind, but you have to admit a big question mark is hanging over Elisabeth Bertolutti. At the moment though, nothing's making sense.'

'And you're hoping I can make things clearer.'

'It'd be nice if you could. It's always been one of my ambitions to be able to tell Polly's parents that we've caught her killer.'

'You've mentioned her first name. I've been given the name Polly Hayes? Murdered in nineteen eighty-eight?'

Hunter nodded.

'Sorry about that.'

'No, it's okay. Long time ago now. Fell in love with Beth and married her.' He rolled his eyes to the sky, studied the scudding clouds for a few seconds and then returned his gaze. 'I'd still like to catch Polly's killer though.'

'Yeah, I would as well.'

'So, Duncan, do you have anything else?'

'I think so. I just want to check back. You said the witness to this saw the murder on web-cam?'

Hunter nodded. 'Yeah, it was Tony Bullars' girlfriend who witnessed it. She was at a friend's flat down in Richmond and was Skyping her when it happened.'

Duncan shook his head, 'Christ man, that must have been a shocker.' He tightened his lips. 'Anyway, why I asked that, is because there's no sign of any computer or laptop in the house. I've found its plug and lead. That was still in the socket next to a low table. I've dusted the table and there's certainly a lot of scuff marks on the surface. Some of those look like the same glove marks I've found on the edge of the door and jamb. None of you lot have taken the computer as evidence?'

Hunter shook his head, 'Nothing's been removed or disturbed. As soon as we found her like that, we left everything as it was.'

'Well, in that case then, it looks like whoever attacked her took it.'

Hunter screwed up his face. 'What did I say about none of this making any sense.'

'I echo that sentiment, Hunter. My initial thought was that this was maybe a burglary gone wrong, but now I don't think so. The body was found on the floor next to the sofa, and her bag's still on the sofa, with her mobile and purse still inside it. Cards and cash in the purse and a cheque book untouched. Also, there doesn't appear to be any signs of a search. In fact, judging by the trail of bloodied footprints, the offender appears to have confined themselves to the room where Elisabeth Bertolutti was killed. And, from what I saw of the body yesterday, she didn't have any injuries to suggest she put up any type of prolonged fight. Sure, she had a few defence injuries to her hands and forearms, but that was all. It was over and done with pretty quickly. If you're wanting my opinion – given the location, and given the circumstances, and the fact that nothing's been disturbed, and it's only her laptop that's been taken, I'd say this looks to me more like a planned attack for the precise purpose of taking her laptop.'

Hunter nodded. He agreed with the SOCO Supervisor's assessment.

'I'd be looking at why just the computer was stolen. Maybe there was something on it he wanted.' After a short pause he asked, 'What job did she do?'

Hunter shrugged his shoulders. 'Something to do with buying and selling artwork. That's what Bully told me. She and Bully's girlfriend were in a partnership.'

'I'm no aficionado of the art world, Hunter, but that doesn't sound like the type of job which would get you murdered, does it?'

Mouth zipped, Hunter nodded in agreement with Duncan's sentiment. Then he said, 'And it doesn't help me resolve what her links are to Polly's murder.'

'I'm afraid I can't help you there.' Duncan placed a hand on Hunter's shoulder. 'Sorry, buddy.'

Hunter let out a deep sigh. He asked, 'Am I okay to have a look round now?'

'Yeah, we're just about ready to start packing up. We've been all through the cottage. Everything evidence-wise is contained within the lounge area. The rest of the rooms appear to be untouched.'

Duncan lifted the entrance flap of the tent and Hunter slipped past him.

Stepping over the threshold onto the first protective plate, which had been set down on the carpeted floor, Hunter paused. A fusty, unpleasant coppery smell, caught at the back of his nose and throat. He immediately knew it was stale blood. Crinkling his nose and only taking shallow breaths, he spent a few moments journeying his eyes around the room.

With its whitewashed plaster walls and beamed low ceiling, he immediately saw that the place had retained its cottage feel. The sitting room was small and cosy. A large Chesterfield sofa, and a dark wood sideboard, took up most of the space. Next to the sofa was a low level table and beside that an upturned framed painting.

Hunter fought back the curious urge to pick it up and view it. *Disturbing evidence.*

A tiled, cast iron Victorian fireplace made for a striking centre piece. Spent ashes in the grate told him it was in regular use. Above the fireplace a large Venetian style mirror helped maximise the light coming in through the left hand side casement window. Around the walls was hung a selection of paintings. He noted that they all appeared to be framed oils, and were an eclectic mix of contemporary and 20th century canvases. He thought he recognised the style of some of the works. He told himself that when the time was right he would spend a bit more time looking around the collection. Right now though, he had to focus on this being a crime scene. And catching sight of the dark stain on the mocha coloured carpet, where Elisabeth's body had lain the previous evening, was his stark reminder of that. Using the stepping plates he skirted past the sideboard to where a door led into a compact dining kitchen. Here, he stepped onto a stone-flagged floor. The room was cold. To Hunter's left the full length of the wall was taken up by pastel green painted units, which were in keeping with the cottage feel. The floor cupboards flowed into an L-shape arrangement set beneath a facing window. It gave him a glimpse over the garden and out across the open countryside. Under different circumstances he would have said the view was even a more beautiful setting than his own outlook from his kitchen window back home, though today the bleak conditions presented only a panoramic palette of dull grey and brown tones. He dragged his eyes away. To the right a wooden staircase led up to the first floor. Hunter climbed the uneven stairs. The landing was long and thin and three doors led off it. The first door was ajar. He stuck his head around it. The room was smaller than he had anticipated. The bedroom walls were covered in pink floral print wallpaper. A large double brass bed and a stand alone wardrobe filled most of the space. He scrutinised the room for a couple of minutes but nothing stood out as warranting further inspection and so he moved on to the second door. This one was closed and he opened it inwards into an even smaller room. A small casement window allowed in a generous helping of light, warming cream painted uneven walls. It held only a single bed. The whiff of oil paint drifted across his nostrils, and he quickly realised why when he spotted the artist easel in the far corner. On it was a townscape featuring a section of bridge and a river. The scene reminded him of a town he had driven through in France. The painting was dull and dark and looked antique. On the floor next to it were several paintings stacked back-to-back. This room looked as though it served as a working studio as well as a bedroom. For a brief moment Hunter's thoughts drifted away. He reflected on some of the paintings he had noticed hanging on the sitting room walls downstairs, and then rewound the conversation with Duncan a few minutes earlier and wondered if Elisabeth Bertolutti's murder was to do with her job. He stored the thought for later. He stepped back into the hallway and checked out what was behind the last door. As he guessed it was the bathroom. It was bijou and fitted out with a white suite, which had seen better days, but it was clean and tidy. Determining that he'd got a feel for the place he returned back down the stairs and made his way outside to the garden.

Duncan Wroe was stepping out of his protective suit.

'Is that you done then now, Duncan?'

'Yes, there's nothing else for me here. The scene's all videoed and photographed. I'll have copies sent across for your morning briefing, and I'll get the prints and DNA samples labelled up by this evening and they'll be sent off to the lab first thing tomorrow.' He pulled out the last leg of his suit, folded it up and dropped it inside an evidence bag. He handed it over to Hunter. 'I'd like to think I can clear up your girlfriend's murder as well as this one.'

It was 6.00 p.m. before Hunter got back to the station. He walked into an MIT office sparse of detectives and relatively quiet.

DI Gerald Scaife was at his desk hunched over a pile of paperwork. Hunter could tell from the colour of the documents that they were witness information forms. He appeared to be slowly checking through them.

DS Mark Gamble, his counterpart, who supervised team two, was leaning against Gemma Cooke's incident board, engaged in conversation with Isobel Stevens from the HOLMES team. Judging by their jerky head movements they appeared to be discussing the content of the information displayed upon the whiteboard. Hunter could see that more had been added to it since the morning briefing.

That couldn't be said for Elisabeth Bertolutti's incident board next to it. Except for her personal details and the two timeframe logs, Tony Bullars' girlfriend witnessing the murder, and the discovery of her body by the police, nothing further had been written.

The only other person in the room was Barry Newstead, and he was in Grace's seat, head down over her desk, his attention seemingly lost in the contents of a very thick file.

Hunter shucked off his coat and dropped it on the corner of his desk. The action startled Barry. His head shot up.

'Oh, hey up, Hunter,' he said, pulling off his reading glasses. 'Just got back from the scene?'

Hunter dropped into his chair, nodded and let out a sigh.

'Drawn a blank?'

'Not exactly drawn a blank, Barry, but I haven't got anything worth shouting about. Duncan's found a couple of footprints in her blood near to where her body was. He thinks the marks are those of trainers or something similar. And he's found glove marks at the point of entry. But other than that, zilch.'

'What about house-to-house?'

'That's not brought up anything either. And that surprises me. I mean, you know what that place is like. The whole of Street is no more than a couple of dozen houses, and there's only one road in and out and yet no one heard or saw anything until we arrived. It's not even as if we can extend it either. I mean the nearest houses to the place are a couple of farms half a mile away. I'm hoping either forensics comes up trumps, or Grace and Bully can get something from their interview.' He picked his coat off the edge of the table and swung it, matador style, over the back of his seat. 'Have you heard from them yet?'

'Spoke to Grace about half an hour ago. They'd just got back. Been a swine on the motorway apparently. They're not expecting to be done before briefing.'

Hunter rolled up his eyes and clucked his tongue. 'Anything from the gaffer?'

'Last I heard she was still trying to find a place to run the incident. She was moaning to the DI earlier about it. And I think she's lost the detectives she'd earmarked to help out because of a murder in Rotherham. A fourteen-year-old girl's body was pulled out of the canal late last night. The rumour is she was mixed up in some kind of sex grooming thing. Could be a paedophile ring. They're throwing everything at it. '

'Just when we didn't need it.'

'I've known worse, mate.'

Hunter dropped his arms onto his blotter. 'Anyway, what are you doing?' Then he sarcastically added, 'That looks like a lot of pages for you to be reading.'

Barry checked him with a scowl. 'I can read joined up writing now you know.'

Hunter couldn't help crack a grin. 'Is it anything to do with this job?'

'It is actually, Hunter.' Barry collapsed the page he had been reading. 'This is the report and summary file into Polly's murder.'

Hunter locked onto Barry's eyes. His colleague had captured his attention.

He tapped the bound file. 'I did this for the District Detective Superintendent back in nineteen eighty-nine. It summarises every bit of evidence we had at the time – witnesses and forensics. As you know we worked on it for almost eighteen months but got nowhere. The enquiries completely dried up and so the Super made the decision to wind it up.' He flattened his hand atop the file. 'Because I've worked on your girlfriend's case, the gaffer told me yesterday afternoon that she was attaching me to your enquiry. She asked me to contact the Cold Case Unit and see if we still had the paperwork for it.' Barry slipped away his hand and dipped it below his desk. Making a jabbing motion with a pointing finger he said, 'One of the civilian investigators from the Unit dropped these off an hour ago.'

Hunter levered himself up from his seat and craned his neck across the adjoining desks. Neatly stacked on the floor beside Barry he saw six archive boxes.

Barry continued, 'They've got everything. By sheer coincidence, Polly's investigation was one of those which had been ear-marked to be re-examined. Apparently, they've been getting excellent results from the nineteen eighties cases of late. Especially with DNA hits. And hers was one of those they've still got all the exhibits for, so we just might get lucky, especially if her killer was not forensically aware – as most of them weren't all those years ago.' He raised one of his shovel-like hands and crossed his fingers. He held the pose for a good few seconds before dropping his hand and returning his eyes to the file in front of him. 'It's such a long time since I put this together that I'm just reacquainting myself with the job.'

'I wouldn't mind having a read of that myself. See what you wrote about me all those years ago.'

Barry gripped the top section of papers and made a motion to close it. 'I can't let you see this, Hunter. You were my number one suspect.'

Hunter narrowed his eyes, 'Yeah, as if.'

With an earnest look he said, 'No seriously, Hunter. I've spoken with the gaffer about it. She's pulling you off the case.'

Hunter pushed himself back in his chair. A vision flashed inside his head. He was back in September 1988. At his home. Barry and another detective were grilling him as if he had killed Polly. He was sitting on the sofa with his parents present. Following that ordeal they searched his room – rifled through all his personal things. He shook away the image.

Back stiffened he said, 'Straight up, Barry.' Hunter checked Barry's look then he caught the edges of his mouth curling up. 'You're winding me up, you shit-hole.'

Barry broke into a laugh. 'That'll teach you, Detective Sergeant Kerr for taking the piss out of a seasoned pro.' He slipped on his reading glasses and dipped his head back into the file. 'Now go and get your Uncle Barry a brew, and no more of your lip, I've got to get up to speed before briefing in half an hour. And if you're really good I'll read it to you before bedtime.'

Hunter slid back his chair.

It would be good to be working alongside his old mentor again, he thought, as he got up to make them both a hot drink.

Detectives began drifting back into the incident room from 6.30 p.m. Thereafter, Hunter checked his watch at almost five minute intervals hoping Grace and Tony would soon join him. He gave up checking at five minutes to seven when SIO Dawn Leggate made her entrance. Unusually she appeared to be ruffled. Her face was flushed and she was struggling with her top coat; tugging at the sleeves while clomping towards the front of the room. Finally dragging it off, she dropped it onto the nearest desk.

Holding up her hands in exasperated fashion she said, 'Sorry everyone, running a little late.' She swung her eyes upon Hunter. 'The Rotherham murder's totally cocked things up. The incident room I'd earmarked for us has been given over for that enquiry and so I've been on the phone most of the afternoon trying to find us another room. You'll be pleased to know I finally got one, and not too far away as well.' Her mouth tightened. 'I've used the word pleased, though I don't think you'll be too impressed when I tell you what I've got.' She paused a good few seconds, as if letting her words sink in. Her eyes remained clamped on Hunter's. 'I've commandeered the Stolen Vehicle Squad office down the corridor.'

Hunter's mouth dropped open.

The Detective Superintendent continued, 'I expected that reaction. I know it's a bit small, so I've also commandeered the rest room next door as well. The admin staff who use it for their breaks are not too impressed, but needs must. It's the only room which has an adjoining door to link both rooms. Until I can find us somewhere else that's going to have to do. Headquarters are sending us a couple of technicians tomorrow to link up the computers, and I've also got the use of the two detectives from the Stolen Vehicle Squad and a detective and a civilian from the Cold Case Unit.' Raising her eyebrows she still held Hunter's gaze. 'I know I told you earlier that I had something of interest to tell you from Elisabeth Bertolutti's PM, well I have, but, I want to hold that off for tonight. Grace and Tony are still interviewing our major witness, and I've been unable to check things back with them, so unless you have anything that's pressing I'm going to suggest we hold off the briefing for the Street Lane job until tomorrow morning and then we'll do a full catch up?'

Keeping his feeling of frustration to himself, Hunter shook his head, 'No, that's fine. Nothing of importance has come up anyway. It's too early for forensics and we haven't got anything from the search of the garden or from house-to-house.'

She acknowledged his response with a brief nod. 'Okay, tomorrow morning it is then. Nine a.m.' The SIO pulled her gaze back to the room and shuffled her eyes around the room. 'Okay, Gemma Cooke.' She levelled her look upon Detective Sergeant Mark Gamble, 'What have we got?'

The DS picked up some scribbled notes from his desk and offered, 'Still no luck with the necklace. We've again spoken with the friends she was out with in Sheffield on the night before she was murdered and she certainly didn't have it on then. In fact one of them showed me some photos, that they took with their mobiles, of their night out for her Facebook page and she certainly didn't have it on then. They all say the same as her mum, that they've never noticed her wearing that necklace. Secondly, me and Mike visited Adam Fields, in Armley prison, this afternoon, and showed it him. He was adamant that he didn't buy it her and he said he'd never seen it before.' He broke off and sought out Mike Sampson's face. 'We believe him.'

Mike supported his statement with a nod and chipped in, 'He certainly seemed puzzled when we asked him about it. And it's not something he's any reason to lie about.'

Picking the thread back up DS Gamble said, 'We've also recovered the clothing that Adam Fields was wearing on the eighteenth. It was still at his mate's flat where he was dossing. It's not been washed or anything. We've checked the T-shirt and jeans against CCTV images from the last pub he was in and it certainly looks to be the same gear he had on. That's been bagged up and will be going off to forensics tomorrow. We've also done a search of the flat where he was staying with SOCO help. They've taped a few items but they haven't found any blood. The place looks clean.'

The moment DS Gamble finished Dawn said, 'Okay, thanks for that Mark,' and looking around the room added, 'What about the taxi she and Tom Hagan came home in?'

From his desk, DC Andy France, at 26, the youngest member of MIT, raised a hand and piped up. 'That's me, boss, tracked the taxi driver down early this morning.' He sprung open his notebook and fixed a page with his finger. Reading from it he said, 'Mohammed Rauf, married, three kids, lives in

Darnall. No form and no intel on him. It's his own cab and it's registered. He's worked the city centre, especially around the front of the City Hall for the last five years.' He looked up and continued, 'He can remember Tom Hagan and Gemma, because it was the first time he'd dropped a fare off in Barnwell. He also said that he can remember Gemma being a bit upset when she first got into the taxi. Going on about someone hassling or following her. He only caught some of the conversation, but thought it was to do with an ex-boyfriend. He said that Tom was telling her that he'd sort it and was calming her down. Very much in line with what DC Hagan has said in his interview. I asked him if there was any argument or anything like that between them. He said no, they were just chatting. He couldn't pick up on the gist of their conversation because they weren't talking that loud. Neither of them appeared to be drunk and they weren't doing anything in the cab to draw attention to themselves. He said it was Tom who asked him to drop them both off outside the pizza place in Barnwell. Tom paid the fare and he saw them both go into the pizza place. He roughly places the time as just after midnight, but can't be exact. That's it. It was a busy night for him so he shot back into Sheffield for more fares.' He closed up his book. 'I also visited the pizza place this after and spoke with the manager. He was working the night of the seventeenth and into the eighteenth but he doesn't remember DC Hagan or Gemma coming in. As he pointed out, one customer is like any other, unless they cause him problems. However, he has got CCTV installed and he let me view the tape for that day. It's not very good quality, but it's good enough to pick out someone when you know who you're looking for. Tom and Gemma did go in there. The video was timed and dated. They went into the pizza place at six minutes past midnight and left at twenty-one minutes past.'

'Okay, Andy, thank you.' Detective Superintendent Leggate bounced her gaze around the room. 'Anything from Sheffield city centre CCTV?'

Mike Sampson offered up, 'It's still being looked through. We've managed to isolate the area she would have walked along to get to the City Hall from her last pub, and we've now got a rough time of when she got into the taxi, so I picked up those discs this morning and left them with two Viewers. I checked in just before I came into briefing and they've gone through the images from four of the cameras but they still have a couple more to go through. They're hoping to have finished them all by lunchtime tomorrow.'

SIO Dawn Leggate clasped a hand around the nearest edge of Gemma Cooke's incident board. She scanned the room, 'Anything else anyone?'

There was no reaction.

She brought the briefing to a close. 'Okay, good work everyone. It certainly tightens up our time-frame. We've still got CCTV work to do and forensics is still with the lab, so if no one has anything else to offer we'll wrap things up for the day and re-convene tomorrow morning at eight a.m.'

Immediately after briefing, Dawn collared DI Scaife, checked with him that he would get the Elisabeth Bertolutti incident board updated, requested that a new one be started for the Polly Hayes cold-case murder, and then left him with the task of ensuring that everything for the two investigations be moved down to the new incident room ready for the following morning's briefing. Then she looked in at her office and made sure there was nothing urgent waiting for her on her desk before heading down the back stairs to her car. She drove the twenty-five minute journey to Michael's running through the day's events inside her head. The radio was on but the music washed over her; she had two recent murders and a cold-case enquiry to grapple with and it wasn't easy separating her thoughts. It was only as she pulled onto the drive did she realise that she hadn't remembered any of her passage home.

Letting herself in with the newly cut key Michael had given her she called out that she was home. Then leaning back against the front door, pushing it closed, she let out a deep sigh and dumped her bag next to the hall table. Kicking it against the skirting, she toe-heeled off her court shoes and made her way through to the kitchen from where the delicious smells of cooking drifted towards her.

'Something smells good,' she said, pulling off her coat and dressing it around the back of one of the high stools by the breakfast bar.

Michael Robshaw glanced back over his shoulder. He was cooking at the range.

'Fillet steak,' he responded, 'with jacket potato and salad,' he added.

'Sounds good I'm starving.'

'There's wine in the fridge, want to pour us some.' He suggested and returned to cooking the steak.

Pulling open the fridge door, Dawn removed a bottle of Chardonnay from the rack, picked out two glasses from a glass fronted dresser, arranged them side-by-side and poured out two generous helpings of chilled wine. 'How's your day been?'

'Nothing like yours I bet. Sorry I couldn't help out with the incident room, the Rotherham job looks as though it's going to be a big one.'

Dawn sidled next to him, handed him a two-thirds filled glass and leaned in and planted a kiss on his cheek. She sneaked a look at the contents of the pan. Michael had basted the fillet in olive oil. It looked and smelled good. She lifted her eyes and caught his look. Then, giving him a 100 watt smile, she responded with, 'It's not your fault.' She stroked his arm, still holding his gaze. A warm glow enveloped her. She felt herself so fortunate. Dawn had met Michael six months earlier, during her pursuit of two sadistic killers, who had brutally murdered four people in her native Scotland and had then fled down to Barnwell in search of another victim. Here they had been finally cornered and captured with the help of Michael's team.

Then, she had been a Detective Chief Inspector, on a career fast-track, involved in high-profile work, with her own CID team, and most importantly no baggage. But then had come the shocking revelation, which had rocked her world. In the midst of the investigation she had learned that her husband Jack had been cheating on her with a girl from his work. When she had first received the news she hadn't wanted to believe it. In fact, at first, she had tried to ignore – as if it would simply go away. But the only thing that went away was her marriage. The lousy, lanky shite had even blamed her for his indiscretions. Said it had happened because she was never there for him. 'Always at your precious work,' he had mocked down the phone, when she had finally tracked him down to 'that bimbo's whorehouse' and demanded to know why. She had wanted to beat him to a pulp with the handset. Instead she had cut him off and slung the receiver across the room, smashing it to smithereens. She had been hurting so much during that investigation and Michael had been the one who had supported her when she had been at her lowest ebb. At the end of the investigation, he had taken her for a celebratory meal and over drinks he had planted the thought in her head about cutting all her ties and starting afresh. He had told her that he had been offered promotion to Detective Chief Superintendent – The Force Crime Manager. It would mean that the position of SIO with Barnwell Major Investigation Team would be becoming vacant and he suggested that she should consider applying for the job. 'You've certainly got all the credentials and more than capable of achieving the post,' he had said, holding her gaze across the dining table. Those sexy blue eyes, and comforting words had been the catalyst and she had applied for the position. Four months ago she had gained promotion to Detective Superintendent and had been elated. Unfortunately, that elation had been tinged with one of sadness as she had said goodbye to her team. In fact the celebrations in the pub had felt like a wake. She had carried herself through the ordeal wearing a mask of false happiness. On the day she had emptied her desk and driven away from the police station at Stirling she had repeatedly told herself 'that it was for the best,' despite the fact she hadn't been truly convinced it was. And she had made the journey down into England with a heavy heart. Since then she had thrown herself into her new job, to ease the pain. In that time Dawn had used Michael as her crutch. Not only as a confidante with whom she could talk through the mess of her broken marriage – he had suffered the same fate years earlier – but also as a colleague to guide her through the different police procedures 'in this neck of the woods.' During those four months she had engaged in many evening chat sessions with him. Some had been on the phone but the majority had been at his place over a bottle of wine. It had amazed her how much they had in common and it hadn't come as a surprise when Michael had asked her to move in. That had been six weeks ago.

'There's a letter come for you.' Michael jerked his head sideways, aiming a look towards a low unit by the back door. 'Personal,' he added.

'Personal?' she repeated, diverting her gaze to where she spied a solitary white envelope propped against the fruit bowl.

Michael nodded and with raised eyebrows said, 'Looks official.'

Dawn took a slug of her wine, set down her glass, and sidled across to the opposite side of the kitchen. Picking up the typed addressed envelope she turned it over, inspecting it, to see if it gave any clues as to where it had come from. There was none. She tore open the flap and lifted out the contents. It was a single sheet of typed paper on headed notepaper.

'It's from Jack's solicitors,' she announced without looking up, immersing herself in the print. Two weeks ago she had filed for a divorce, citing adultery as the reason. As her eyes danced across the words and she began to take in the thread of the letter she could feel herself getting anxious. As she finished reading the last paragraph that feeling of anxiousness had turned to one of anger. Her chest tightened and with a viperous cry she loudly spat out, 'The bastard.'

Michael met her hate-filled eyes. 'What's he done?'

'What's he done. What's he fucking done!' she took a deep breath. 'He's only cited me for unreasonable behaviour. Unreasonable fucking behaviour. And he wants half my fucking house. He didn't even put a penny into it. My gran left me that house. That's my house.' Crushing the letter and envelope in a vice-like grip she marched back to where she had set down her glass. She snatched it up and downed the remainder of her wine in one gulp.

She heaved an exasperated sigh. 'To be honest, I suppose I should have expected this.'

'Oh why's that.'

'He tried to call me a couple of times but I've cut him off. And he text me last weekend. He's been made redundant and he asked if he could move back into the house as I wasn't using it.'

Michael tilted his head. 'And?'

'I'm afraid I wasn't very polite to him. I told him to go forth and multiply.'

Michael smiled. 'That's my girl.'

She snapped, 'I could strangle the scrawny fucker!' Setting down her glass, she pushed it forward, inviting Michael to pour another. 'Well he's going to get an almighty fucking shock coming.'

Michael poured out another measure of wine. 'I don't want to add to your burden, but he just might be able to claim half of it. That happened with me when I divorced.'

Dawn flashed a wicked smile. 'Nae chance. I tied it up years ago in trust for my goddaughter. Better than any pre-nuptual.'

Michael checked the food he had been stirring and turned down the gas. He returned his gaze. 'If it's any help, I know a good hit-man. Cheaper than a solicitor.'

Taking in his words she examined his face over the rim of her once more empty glass. The look he displayed was earnest. But it was only momentarily. Within a few seconds his expression had cracked to be replaced by one displaying a wide grin.

'And do you know, for a minute there I was going to take to take you up on your offer.'

They both started to laugh.

For Dawn the laughter had been a long time coming.

Then the phone rang in the hall.

- ooOoo -

CHAPTER ELEVEN

Day Ten: 27th March.

The office was deserted. Hunter was the first one in.

Closing the door to with one shoulder, for a brief moment he rested against the set of double-doors, his eyes panning around the office, taking in the peace and calm, though he knew that in another half hour this place would be anything but. Once the troops got in it would become a beehive of activity; workers at their desks, sifting through statements and evidence, making phone calls, discussing tactics, and all of them with one determined focus – catching a killer, or given recent events, two killers.

Suddenly his eyes stalled. At the front of the room, standing shoulder-to-shoulder were the incident boards detailing the murders of Gemma Cooke, Elisabeth Bertolutti and his once beloved Polly Hayes. The sight of them together took him by surprise. He had expected Elisabeth's and Polly's to have been transferred to the new incident room, in readiness for the morning briefing.

As he scrutinised them he let out a crestfallen sigh. It looked as though there was going to be a delay again he mumbled to himself. Though, he was pleased about one thing, he saw that the boards had been updated. As well as full victim details, time-frames had been revised, and appendant to the information were photographs. In the case of Polly's board, though he couldn't make out the contents written upon it, there certainly appeared to be a lot of information on there. He rocked himself forward and set off across the room to get a closer look.

Hunter had just made it to the front of the room when he heard the office doors clatter behind him. Snatching a glance back over his shoulder he hadn't expected to be seeing Detective Superintendent Leggate coming through the gap; she didn't normally come in this early. He saw that her arms were laden with paperwork and she was using a crooked elbow to keep one door open while she edged through.

'Morning, Hunter, I thought you'd be first in,' she greeted, forging her way towards him with a spring in her step. She stopped close by his side, letting out a groan as she dropped the bundle of papers on a nearby desk. Then she began unbuttoning her cashmere coat.

'Glad I've caught you alone.' She nodded towards the wipe boards, 'I bet you're wondering why all three incident boards are still here, aren't you?'

Hunter locked onto her eyes. 'I was actually, yes. Don't tell me we've lost the new incident room, just like we did at Rotherham?'

She returned a grin, 'No, nothing of the sort. I got a phone call last night from DI Scaife. They've been left here for a reason. There's a strong possibility we could be looking at one job.'

'One job!'

Dawn finished unbuttoning her overcoat and heaved it off her shoulders. Then folding it she placed it over her one arm and picked back up her pile of papers. 'It's looking that way. He's doing some of the briefing this morning so I don't want to steal his thunder.' She still held Hunter's gaze. 'Are you going to be all right working on Polly's murder?'

'Yeah sure, why?' He gave her an apprehensive look. 'You're not worried about my involvement in the Tom Hagan incident, are you?'

She shook her head. 'Goodness me, no. That wasn't your doing. What DC Hagan did was of his own doing.'

'Are you referring to what happened with Adam Fields? I can assure you I've learned my lesson, boss. I won't be going off on one again.'

'No it wasn't that either I was thinking about. Though now you've raised it, I bloody well hope you won't. No I was thinking about you. I need you focussed on this and I know from what Barry's told me that you were pretty well gutted by what happened to her.'

He stole his eyes away from his SIO's gaze and fixed them on Polly's incident board. He couldn't help but be drawn in by the black and white photograph in the top right hand corner. It was of Polly's lifeless form lying face down amongst tall grasses. Around her cloaked torso the ground was stained. Despite the image being in black and white he knew he was looking at blood. Barry had told him what had happened to her all those years ago but this was the first time he had been able to see for himself how her killer had left her. He felt the hairs bristle at the back of his neck. 'It was a long time ago, boss. Twenty-one years in fact. I was a teenager. I can handle it.'

'Well listen, Hunter, if it gets too much for you don't be afraid to come and talk to me, will you.'

He met the Detective Superintendent's concerned look. 'I won't, boss, thank you.'

'Good. Welfare chat over. Now stick the kettle on, Hunter, I've got to plough through this lot before briefing.' She clutched the wedge of documents tight to her chest and turned on her heels.

By 8.00 a.m. the MIT team had assembled, their ranks swollen by the additional officers drawn from the Stolen Vehicle Squad and the Cold Case Unit.

There was an air of expectation in the room. Desk phones had been diverted across to voicemail, and mobile phones switched to silent, everyone paying attention as Detective Superintendent Dawn Leggate took up centre stage at the front of the room. Detective Inspector Gerald Scaife, left his desk and quickly shuffled beside her, lowering his head to scan the contents of several sheets of paper, which he was rearranging in his hands.

She called the room to order. 'Okay let's listen up everyone, quite a bit to be going through this morning, so I need your fullest attention.' She aimed a quick glance at her Office Manager. 'I'm going to immediately hand over to the DI for the first part of this session and once he's done I'll pick things back up.' She threw him a nod. 'The floor's all yours.'

The DI stepped forward and made for the wide-screen TV in the corner of the room. He picked up the remote and fired up the TV. A blue screen appeared.

Facing the team, in his broad Yorkshire accent he said, 'Okay everyone, eyeballs wide for this bit, I've got some interesting CCTV evidence to show you.' He tapped the remote. 'As you know for the last couple of days our Viewers have been checking CCTV from the pubs, and also footage from the cameras in and around the streets of Sheffield where we know Gemma was on St Patrick's night. One of the things we picked up on, from what her mates have said, is that Gemma had an altercation with a man in the Frog & Parrot, the last pub she was in. What we've been able to piece together, from what Gemma told her friends, is that a man apparently pinched her backside while she was coming back from the toilets and she slapped his face and gave him a bit of a slagging for it. None of her friends saw the incident, but one of them did see Gemma having a go at a guy in the corridor near the toilets and stepped in and dragged her away. Unfortunately that part of the pub is not covered by CCTV, and the girl who dragged Gemma away didn't get a good look of him. So, we've only got the most basics of a description, and that is, a white male, clean shaven, probably mid, to late thirties, and tall and slim. That's it. She'd had quite a bit to drink and just wanted to get Gemma back to their party. So in respect of picking anyone out from the pub CCTV over this incident, we haven't had any luck. However, what we have found is this.' He targeted the remote in on the TV and it buzzed into life. Onto the 42 inch screen a street scene appeared. There were tall buildings in the background, while in the foreground half a dozen young people milled around a large, open paved area. None of them appeared to be in any hurry to be anywhere. The scene was a typical one of a mixed crowd out for the night, enjoying themselves. The image was in colour, but it was night time and the tones were muted. Street lamps, dotted around, cast haloes of yellow light, blurring edges, and left the lower parts of buildings in deep shadow.

'The scene you are looking at is from the camera located opposite the City Hall in Barker's Pool.' Using the remote he aimed left of the screen. 'And this narrow street here connects West Street to Division Street. It also goes behind the City

Hall.' Edging the remote sideways, he pointed out a large building with stone steps leading up to a pillared frontage. Its architecture was in the Corinthian style. 'This is the City Hall.' He announced. 'In two seconds you will see Gemma Cooke appear.' Just as the DI had finished his sentence the slim, petite figure of their murder victim came into view, left of screen. She had her head down, eyeing the ground before her. A few paces in, she stopped abruptly and flicked up her head, spinning her gaze away, shooting it in the direction of the narrow road, which led off towards Division Street. She stood stock-still, as if rooted to the spot, for the best part of ten seconds, and then spurred into life and with a pace somewhere between a walk and a jog, she crossed in front of the City Hall and disappeared off screen. The DI froze the picture. 'Without showing you further footage from another camera, I can tell you, she makes straight for the taxi rank where she meets up with DC Tom Hagan. If you recall, she told Tom that she thought she was being followed. Having seen her reaction on that clip we did some further digging and found this.' He rewound the film, back to the part where Gemma was staring down the narrow road towards Division Street. There, he halted its progress and zoomed in. After several seconds he froze the picture. Although the screen was fuzzy, there was enough clarity within the exposure to make out the silhouette of a figure hiding amongst the shadow projected by a nearby building. The grainy character had on dark clothing and was wearing what appeared to be a peaked cap, similar to a baseball hat. DI Scaife faced the room.

A sea of detectives' faces were staring beyond him, their eyes glued to the TV.

'Said it was interesting. And, it gets better.' He re-started the film and the scene changed. A long, well lit street appeared and it was teaming with people. 'This is Division Street. For those who don't know this is one of the busiest streets in Sheffield at night-times. It's full of pubs and fast-food outlets, hence the crowd of people you can see. When we found that image of that person hiding, we knew that there was only two ways that they could come out. One way was into Barker's Pool by the City Hall and the other way was onto Division

Street. We checked the cameras both sides of the connecting street and we found this.' The DI turned his head towards the TV just as a shadowy figure appeared left on screen. The darksome individual was hunched forward, chin tucked into what appeared to be a hooded top. As the character entered the centre of the screen it stopped and slowly lifted its head. It deliberately sought out the CCTV camera and stared directly into the lens. The figure was wearing a mask. Torn eyelets in hessian sacking gave insight into two black holes, and where the mouth should be, a ripped gash had been sewn haphazardly with thick black wool. It looked, every inch, as if the mask was mocking them.

'Freeze the picture there, would you Gerry,' interjected Dawn Leggate.

The image was suspended.

With outstretched arm the Detective Superintendent pointed towards the large flat screen. 'This changes everything.' Her eyes swept the room. None of her team's faces left the TV to look at her. They were hypnotised by the 2D monster before them.

Though she was excited by this latest development she took in a large breath and deliberately controlled the pace of her speech. 'Gemma Cooke told DC Tom Hagan, that she thought she was being followed, and if you recall, she initially thought it might have been something to do with Adam Fields. But let's not also forget, we now have the incident that night in the pub with the guy who pinched her bum. Putting those incidents to one side there is no doubt from that CCTV evidence that someone is hiding and Gemma has spotted them. What we don't know is what happened next. Whether this person followed Gemma or not because that is the last we see of whoever this person is. We lose him or her in the back streets. We are currently trawling through car park cameras to see if this individual gets into a vehicle. We don't know yet if the taxi Gemma and Tom got into was followed. If our masked individual here did follow the taxi, then this is a whole different ball game. And, although it doesn't exactly let DC Hagan or Adam Fields off the hook, it certainly means we have another suspect we need to look at.' She swung her arm towards the furthest whiteboard. 'So armed with this latest CCTV evidence, our first victim, Gemma Cooke.' She paused as if waiting for the name to cement in everyone's mind and then in her Scottish brogue said, 'Okay, now let's re-focus. From the CCTV outside the City Hall we've got a definite time for her and DC Tom Hagan getting into the taxi, and similarly, we also know, from CCTV footage, that she and DC Hagan were inside the pizza place on Barnwell High Street where they ordered a pizza to take out. We know that at twelve twenty-six a.m. on the morning of the eighteenth, when Gemma and Tom Hagan walked out of the pizza place, she was alive. That is concrete evidence.' She broke her eyes away from the incident board and scoured the room as if searching for an acknowledgment. She checked a few nodding heads and then snatched her gaze back to the whiteboard. 'After that we only have DC Tom Hagan's word as to what happened back at her house, including what time he left. He says that Gemma let him out of the back door at approximately quarter to two and that he made his way home via the back streets because he was embarrassed and didn't want to be seen. And although he states he arrived home somewhere around two a.m., we only have his word for it.' She returned her eyes back into the room and honed them in on DC Andy France. 'I believe you've taken the route DC Hagan says he took to get home?'

Andy France replied, 'Yes, boss. He said he did it at a brisk walk. I did it yesterday morning and it took me just over eighteen minutes to walk from Gemma's place to the front of Tom's house.'

Taking back the briefing she said, 'Okay, time-wise that's roughly in line with what he's said.' She returned eye contact back on Gemma's board. 'The next concrete piece of evidence we have is from the statement of neighbour, Valerie Bryce, who telephoned three-nine's at two eleven a.m., stating that she could hear shouting, banging and then breaking glass coming from the rear of Gemma's. She identified Adam Fields as being the person who she saw running from out the alleyway at the side of Gemma's and taking off in the direction of the industrial estate. She finished her phone call with the police operator at two thirteen a.m. A two minute window.' She broke off and scanned the room. 'It's a very tight time-frame, but it's enough time for him to have stabbed Gemma. We know that Adam was certainly angry that night, and he has got form for violence against women and he has admitted to assaulting Gemma previously. The thing in his favour is that we have recovered his clothing, which he had on that night, and early indications are that none of it is bloodstained.' She jabbed a finger back towards the incident board. 'We can see from the crime scene photos that this was a vicious attack. Blood was everywhere. If Adam Fields had killed Gemma then surely he would have been covered in blood.' Dawn waited for her comments to sink in and then diverted the direction of her arrowed finger to the photograph of the kitchen knife. 'The one thing that we can't get away from, and again it's concrete evidence, is the fact DC Hagan's fingerprints are all over the murder weapon. I know he can account for that, because he told Hunter and Grace in interview that he had used that knife to cut up the pizza. But I think any one of us in this room would have thought up a similar answer given the same circumstances.' She took a longer than normal pause before continuing, 'However...,' she pointed towards the TV, '...if we now bring in this individual as a prime suspect, and surmise that after disappearing off camera, he or she got into a vehicle and followed Gemma and Tom's taxi, then we have a bigger time-frame to focus on.' She surveyed the room. 'Between DC Hagan leaving Gemma Cooke's house and Adam Fields arriving we have a twenty-one minute time-frame. And I think you would all agree that is a more realistic time-frame for this vicious attack to have happened in.' She held up a hand. 'So, let's just speculate a moment. Let's say that Gemma lets DC Hagan out of the house, and then, as one would normally do, locks up. This masked suspect here, has followed Gemma and Tom Hagan home and is waiting somewhere nearby, until he sees Tom leave, and then he makes his way to the back door and knocks. Gemma thinks it's DC Hagan who's come back, and so, without checking, opens up and lets this killer in. Gemma, confronted by our masked psychopath here, would no doubt go into a panic, there's a bit of a scuffle, and in the midst of that scuffle, he or she picks up the kitchen knife, which was on the side, and stabs Gemma repeatedly. They then leave locking the door behind them. We know Gemma's door has a yale lock which locks automatically. The next thing that happens is Adam Fields turns up, an angry man, because a mate of his has seen Gemma and Tom going into the house together and has rung him. Remember, in interview, he said the kitchen light was on and the back door was locked, and so after getting no response to his banging, he kicks it in. He said that as he pushed the door open he saw that there was blood everywhere and then he found Gemma dead on the kitchen floor.' She bounced her gaze around the room. She noted that quite a few of the team were nodding. 'So, let's just hold onto what I've just said, because I want to introduce a few other pieces of evidence which will firm up that speculation. I'm going to switch to our most recent murder.' She speared a finger towards the middle incident board. 'Elisabeth Bertolutti.' Dawn dotted her look around the room and then homed in on DC Bullars. 'I'm going to ask Tony to update us on the interview he and Grace had with Linane Brazier yesterday evening.'

Tony had been fiddling with his pen. He stopped rolling it between his fingers and clamped it between both hands. He exchanged a glance with Grace and then faced his colleagues. 'As you know, yesterday, Grace and I went down to Richmond upon Thames, to pick up Linane Brazier who'd actually witnessed Elisabeth being killed while she was Skyping her.' He paused, then continued, 'It's no secret that Linane is my girlfriend – we've been seeing one another for almost four months.' He glanced at his hands, released the pen from his grasp, laid it carefully on his desk, and returned his gaze into the room. 'Because of that I can give you some brief background as to their relationship. Linane and Elisabeth were not only good friends they were partners in business. They bought art, mainly old paintings, restored them sometimes and then sold them on to dealers or private collectors. They've been doing that for almost two years.' He thumbed the edge of his chin. 'Linane first met Elisabeth eight years ago, when they were both at university. They were on the same fine art course. As you've probably guessed Elisabeth is not English. She's Italian. She comes from Venice. Her parents own a gallery there and wanted her to be involved in the business from the restoration point. The initial idea was that after getting her degree she would take up employment with a gallery in London and learn the technique of restoration. That's where Linane met Elisabeth. They were both taken on by the same gallery...' He broke off while he checked some notes he had written. He scanned them for several seconds. Then he continued, '...six years ago. They became friends and apparently Elisabeth invited her to a couple of auctions where she bought old paintings, Italian scenes, for her parents' gallery, restored them and shipped them over. Linane used to help with the restoration to earn some extra money. After doing it for a couple of years they both realised they could make quite a tidy profit between them and so they decided to give it a go. They got a base in London three years ago and began their own business of buying and restoring paintings.'

'So how did Elisabeth and Linane end up here?' interrupted Mike Sampson.

'The rent of their place in London kept going up and was eating well into their profits so they decided to look elsewhere. They'd built up a good business using the internet and so realised they didn't need to be actually based in London. Linane is from round here. Her parents own a restaurant in Sheffield. They're French, but Linane was born here. Her dad shoots with the Estate Manager at Wentworth and he got her the cottage at Street, just over a year ago. They ran the business from there.' Tony paused, checked he still had everyone's attention and continued. 'They still needed the London auction houses and so would take it in turns to go down there whenever they needed to. That was why Linane was down there yesterday. She'd been to a sale and was staying over at a friend's flat in Richmond. Elisabeth had apparently been down to Somerset yesterday to view a painting which they'd been offered privately. She'd just got back when the attack happened. That's how Linane managed to be Skyping her. Elisabeth was showing her the painting she'd just bought.' Tony relayed the specific details of the attack as witnessed by Linane Brazier. He added, 'I believe this is where I now reveal my interesting piece of evidence. He scanned some of his colleagues' faces. 'Linane was unable to identify Elisabeth's attacker. The person was dressed in dark clothing and was wearing a mask.' He broke off for a few seconds, to let what he had just revealed sink in. He nodded towards the image still displayed on the flat screen TV. 'Linane described the mask as being made of a sacking material. Something similar to hessian. She said that in a way it reminded her of the one the Elephant Man wore in the film, but that the mouth was stitched with dark thread. She said it made it look as though there were jagged teeth.'

SIO Dawn Leggate chirped up, 'Thank you Tony, if you don't mind I'll come in at that point.' She explored the faces of her team. 'You don't need me to say that this is just too much of a coincidence. We have two vicious murders of females, both of them stabbings, in the space of a week of one another, and in both of them a masked individual features. I used the word speculation earlier on, when I ran through the sequence of events leading up to and including the attack upon Gemma Cooke. I would now like to put the word speculation to bed and focus on this being relevant evidence. I also want to introduce something else I learned yesterday from the post-mortem on Elisabeth Bertolutti. Tony hasn't mentioned it because I asked him not to.' She zeroed in on DS Kerr. 'Hunter, this will go some way to solve the puzzle of why Polly Hayes T-shirt was on Elisabeth Bertolutti's body.' She returned her gaze into the room. 'First of all, as you've heard, Tony has told us in detail about the attack upon Elisabeth as witnessed by Linane. During her interview the specific question was asked as to what top Elisabeth was wearing at the time she was attacked, and I can tell you she wasn't wearing the Bon Jovi T-shirt she was found in. Linane is adamant that Elisabeth was wearing a white cotton blouse at the time.' Her face took on a stern expression. 'We have not found that white blouse.' She let the detectives' take in what she had said, before continuing. 'I said some way to resolve the mystery of why Polly's T shirt was Elisabeth's body because Professor Lizzie McCormack, who carried out Elisabeth's post-mortem, states that the Bon Jovi T-shirt was put on after the attack. That T-shirt has old, dry bloodstains upon it, as well as fresh bloodstains from Elisabeth's wounds, and the knife tears in the fabric do not line up with the stab sites upon Elisabeth's body. Barry's already told me that when Polly's body was found, back in nineteen eighty-eight, it had been wrapped in a dark green cloak. I think this has solved that puzzle.' Dawn's eyes diverted away from Hunter and roamed the room. She could see she had everyone's fullest attention. 'Unless anyone wishes to correct me, I think what we have here is a killer who is a trophy collector, who is switching items between his kills. For me, it's not just the T-shirt business, but the necklace found on Gemma's body which reinforces my thought. That necklace has been a puzzle since her parents mentioned it didn't belong to her, and of course, as we know, it had the wrong initials inside.' She raised her eyebrows. 'I'm guessing we still haven't found anything out about the necklace?'

Mike Sampson responded, 'That was my job, boss. And no we haven't. I can't find anyone who has seen that necklace before, or knows where it came from. I've shown it to a few local jewellers. They tell me it's sterling silver – not an expensive one, and it's a good few years old – its date stamp is nineteen ninety-five.'

For a brief moment Dawn played with her bottom lip. 'Okay, I still want some digging around with that enquiry. Let's contact other forces, see if they have anything outstanding, murders or attacks on women where jewellery has been taken. I also want Adam Fields' mate re-visiting. The one who lives on Manvers Terrace, and who rang Adam when he saw Gemma and Tom going into her house. I want to know if he saw anyone else on the street. Do the same with Gemma's neighbour, Valerie Bryce. And let's get hold of the cloak that Polly Hayes was found wearing when she was killed and make some fresh enquiries. We have an M.O. here of a very dangerous individual that needs following up. We know he's killed at least three times, one of those was twenty one years ago.' With an earnest look she said, 'Something tells me there are more bodies out there.'

- ooOoo –

CHAPTER TWELVE

Day Eleven: 28th March.

Hands clasped behind his head, steadying his heaving breath, Hunter stood roughly at the spot where they had found Polly's body, twenty-one years ago, staring out across the landscape. He had been stationary for only a few minutes but already the cold was beginning to creep through his running gear. He stamped his feet to release the tightening in his calves and a sharp pain, like an electric shock, jolted his ankles. The ground was solid. There had been an acute temperature drop overnight and this morning a hoar frost decorated everything.

He unhooked his fingers and dropped his hands down by his side. Taking a deep breath, he held it.

The pangs of guilt are back.

He had set off on his normal route into work, but a mile into his jog, the haunting image of Elisabeth Bertolutti's bloodied body, dressed in Polly's T-shirt, had invaded his thoughts, and he had deviated into the woods and followed the trail up to where he was now.

He released a pent-up breath. A silvery shroud left his mouth and wavered on the still, cold air. It caught his attention. Pulling back his gaze from his panoramic view of the Dearne Valley, he watched it drift away. Then, for no apparent reason, the black and white crime scene photographs, from Polly's murder file, wormed their way inside his head, and he glanced down at the ground, as if expecting to see her lifeless form laid out before him. He felt the hairs prickle at the back of his neck. Sometimes he wished he could switch his brain off.

Pinching the bridge of his nose and closing his eyes, he tried to rid himself of the images, but they hung around. *This was one of those moments.*

He had been here before. Many times. Though not in recent years. He had locked away his thoughts and memories of Polly a long time ago. Now, they were centre stage in his life again.

He knew that what had happened three days ago was the reason behind it. That vision back in the cottage in Street had also been a stark reminder of his past wrongdoing.

He snapped open his eyes. *You have to stop doing this to yourself, Hunter Kerr. You can make amends by catching her killer.*

In the distance the morning sun was making its appearance above a hillside. A warm glow lit up the horizon. He began a gentle jog on the spot – re-invigorating the circulation in his lower limbs.

Time for work.

Today he had the task of visiting Polly's parents to inform them of the investigation. It wasn't something he was looking forward to.

He pulled up the hood of his training top and stepped back onto the path.

Hand poised, ready to deliver a knock, Hunter froze. A sudden feeling of dread engulfed him. He stared into the patterned glass panel of Peter and Lynda Hayes front door. His own shadowy image reflected back. He could feel his skin becoming clammy. Although he had visited this address dozens of times in the past this was one visit he hadn't thought about making.

Taking a deep breath he rapped. He did his best to make it sound nothing like his policeman's knock.

Within twenty seconds Peter Hayes answered the door. A look of surprise registered on his face.

'Hello, Hunter…' Then his voice broke off.

Hunter watched Peter's pale blue eyes stray over his shoulder. His face changed to an earnest look. Hunter knew he had clocked Grace following him down the driveway.

He returned his gaze to Hunter. 'This is about Polly, isn't it?'

'Yes it is. Can we come in?'

Peter Hayes turned and shuffled away down the hall, leaving the door open.

Hunter and Grace traipsed in after him, following him into the lounge. When they entered Peter and his wife, Lynda, were standing close together. Lynda was grasping her husband's arm.

She said, 'Is it about what's been on the news. That woman's murder?'

Hunter thought he saw pain register in her eyes. He threw her a concerned look, nodded, and clarified with, 'The one near Wentworth.' He pointed out the sofa behind them, indicating that he wished them to sit. He chose one of the armchairs. It was a chair he had sat in on many occasions. He tried to remember the last time. When Polly had first been killed his visits had been almost on a weekly basis. Then, when he had joined the police he had called in every few months or so, while on the beat, to remind them he hadn't forgotten them and that he was still making his own enquiries into Polly's murder. The visits had slowed down when he had entered CID, and more so, when Jonathan and Daniel had come along. If truth be told he'd felt uncomfortable since he'd met and then married Beth. As if he was betraying them. Now he couldn't remember the last time he had been here. It must be well over a year ago, he thought to himself. Suddenly, he felt guilty again.

As he watched them sink into the cushions, exchanging glances and reassuring one another, he couldn't help but notice how the pair had aged. The blue in their eyes was no longer as intense and bright and their faces were heavily lined. Peter's once brown hair was greying towards white.

Hunter quickly scanned the room. Except for a change in decor it was still very much how he remembered it. The three-piece suite was the same, as was the sideboard, and that was still cluttered with the pottery clowns, which Lynda collected. Hung above the stone fireplace was the Cornish seascape he had painted when he first dated their daughter; they had supplied him with one of their holiday snaps and he had gifted them with it. It seemed such a naïve piece now, but he had been so proud of it at the time. He could still visualise how their faces had lit up when he had presented it to them. He was so glad they still appreciated it enough to display it on their wall. Close to it, in one alcove, was a large selection of framed photographs, featuring Polly. Her smiling features pricked his conscience. He dragged his eyes from them back to Peter and Lynda and said, 'I wanted to come and see you personally to tell you this. I always said if I ever had any news about Polly's murder I'd make sure I was the first to tell you.' He met their curious and expectant looks. 'We're re-investigating Polly's case.'

Lynda offered him a puzzled frown, 'Hunter, that's really good news, but what's Polly's murder got to do with that woman's in Wentworth. Do we know her?'

Hunter shook his head, 'No, I don't think so.' He paused and checked their faces. 'What I'm going to tell you now mustn't go outside this room.'

They nodded an acknowledgment of understanding.

'It's not that I don't trust you. I do. But we don't want the press to get hold of what I'm going to tell you. Not yet anyway. They'll get hold of it soon enough and then we'll have our hands full.'

Peter replied, 'You know you can trust us.'

Hunter settled his gaze upon Lynda. 'As you've already mentioned, it is about what's been on the news. The murder near Wentworth.'

Lynda exhibited a puzzled look. 'You've just said we don't know this other woman that's been killed.' Her expression changed. 'Then is it to do with who killed her? Is it the same person who killed them both?'

Hunter assented with a brief dip of his head. 'That's something we're looking into. It's a strong possibility.' Then he said, 'Remember that day she was killed?'

Lynda quickly delivered, 'I've never forgotten it.'

Hunter checked himself, 'Course not, forgive me.' Then with a qualifying look he added, 'I don't want to upset you with any of this but we'll be going back over every statement ever made in that enquiry, and then be re-visiting every witness to see if anything different or fresh springs to mind. You are the first to be seen. Are you okay to go back over things?'

Peter and Lynda both returned a nod.

Peter said, 'Anything that will help catch her killer.'

'Fingers crossed,' replied Hunter. 'Okay, now about your original statement. In it you told detectives that the last time you'd seen her she was wearing that Bon Jovi T-shirt she'd got at that concert we went to and a pair of jeans.'

Lynda replied, 'Yeah, I was the last to see her here. Peter was on days. It was just after nine that morning. I called up to her to tell her I was off out soon and asked her if she wanted a drink bringing up. She shouted down that she didn't, and then a couple of minutes later she appeared and said she was going to grab some cereal. She was wearing the T-shirt over her pants. It looked as though she'd slept in it. To be honest, I was sick of seeing her with it on. I told her, wasn't it time she washed the thing. She just laughed and kissed the front of it. Right over that singer's autograph she'd sewn over. I remember what she said as well. She said he was nearly as gorgeous as her boyfriend.'

Hunter felt his face flush. He caught a smile light up Lynda's face.

'Anyway, I was just going off to the Mother and Toddler Group, you remember, which I ran down at the community centre. I asked her what she was going to do that day, and she said she was gonna give you a call and then take Mollie for a walk. She knew I always got back around noon, and so she said she'd make me a sandwich for lunch and see me later. I left about half-nine. Toddler Group started at ten.' For a second her eyes drifted away. Her face took on a studious look. Then she snapped her gaze back, nodding, 'That's exactly as it was.'

Suddenly, the room started closing in on Hunter. What Lynda had just said triggered another flashback. That Thursday was back inside his head. Like Lynda, he'd never forgotten that day. In the early years the thoughts of what had happened to Polly had haunted him. Over time the burden had lessened, though the regret hadn't. The crux of it all was that he knew he should have been with Polly during that walk with her dog. Instead, when she'd telephoned him that morning, he'd told her he couldn't and had gone and had a kick-about with his mates. If he hadn't have been so selfish she no doubt would still have been alive today. He caught Lynda's gaze. He wondered if she laid any of the blame on him.

Peter's voice brought his thoughts back.

'When they found Polly, you know she was wrapped in a cloak, don't you, Hunter? They never found her Bon Jovi T-shirt.'

'Yes, I'm aware of that. That's what this is about. We've found Polly's T-shirt.'

'What,' Peter spluttered out the words. He swapped glances with his wife.

'You'll appreciate, at this moment, I can't go into any details about the circumstances of how we've found it, but I can definitely tell you it's her T-shirt all right. We've checked it and her DNA's on it. That's why we're re-opening Polly's case.'

'Where did you find it?'

'I'm afraid I can't go into that either at the moment. Sorry. But I can tell you that it was found in circumstances which lead us to believe that whoever killed the woman near Wentworth also murdered Polly.' Hunter fixed their looks. 'But as I said earlier. That has to be strictly between us, for now. You mustn't tell anybody. Not your closest friend. Not even a relative, until we officially release it.'

Lynda made a cross over her heart and mouthed the word 'promise.'

'There's a couple of other things I'd like to go back over with you. Are you okay to do that? I fully understand if you don't want to. I guess I've delivered something you hadn't expected, so I can always come back if it's too much to grasp?'

'No it isn't, Hunter. It's good of you to come and give us the news. It can't be easy for you as well, it being about Polly.' Lynda gave her husband a sideways glance. 'We want to help. We won't settle until you've caught whoever did this to her. And this other poor woman, of course.' She locked onto Hunter's eyes. 'We've never forgotten that day. People have told us that it gets easier.' She shook her head. 'Load of rubbish. There's not a day goes by without me thinking about Polly.'

Pursing his mouth Hunter replied, 'Of course. I've not forgotten it either. Sometimes I wish I could turn back the clock.'

'You can't,' Lynda said softly. 'No one can. But it would be nice if you could catch her killer after all this time. We'll all maybe be able to settle then.'

Hunter nodded, 'That's what we're hoping. Forensic techniques have moved on so much now that we're hoping that whoever killed her slipped up.'

'So what help do you want from us?' asked Peter.

'I just want to run through things with you again and check out one or two other things.'

Peter exchanged glances with his wife and then returned his gaze to Hunter. 'Fire away.'

'Lynda, you said you last saw Polly at about half nine that morning.'

'Yes. As you know she'd still got another week off before she went back to college. She'd taken to walking Mollie regularly for us, with us both out at work. It was a lovely morning and she said she fancied a long walk in the woods and was going to give you a ring.'

Hunter tugged at the collar of his shirt. He responded, 'She rang me just after ten, but unfortunately I'd agreed to meet up with a couple of mates, so I told her I'd see her that afternoon.' He paused as he explored Peter and Lynda's faces. There didn't appear to be any blame in their looks. Continuing, he said, 'Did she normally go out walking with anyone else?'

'Varied. If she wasn't with either of us two, or yourself, she'd sometimes go out with Lucy Stringer, or Amy Parker. Remember them?'

'Yes, I do.' An image flashed inside Hunter's head. The four of them listening to cassette tapes in Polly's bedroom. They'd take it in turns to record the top twenty pop charts every Sunday evening and then play them when they got together.

Lynda disturbed his daydream. 'But they were both on holiday that week.'

'So she would have gone up to the woods alone.' It was a rhetorical question. Hunter already knew from the police statements he had read that there were half a dozen sightings of her that morning during her journey up to Barnwell Woods. They even had a sighting of her in the woods itself. A female dog walker had stopped and exchanged pleasantries with Polly before going her separate way. The last time she was seen was at 11.15 a.m. 'And she was found just after three p.m. the same day?'

Grim-faced, Lynda Hayes nodded. 'She was found the other side of the woods, lying in a ditch by the edge of a field. Two women out jogging heard Mollie barking. She'd stayed with her. Looking after her.' Lynda's eyes started to glass over.

Hunter watched her wipe her eyes. He gave her a couple of seconds. 'I've seen in your statement that you called the police at roughly two o'clock that Thursday.'

'Yeah. Once she hadn't come in by twelve thirty I started to panic. It wasn't like her. I first rang Peter at work, to see if he'd heard from her, then I rang her gran. Then I rang you.'

'Yes, I remember. I came straight round and we went out looking for her. We stopped a few people in the woods and asked them if they'd seen her. No one had. Then we came back here and you phoned the police.'

Tight-lipped, Linda made a sharp sucking noise, as if holding back a sob.

Hunter gave her some more time to gather her composure. 'I know you'll have been asked this already. And probably dozens of times. But I need to ask you again. That cloak. You said in your statement that you'd never seen it before?'

Peter leaned forward, clasping his hands. 'We hadn't. As you know Lynda reported her missing and gave the police her description. They said they normally didn't bother doing anything until someone of her age had been missing for twenty-four hours, but I insisted this was way out of character for her and so they promised to send an officer. Two detectives came round at tea time, and I thought it was to take my report, but it wasn't. It was to break the news that they'd found Polly. They kept asking us about the clothing she'd gone out in. At first we couldn't fathom out why and then a couple of days later they told us that when they'd found her she had this dark green cloak wrapped around her. They showed it to us and asked us if we'd seen it before. Neither of us had. We don't know where it came from.'

Lynda interposed, 'The other thing was that it was far too big for Polly. Polly was only size ten.'

'And you still have no thoughts of where it could have come from.'

Lynda shook her head. 'Polly wouldn't have been seen dead in it.' She pulled herself up and gulped. 'That was a wrong turn of phrase wasn't it, but you know what I mean. Polly was very fashion conscious, as you know, Hunter. It looked like the type of cloak a monk would wear.'

Hunter interlaced his fingers. With a steadying voice he said, 'I'm sure you might have been asked this before as well, but a long time has passed now, and I just wonder if you ever heard a whisper that she might have been seeing someone else?' He paused and added, 'Other than me.'

Lynda shook her head vigorously. 'Definitely not, Hunter. You could read our Polly like a book. She thought the world of you. You recall, we took her camping in Cornwall, with Lucy, in July that year. Well, halfway into the holiday they got chatting to a couple of lads, who took it the wrong way, and kept chatting them up at every opportune moment, but Polly sent them packing. Told them where to get off, in no uncertain terms. Me and Peter had a good laugh about it. No, you were the only one for her.'

'Just one other question. I know it's such a long time ago now but did anything unusual happen leading up to Polly's death. It could be days, even weeks. Anything out of the ordinary?'

Peter crooked his head to one side. Thought for a couple of seconds and then said, 'Do you mean the nuisance phone calls?'

'Phone calls?' Hunter glanced at Grace. She shrugged her shoulders. He returned his gaze. 'I don't recall anything about nuisance phone calls in your statements.'

Peter exchanged a look with his wife. 'Well, we told the detectives about it. They said they'd look into them.'

138

'Unless I've missed something when I've read through the file, I can't recall any mention of nuisance phone calls. Tell me about them.'

'Well, I suppose on the face of it they were nothing. There were only a couple. Maybe three or four at most.'

'What was the nature of them?'

'It was Polly who brought it to our attention. She told us she'd had a couple of crank calls one day. I asked her what she meant by that and she said, "just crank calls." She joked about it and said she'd shouted perv down the phone and then hung up. She didn't elaborate on the nature of them. Then one night I answered and I just got silence. I think I shouted down the phone. Told them, whoever it was to stop it, otherwise I was going to the police. Then Lynda got one.' He shot a sideways look.

Prompted by her husband's glance Lynda said, 'Mine was a silent one as well. I didn't hang up straight away, I listened for a good couple of seconds. I tried to hear if there was anything I could recognise. I could hear whoever it was breathing. Not deeply or anything, just breathing. I eventually told them it wasn't funny, and to grow up and then hung up.'

Peter interjected, 'And then Polly took one, one evening. She shouted to me that it was him on the phone. I told her to give it to me, but by the time I'd got there, they'd hung up. Polly said he'd spoken to her.'

'Did she recognise who it was?'

Peter shook his head. 'Well, when I say he'd spoken to her. It wasn't exactly that. She said, and these were her words, the weirdo was whispering. It sounded like he was counting backwards.'

'She said it was a "he?"'

'Definitely. I asked her what she meant, when she said the weirdo was counting backwards. And she said, "you know, counting down Dad, like when we used to play hide and seek." That was it.'

'Counting down. That was all? No threats or anything?'

'No threats. That was it. We got no more calls after that one.'

'What time span was this before what happened to Polly?'

Peter screwed up his face, thought for a few seconds and responded with, 'Week, maybe ten days.'

'And you told detectives about them.'

Peter nodded, 'Yes, they said they were going to check them up.'

'Okay, that's great. I'll follow that up. We've got someone on the team who was involved in her case. I'll have a word with him.' Hunter met his partner's gaze, gave her an enquiring look, as if to say, 'is there anything you want to ask.' She shook her head.

He settled his eyes back upon Peter and Lynda and smiled. 'Okay, that's great. Except for the information about the phone calls I think that's confirmed everything that was in your statement.' He started to push himself up and then caught himself. 'Oh, there is one thing. Again, I know it's a long time ago, but did detectives search Polly's room. Go through her things.'

'Yes, they took a few of her belongings away. Some photos of her with her friends, a couple of letters. I think some were from you. And a diary and address book.'

'Were those ever handed back?'

'No. We never got them back. Why, haven't you got them?'

'To be honest I don't know. I've only read Polly's file. The statements etcetera. I'll chase up where they are so that we can go through them again.' Hunter straightened himself. 'In the meantime if you bear in mind what I said earlier. We have opened up Polly's case. If anything else springs to mind, no matter how small or inconsequential you think it might be, you know where I am.'

Hunter reached out and offered Peter his hand. He caught sight of his eyes welling up.

On a brittle note Peter said, 'Catch the bastard, Hunter. For Polly. For us.'

Unable to get hold of Barry Newstead, who was out on enquiries, Hunter spent the rest of the afternoon chasing up the exhibits from Polly's case. He tracked down the cloak, she had been found wrapped in, to the Forensics Laboratory at Wetherby. It had been archived with other samples from the case. He made a request for them to be examined and spent an hour completing the paperwork. Then, he made further phone calls to determine the whereabouts of the personal things detectives had removed from Polly's room. He had a breakthrough with those as well. He discovered that her diary, address book, photographs and letters had all been packed away in a storage box, and were held in a warehouse facility, amongst other exhibits from all unsolved cases investigated by South Yorkshire Police. He arranged for them to be delivered.

At evening debrief Hunter fed in his and Grace's visit to Polly's parents and reported on his success at finding all the original exhibits from the investigation. He didn't raise the matter of the nuisance telephone calls because he hadn't been able to quiz Barry about them. He had a doctor's appointment and had booked off duty without coming back to the station. Hunter had decided to speak with him first, and determine if the calls issue had been resolved during the original investigation, before introducing them.

No one else brought anything new to the proceedings.

That night, before going home, Hunter stopped off at the churchyard. He felt the need to visit Polly's grave. It had been a long time since he'd done so. Negotiating the criss-cross of paths around the sides of the church he discovered, that aside from him, the graveyard was empty. Eerily silent. The light was starting to go; dusk had descended, throwing everything into shadow, confusing his bearings, and he found himself doubling-back on more than one occasion as he searched out her headstone. He eventually found it. The grave site was still pin-neat tidy; an obvious sign that it was being regularly visited and maintained. A rose bowl containing a bunch of fake flowers had been placed in front of the dark grey marble headstone. It gave colour to the drab backdrop. He stared at the carved inscription. It read, *'Polly Ann Hayes, 16 years, 25th July 1972, 1st September 1988. Taken from us'*. He dipped his head and a kaleidoscope of happy images tumbled inside his head; things they had done during the ten months they had been together. Kindred spirits. For a moment he wondered how it might be if she hadn't died that day. His spine tingled and he shook himself. Beth and the boys were his life now. He said a silent goodbye, turned and made his way back down the path to where he had left his car.

He didn't drive immediately home, instead he stopped off at his parents' house, and over a cup of tea, told them about the investigation. He also wanted to check out their garage, and see if the box, he had tucked away all those years ago, was still there.

It was. He found it hidden away amongst cans of old paint, high up on a shelf. He picked it down and brushed away the years of dust. The lid was still Sellotaped. He knew he should have binned the box ages ago, but he'd never been able to bring himself to do it.

He took it to his car, put it to the back of the boot and drove home.

- ooOoo –

CHAPTER THIRTEEN

Day Twelve: 29th March.

Detective Superintendent Dawn Leggate added a quick signature to the last of her urgent paperwork, placed the cap back on her pen and checked her watch – briefing in ten minutes. Her timing was perfect. She would even have time to grab a quick coffee she told herself. As she pushed back her chair, her personal mobile rang. Not recognising the number, and thinking about having that coffee before briefing, she was in two minds whether to answer. She decided she had enough time and took the call.

'Hi, Dawn.'

As soon as she heard the voice she regretted her decision.

Taking a deep breath she said, 'What do you want, Jack?'

'Just to talk.'

'We've done talking.'

'Just hear me out please.'

Clenching her teeth together she said, 'You've got two minutes.'

'I just want to apologise. I know you're angry with me, but I realise now what a stupid mistake I've made.' There was a couple of seconds pause and then he said, 'I realise just how much I miss you. I can't live without you.'

'Well you should have thought about that before you decided to shag that bimbo secretary of yours.'

'We've finished. I've ended it. It's you I really love.'

'I don't love you anymore.'

'Please, Dawn.'

'No. I'm happy now.' She paused. She could feel her heart fluttering. She took a deep breath. 'Jack, I want you to leave me alone. I've moved on.'

'That's not the Dawn I once knew talking. The job's changed you.'

Suddenly, the anger welled up. She bit down on her lip. 'Don't you dare blame the job, Jack. This is your fault.' She took another deep breath. 'This conversation is over. I don't want you ever ringing me again.'

'Please, Dawn, you don't mean this.'

'Yes I do, Jack. I'm hanging up.'

'Don't.'

She ended the call and glanced at the screen. Suddenly, her chest tightened. She could hear the blood rushing between her ears. Gripping the edge of her desk she steadied herself. Then, saving the number, so she could ignore it the next time it rang, she switched off her mobile and slung it across her desk.

For a few seconds she stared aimlessly around the room, trying to pull herself together. She could feel the start of a panic attack. She caught herself and steadied her breathing.

I'm not going to let that bastard ruin my day.

She forced herself out of her chair, picked up her briefing notes and walked out of the office.

'Heads up everyone, lot to get through this morning,' she shouted, weaving between the desks, to the front of the room.

Upon reaching DC Carol Ragen's desk, she offered her a quick smile, moved aside some of her paperwork and deposited herself gracefully on a corner. Hitching up her dark blue pencil skirt she shuffled into a comfortable position. Dawn could feel her composure returning. 'Okay, just a quick reminder.' She did a quick recce around the room – checked that she had everyone's attention. 'We're now linking the murder of Polly Hayes, in nineteen eighty-eight, to the murder of Elisabeth Bertolutti, four days ago, by the fact that Polly's T-shirt has turned up on Elisabeth's body. And we're linking Elisabeth's murder to that of Gemma Cooke, eleven days ago, by the fact that a masked man was identified as being responsible for killing Elisabeth, and a masked man, as we have seen on CCTV, was seen following Gemma only hours before her body was found. Our main suspects to date are, as you know, Adam Fields and DC Tom Hagan. Both have been interviewed and neither of them have solid alibis for the time period in which we believe she was killed. And, so to that end, although I'm not completely dismissing them yet...' she swung out an arm, and aimed it at an A4 size still CCTV image of the grotesque masked head, Blu Tacked to Gemma Cooke's incident board. '…my feelings are that whoever that masked man is, is the person we need to be focussed upon.' Dawn glanced down at her lap, flicked away a piece of fluff, crossed one shapely leg over the other and raised her eyes. 'As you know, for now, I'm running on the theory that what we have here is a serial killer, who is a trophy taker and who is then transferring his trophies between his victims. And with that in mind, I want us to focus on several things. Firstly, the green cloak, which Polly Hayes was found wrapped in. That is currently with Forensics and is being fast-tracked for DNA etcetera. I want it photographed and sent out to all Forces. See if any of them have any outstanding murders or attacks where the victim had a similar cloak taken. Remember we're looking at a time-period during the nineteen eighties, maybe even earlier.' She directed a pointed finger at Gemma Cooke's board. 'The second item of interest is the locket found on Gemma's body. Again I want the same doing with that and see if anything comes back.'

She returned her eyes into the room. 'One more thing before we move on. While we're still on the subject of trophy taking, who had the assignment of seeing if anything was missing from Gemma's?'

'That was me, boss,' the call came from the room. Mike Sampson had his hand raised. He put it down when the SIO looked his way. 'I learned that Mrs Cooke cleaned the house occasionally for Gemma, when she was pulled out with work, so I took Gemma's mum up to the house yesterday, and we checked each room and went through her things together. I asked her to see if anything was missing from its normal place. I have to say, it was actually Tom Hagan who gave me the clue of what to look out for. In interview, if you recall, he mentioned that Gemma had been wearing a watch, which caught him, and so she took it off and left it on the coffee table. We searched the whole house but we couldn't find a watch anywhere. I asked her mum if she knew what it looked like. Although she was vague she can remember Gemma wearing a certain type of watch on a regular basis. She described it to me as having a white face, with crystals around the glass and it had a white leather strap. I've asked her to have a look on the internet to see if she can come up with a possible make and style.'

'Good. Well done, Mike,' Dawn interjected. 'Let me know the minute you get a result. We'll circulate that to all Forces as well, just in case another body turns up. And while we're at it, let's not forget the blouse Elisabeth was wearing.' She pointed towards Tony Bullars. 'See if Linane can give us a better description of it, or if she has any photos of Elisabeth wearing it, which would be a bonus and get that circulated as well.' She paused and shuffled her gaze between the faces of her team. 'There was another task I asked to be done. Following my theory that Gemma and Tom Hagan were followed from Sheffield, I want someone to visit the guy, on Manvers Terrace, who revved up Adam Fields with the phone call, on the night of her murder, telling him that he'd seen Tom Hagan go into Gemma's house. Also, the neighbour, Valerie Bryce. To see if either had them had seen anyone hanging around on the street.'

'That was me,' called out DC Paula Clarke. 'I drew a blank with Valerie. It's as per her statement. She can only recall seeing Adam running off towards the industrial estate. But I did have a stroke of luck speaking with Paul Rose, the mate who rang up Adam. He wasn't forthcoming at first. Said he didn't want to get involved. However, after a little gentle persuasion, he did remember seeing someone on the street. He told me, he saw someone hanging back in one of the alleyways opposite Gemma's house. He said, he thought at first it was Adam, waiting for Tom Hagan to come out of the house, but then just like Valerie Bryce, he also saw Adam running off down the street towards the industrial estate and when he looked back there was no sign of the person.'

From a slouched position, Dawn Leggate straightened. 'Any description?'

DC Clarke shook her head, 'No, boss. He says that whoever it was, was mostly in shadow. He describes the person as being half-in, half-out of the alleyway and they were too far away for him to get a good view.'

'That's a shame. But it takes us a step further. It puts someone else in that location at around the time of Gemma's murder. And it strengthens my theory.' The Detective Superintendent tapped the palm of a hand. 'Let's get this Paul Rose to point out exactly where he saw this person, and get SOCO back to check out the alleyway. Then I want some more house-to-house nearby.' She supported herself on her hands and launched herself off the edge of the desk. 'Right, I need everyone's undivided attention for the next bit.' She stepped toward a laptop that was set up on a trolley, close by and hit the touchpad mouse. The screen lit up, displaying the Force crest. She addressed the room, 'I'm going to play you something which was brought to my attention yesterday evening. As you know the technicians have been going through Elisabeth Bertolutti's mobile to see who was in her contacts and what was in her calls list. Well, as a result, they found that at three forty on the afternoon of the day she was killed, she had made a three-nines call to West Midlands Police.' She watched the expectant expressions appear on the faces of her team. 'We got on to them yesterday and they've sent us a disc with a recording of that call.' With the tip of her forefinger Dawn scrolled across to an icon on the screen and tapped the touchpad. The screen format changed. She selected a folder, opened it and tapped again. After several seconds a female voice broke the hush.

'Emergency Helpline, which service do you require?'

Elisabeth Bertolutti's anxious voice replied, 'Police, please.'

Following a short ringing tone, signifying the transfer of the call, a male voice answered, 'West Midlands Police, can I help you?'

'I think I'm being followed.'

'Who am I talking with?'

'Elisabeth Bertolutti.'

'How do you spell that?'

She spelled out her name slowly.

'And is this number you're calling from your own number?'

'Yes, it's my mobile.'

'And what is your address?'

She gave the Call Handler the address in Street.

'And where are you calling from?'

'Leicester Forest Service Station.'

'And you say you're being followed?'

'Yes. Well, I think I am.'

'What makes you sure you're being followed. Has this happened before?'

'No, it's not happened before. It's just that I almost bumped into this man I know. Well, I briefly know. He surprised me because I didn't expect to see him up here. He lives in London, you see, or I think he does.'

'So it's someone you know?'

'Not exactly. I think it's someone I've had hassle with recently. I'm not being helpful am I? It's just that it's unnerved me.'

'I can tell that. Just calm yourself down, Miss Bertolutti. You're talking to the police. Are there people around you? Are you still inside the service station?'

'Yes. I'm in the ladies toilets.'

'So you're safe then?'

'Yes.'

'Good. So take your time. Do you know the name of this man, who you say is following you?'

'I think his name's Dale. I don't know him that well.'

'Do you know where he lives?'

'No. Only that he's from London. I think. I don't know him that well.'

'And you say this has never happened before?'

'No.'

'So, what makes you think you're being followed by this man?'

'Well, there's no reason for him to be here, is there?'

'I'm afraid I can't answer that, Miss Bertolutti.'

'Do you think I'm overreacting?'

'I'm not saying that. If you're saying this has not happened before, what makes you certain you're being followed now?'

'Just that he shouldn't be here.'

'Do you think it might be a coincidence?'

There was a pause, then Elisabeth said, 'Do you think it might be a coincidence?'

'Well has this man said anything to you, or done anything?'

'No, we just almost bumped into one another, that's all. Then I've come into the toilets to phone you.'

'Can I make a suggestion, Miss Bertolutti?'

'Yes.'

'When you leave the toilets, have a good look around, and if you feel unsafe, or you're unsure, and you see this man hanging around, then don't hesitate to call us and I'll send out a police officer straight away. Does that sound okay?'

'Yes. Yes, I'll do that.'

'Also, in the meantime, I'm guessing you're on your way home to Yorkshire?'

'Yes.'

'Well, while you're driving, if you see anything suspicious, a car following you for instance, for too long, slow down and let it pass. If you see it after that, pull onto the hard shoulder and call us immediately. We'll dispatch an officer to you straight away. Is that okay?'

'Yes, thank you for your help. I'm sorry to trouble you.'

'No trouble, Miss Bertolutti.'

The call ended.

Dawn checked out the looks on her investigators' faces, as they exchanged glances with one another, across desks and across the room. She brought back their focus with, 'Now that's what I call a breakthrough.' She bounced her gaze around the department. Then she aimed a finger at the laptop. 'I don't know about you lot but something tells me that was no coincidence. Bumping into a man who she'd recently had hassle with at a motorway service station. And then a few hours later she's attacked and murdered at her home.' She slowly shook her head, 'No, this looks to me like this was meant to happen. Unless anyone can come up with a different suggestion, it's my guess, this man is our killer.' She saw a few nodding her way. Clasping her hands and rubbing them together she fastened her eyes upon Tony Bullars. 'Tony, as the only person in this room who knew Elisabeth, does anything of what you've just heard ring any bells?'

Biting down on his lower lip, Tony screwed up his face. 'Do you know, it might do.'

All heads turned towards him.

'I first met my girlfriend, Linane, as a result of a bust-up she and Elisabeth had with a couple of guys in a bar near Covent Garden.'

'You have a captive audience, Tony, tell us more.'

'To be honest there isn't that much to tell. This happened six months, or so, ago; September time. I'll have to check the date. I went down to London for a long weekend to catch up with my sister and her husband and they took me to a matinee show of 'We Will Rock You,' on the Saturday afternoon. Afterwards we went for a pizza and then for a beer. I'd just got to the bar, in this pub, near the restaurant we'd been to and this argument kicked off behind me. I looked round and saw Linane and Elisabeth in the middle of this almighty bust-up with a couple of blokes. There was a fair bit of shouting and pushing going on and then I saw Elisabeth backhand one of them, and I could see he was about to crack her one back, so I jumped in and grabbed hold of his wrist. Me and this guy had a little bit of a tussle, well, to be honest, it was more of a handbags at dawn, than a tussle and then a couple of bouncers appeared. I flashed my warrant card and the two blokes Linane and Elisabeth had been arguing with were thrown out. That was it. End of. As a result of the shenanigans, I'd got some drink spilled on me and Linane offered to get it cleaned. That was how we met.'

A couple of wolf-whistles erupted.

Child-like, Mike Sampson issued, 'Ooh, my knight in shining armour.'

Tony blushed.

With a shake of her head and through a smile, the Detective Superintendent said to her audience, 'Bunch of reprobates. Some of you just can't help yourself, can you?' She waited for the sniggers to die away, then said, 'Carry on, Tony.'

'As I say, that was it as far as I was concerned. It was over and done within seconds. I got chatting to them both, mainly with Linane, asked them what it was all about, and all she said was that one of the guys had been hassling Elisabeth for a date, but she didn't fancy him.' He shrugged his shoulders. 'That's the only thing that comes to mind.'

'What about descriptions?' asked Dawn.

Tony's eyebrows knitted together. For a few seconds his gaze drifted up to the ceiling. Then, he brought it back down and shook his head. 'I'm afraid I'm not going to be much help here. As I say the incident was over and done with in less than a minute. I never saw the two guys again. All I can remember is that they were both white, mid to late thirties, the pair were roughly my height – six foot, and medium build, with short dark hair. Oh and the guy whose wrist I grabbed had dark brown eyes. He gave me this really evil stare.' His lips tightened. 'That's it, I'm afraid.'

'Okay, never mind. See if you can sit down with SOCO and come up with an e-fit of any of them.'

'Yeah, will do, boss. I'll give it some thought.'

'And in the mean time I want you and Grace to do another video interview with Linane. Get her to go through the incident. See if it was involving this Dale, whatever his name is, and if it was, what it was all about and what exactly was the type of hassle Elisabeth was getting from him. And, see if she's taken any of their photos on her phone, or check out if they're on Facebook. Failing that, get her to do an e-fit.' Dawn threw her gaze wider, scrutinising the faces of her team. 'And, it's a long shot but I want someone to get onto Leicester Forest Services and see if they've still got the CCTV from that day. This just might be what we've been waiting for.'

At his desk, using an elbow as support, Hunter propped his face in one hand. With his free hand he was indexing the pages of Polly's five-year diary as he pored over her entries. It was a red, faux-leather-backed affair, A5 in size, one week spanning across two pages. The exhibit had arrived shortly after his partner, Grace, had disappeared with Tony Bullars to interview Linane Brazier. Along with the diary had come her address book and two letters. The letters, addressed to Polly, were from him. Seeing them had taken him by surprise. And with them had come happy thoughts. He remembered he had written them when Polly had gone on holiday to Cornwall, with her parents and her best friend Lucy Stringer, in the summer of 1988. Before taking them out of their envelopes he had checked the postmarks. They had been date-stamped, the fourth and eleventh of July – less than two months before she had been found murdered. Having long forgotten their slushy content he had felt himself colouring while perusing them. Especially in the manner he had signed each one off. The first one bore the acronym H.O.L.L.A.N.D. Beside the word was an artistically drawn bleeding heart. And the second letter had been finished with the caption I.T.A.L.Y. He mouthed the words – he still remembered their sentiments – 'Hope Our Love Lives And Never Dies,' and 'I'll Truly Always Love You.' He couldn't help but crack a smile as he'd finished each letter. In both he'd creatively expressed, how much he was missing her and vowed his undying love. Under normal circumstances he would have classed them as drivel, but these were different. These were a part of him, and although the letters were full of naïve prose, he knew that when he had written them, they were the truthful words of a person who had found love for the first time. He had read them through three times before putting them to one side. He knew he would be reading them again in a day or so. Then he had picked up Polly's diary and instantly become hooked by her almost mirrored response. Where, she had described her similar feelings towards him, he had hung onto every crisp word. The first recorded entry, which had grabbed him, had been written two months before their first official date.

On Wednesday the 23rd September 1987, she had scribed:-

Went to netball practice today, just so I could see Hunter at football training.

That had amused him. He had never known that.

Then he had found the entry in November that year. The day before their first 'going out':

Hunter walked me home from the youth club. He kissed me on our street. It made me go all jellyfied! Then he asked me to go to the pictures with him tomorrow. I'm in love. The record had instantly triggered the recovery of another buried memory. He remembered that first kiss. Her mouth had been so soft and warm. It had seemed as if it had lasted forever and that evening he had walked home floating on air. When he'd read it, a chuckle had almost burst forth, provoking a feeling of child-like embarrassment. Quickly zipping his mouth, he had instantly explored the room, and been relieved when he had seen that no one had been looking his way.

He was currently beginning the month of June 1988 and he could feel a strain beginning behind his eyes. He closed them and pinched the bridge of his nose. Just as he was thinking about the possibility of needing glasses he caught the sound of the office doors crack, and snapping open his eyes, he clocked Barry Newstead barging through, while simultaneously wrestling with the sleeve of his overcoat, trying to release an arm. He was chuntering to himself, but loudly.

Securing the page with his forefinger Hunter sought out Barry's gaze. 'You're just the person I need to talk to.' He caught a strange look appear on Barry's face. He turned Polly's diary over, trapping it face-down to save the page and pushed himself back in his seat.

Still struggling with his overcoat, Barry glided past him without making eye contact. 'Oh aye, what have I done now,' he said gruffly. As he neared his desk he finally extricated himself from his mac, threw it across his paperwork, and kicking out his chair, dumped himself into its upholstery.

Hunter took another look at Barry. He thought that his expression appeared to be unusually downcast.

There's something wrong with him.

Jettisoning himself out of his chair he made his way across the room to where Barry was seated. The desk opposite, normally occupied by Mike Sampson, was empty. Hunter plonked himself down. 'What's up?'

'Nothing's up.' Barry still avoided eye contact. He pushed aside his coat and picked up some loose papers.

Then Hunter remembered that Barry had been to the doctors. Not just that morning, but he recalled he had also had an appointment the previous evening. That's why he'd not been able to get hold of him. He took a deep breath. 'You've been to the doctors.'

'No secret.'

'I know. Is everything okay?'

'Why shouldn't it be. Just my annual check-up.'

'Barry, you know Beth's a nurse. And I know that an annual check-up does not run to two sessions back-to-back. This is your pal talking to you.'

Barry lifted his head. 'I've got angina.' Suddenly his eyes glistened.

Hunter was silent for a moment. Then he said, 'Okay, I know about angina. Have they said how bad?'

'I've had all the tests. They've put me on medication – tablets.'

'Tablets are okay, Barry. Tablets mean it's not too serious – doesn't it?' Very quickly, Hunter realised what he had just said. He added, 'You know what I mean, Barry.'

'Yeah, I know, Hunter.'

'Did the doc say anything else?'

'She told me my blood pressure was high as well. I've been given tablets for that as well. And she gave me a few leaflets and told me I need to make some lifestyle changes. The usual crap.'

'It's not crap, Barry. Look, if you want I can ask Beth to have a chat with you. She might explain it better.' He paused and then said, 'I bet it's been a bit of a shocker for you.'

Barry wiped his mouth and licked his lips. 'To be honest, I know something hasn't been right with me for a couple of months now. I've been having chest pains a while now. That do with Adam Fields was a shot across the bows.' He caught Hunter's eyes. 'But I'm not ready to peg it yet. She says if I do as I'm told I've got a good few years of collecting my police pension still.' He cracked a grin.

Hunter felt the mood had lightened.

'Did the doc say anything else?'

'She said if I changed my diet and lost some weight it would help. I guess it's my own fault. I've burned the candle at both ends for far too long. It's finally caught me up.'

Hunter pushed himself up. 'Look, I'll get Beth to sit down with you and go through everything. Put your mind at ease.' He slipped out from behind the desk. 'In the meantime I'll stick the kettle on, cos I've got some questions to ask about Polly's case.' As he passed Barry, he rested a hand on his shoulder. 'You'll be fine, mate. In a couple of weeks' time you'll be back to your old self. You watch.'

As Hunter walked towards the tea-making facilities he glanced back over his shoulder. He caught Barry wiping his eyes with the back of his hand. Suddenly, he felt for him. As he started up the kettle, he shot back another glance. Barry had his head resting in his hands and was staring into space. Hunter returned his gaze to the gurgling kettle. His thoughts drifted. Barry was the one of hardest men he'd come across but he could tell this news had floored him. He knew that he would be worrying about the long term implications of this diagnosis. Barry's life revolved around policing. He thought about how he could settle the big man's turmoil. As the kettle went into its final burst he determined that he would speak with Beth first for advice and then, like he'd done with him in the past, take him down to the pub to talk things through.

Five minutes later, holding two freshly brewed cups of tea, Hunter returned to Mike Sampson's desk and seated himself opposite Barry. He pushed across a steaming mug.

'I went to see Peter and Lynda Hayes yesterday.'

'Yeah, I saw that you and Grace had been given the task. How are they doing? I bet they got a surprise when you told them we're re-investigating Polly's murder.'

'A bit, but I think they were more pleased than anything.' He took a sip of his tea. 'While I was talking to them something cropped up about some nuisance telephone calls they'd had, which started a week or so before Polly's murder. But I couldn't find anything about them in the statements they made.'

Barry's eyes narrowed. 'Oh, yeah. I remember that enquiry. There weren't just them who received them. Her best mate, Lucy Stringer, reported, or at least her parents reported, having received some as well. We looked into both reports. In Lucy's case the calls were just silent. I think she had a half a dozen in total. And, as you're aware, Polly had four, one of which she mentioned that she heard a male voice counting backwards.'

Hunter nodded. 'Did you manage to trace them?'

'Yeah we did. To a call box next to the main post office.'

'And did you get anywhere with them? Find out who made them?'

'Barry shook his head. 'Drew a complete blank. They were brought up on quite a few occasions during the investigation, but we couldn't bottom them. And as they weren't threatening or anything, and the fact that they stopped, we were never able to follow them up.'

The minute Hunter walked in through the front door he was ambushed by his youngest son.

Daniel squealed, 'Daddy,' and wrapped his skinny arms around one of Hunter's legs, as if holding onto a tree trunk. He planted his bottom onto his foot.

Hunter dropped down his briefcase and clomped Daniel elephant-like towards the kitchen. He deposited him in the doorway. 'Daniel Kerr, you're getting far too heavy for me to be doing this.'

His youngest looked up at him and flashed him his twinkling blue eyes. Daniel chuckled and dashed away towards the stairs. 'Want a game of FIFA, Dad?'

Hunter caught sight of Beth washing pots at the sink. He shouted back over his shoulder. 'Fire it up, young man, I'm just going to have a quick word with your mum, and then I'll be up them stairs to whup the backside off you.' From the upstairs landing he heard Daniel give out a giggle. He called up to him, 'Load me up as Scotland.'

Shucking off his jacket, he draped it over the back of a chair and moved in behind his wife. He slipped his arms around her waist and nuzzled the nape of her neck. He caught the floral aroma of her perfume.

She half-turned her head and blew him a kiss. 'My hands are wet,' she said, wiggling her fingers and dipped them back into the soapy water. Continuing to wash a plate, she added, 'You're home early. You should have let me know, I'd have got you something to eat. Jonathan and Daniel have just finished theirs.'

'I promised I'd get done early.'

She threw him a questioning look. 'Now, how many times have I heard that, Hunter Kerr?'

Hunter smirked, pulled away his hands and tapped her bottom. 'Cheeky mare,' he said and went to the fridge. Pulling out a carton of orange juice, he took a swig, stopping mid-gulp as he caught Beth send a scowl his way. He removed the neck of the carton from his mouth, offered back a child-like look of innocence, before seeking out a glass from the side. Sarcastically, he showed her the glass, poured himself some juice and took a long gulp. 'I'm not bothered about anything to eat just yet. I had a late lunch. I'll get myself something later.' He took another drink. 'I said I'd be home, because aren't you out with the girls from work tonight?'

Beth placed the wet plate onto the draining board, picked up a towel, and turned around drying her hands. 'We're trying out a new place that's just opened up. The menu looks pretty good. You didn't need to rush home though you know. I was going to get your mum to come round and babysit.'

'Well, I'm here now so you can get yourself sorted, can't you.' He checked his watch and with a dead-pan look said, 'You've got bags of time to put your slap on. And believe me you need it. Them wrinkles are really starting to show now.'

Beth scrunched up the towel and slung it at him. 'Cheeky sod,' she smirked as she marched away. Calling back she added, 'And just for that you can bath them and sort out their supper. They're on form today.'

Hunter laughed after Beth as she disappeared out of the kitchen. He drained his glass and followed. He wanted to tell her about Barry while she was getting ready.

Beth had been picked up by a colleague at 8.00 p.m. leaving him to sort out the boys. Thankfully, Jonathan and Daniel had gone off to bed without any fuss. After reading them a story he'd climbed into the shower and changed into a T-shirt and joggers. Now he was getting himself settled down for the evening, and with that, he decided he could do with a drink to help him unwind. He selected his favourite Islay, single malt, and added a generous measure of whisky to the three chunks of ice in his tumbler. He flopped down onto the sofa and swirled the contents around under his nose. The peaty aroma teased his nostrils. He took a sip, and the amber fluid caught the back of his throat, instantly warming his gullet. It was a pleasing sensation. Cradling the glass mid-chest, he rested back his head and listened to the sounds of the heating system ticking around him. He closed his eyes, but only momentarily. Flicking them open, he rested his gaze upon the cardboard box, on the coffee table, which he'd recovered earlier from the boot of his car. Beth, going out, had given him the ideal opportunity to check its contents. It had been so long ago that he could no longer remember what was in there. He took another slug of his drink, set down the glass on the coffee table and dragged the box towards him.

Glancing downwards, the road glistened before him, washed by the sudden downpour ten minutes earlier. His thoughts started to drift. For a moment he questioned what he was doing here, then, the sound of sloshing car tyres drew back his attention and he caught sight of her car coming into view.

His breath tightened as it slowed before him. He followed its progress as it swung into the driveway directly opposite from where he was watching.

The security lamp above the garage activated, lighting up the whole of her Audi TT, and reflected brightly in the puddles on the drive and front garden.

He tensed and checked his watch.

She was later than usual.

Pulling the hood of his waterproof further over his face, he slunk back into the shadows.

From his hiding place, across the road, he heard the engine cease and saw the interior light come on as she pushed open the driver's door. He took a deep breath and held it, scrutinising her as she eased herself out of the low-roofed sports car.

Leaning back into the car, she dragged out her work bag, and then as she slammed the car door she looked over her shoulder.

In his direction.

He froze.

The glance was momentary. She checked her bag was fastened, straightened her top coat and then walked towards the front door.

He heard the clip and splash of her heels on the concrete path, and caught sight of her slender calves. He thought she'd lost some weight. And she'd grown her hair. He strained his eyes to get a better look. She'd altered the style as well. He watched her put the key in the lock, push the door open and step into the brightly lit hallway. As she closed the door, he let out the breath he had been holding. For a minute stars danced before his eyes and he went light-headed. He had held it too long. He took a couple of shallow breaths and very quickly his sight readjusted. Poking his head out from the shadows he was just in time to see her pass by the lounge window. He caught her embrace the man who lived there.

Her Lover.

He could feel his heart beginning to palpitate as an icy fury flooded through him..

Who did she think she was? The fucking bitch. He'd show her. She was soon going to get her comeuppance. Make no mistake.

- ooOoo -

159

CHAPTER FOURTEEN

Day Thirteen: 30th March.

The noise in the MIT room fell to a hush as Detective Superintendent Leggate made her way to the front of the room. She stopped beside the three incident boards. They had all been updated with the previous day's information. And an arrangement of new photographs provided a montage around the black ink timelines. On Elisabeth Bertolutti's board two coloured, computer generated, e-fit photographs took centre stage. They were a head-and-shoulder composition of two white men – clean shaven with short, dark hair. Both bore similar features.

Dawn Leggate picked up a marker pen and took her time scribing beneath each picture. She pulled her head back to check her handwriting. She had written the names DALE and SCOTT in bold.

She underlined the names, tapped the e-fits and faced the squad. 'Our latest suspects,' she announced. 'If you think they look similar, it's because they are. We think the pair are brothers. Our witness, Linane Brazier helped put these together yesterday afternoon after speaking with Tony and Grace.' She zeroed in on Tony Bullars. 'Do you want to tell us about your interview with her?'

Tony pulled himself out of his slouch. Pushing a comb of fingers through his light brown hair he ran his eyes amongst his colleagues. 'As you know, following the discovery of Elisabeth's calls to West Midlands Police, me and Grace did another video interview with Linane. We played that recording of Elisabeth's nine-nine-nine call, and without any prompting she instantly volunteered those two names to us. She also told us that the first thing Elisabeth had said, when she Skyped her, was something to the effect of, "You won't believe what's happened to me today" and that she'd tell her later. She wasn't able to tell her later, because, as we all know, she was murdered. As soon as Linane mentioned that, we all felt

Elisabeth was referring to the incident of her being followed,' he pointed to the e-fit pictures, 'by the one calling himself Dale.' He paused and then continued, 'And, the reason she said that is because of the incident in the bar, in which I got involved. That is the only thing, out of the ordinary, that has happened to either of them. Linane told us that she and Elisabeth first came across those two a couple of months ago. They met the pair in a bar near one of the theatres they'd been to in London. They approached them bold as brass, introduced themselves, and offered to buy Linane and Elisabeth a drink. But they'd already made arrangements to meet up with some friends for a bite to eat at an Italian and so turned them down. They did chat with them for a while, mainly about the show they'd been to. Then, they finished their drinks and left. It was during that first meeting that they found out the pair were brothers. As far as Linane was concerned that was it. Then, about a week later, they bumped into them again, in a different bar. She thinks it was in Covent Garden this time. After that, they'd bump into them almost every weekend, have a couple of drinks, but after an hour of chatting, Linane and Elisabeth would meet up with their friends, as arranged, and these two guys would make their excuses and disappear. Then after the fourth, or fifth time of bumping into one another Dale made it quite obvious he fancied Elisabeth. Linane says that one night he chatted up Elisabeth big style, but she made it quite plain she wasn't interested. He wasn't her type. He was loud, self-opinionated and a bit arrogant, as Linane put it. On that occasion he wrote his mobile number on the back of her hand and told her to give him a ring. She never did. Apparently the argument they had in the bar, where I first met Linane, was because of that. It appears that Dale came up to Elisabeth, much the worse for wear for drink, and asked her why she hadn't rung him. She told him she wasn't interested and to leave her alone. He called her a "stuck up bitch" and she swiped out at him, and that's where I came in.' Tony danced his gaze around the room. 'You know the rest from yesterday's briefing.' He dipped his head towards Elisabeth Bertolutti's incident board. 'I'm afraid though, that although Linane says those e-fits are a reasonable likeness, and the fact that Dale and Scott are brothers, that's where it ends. She knows very little about the pair. She's no idea of where they live or where they're from, other than she got the impression they lived somewhere in the London area. Though, she doesn't recall if that came out in a conversation or not.' Tony nodded towards Detective Superintendent Leggate; an indication that he was done.

Marker pen still in hand, she tapped Dale's e-fit picture. 'Okay, today's assignment, we try and find out who these two are. Run their names through the computer. PNC and CIS checks. See if anything comes up. And I want these two pictures circulating. All Forces.' She set the pen down. 'I've spoken with Headquarters and with the Press Office. We're arranging a press conference for this afternoon. It'll be going out on the local and national news this evening. I'm more than convinced that our crimes are linked, and that we are searching for the same killer, and that's what I'm going to reveal. Once I make that announcement there's a fair bet we'll be inundated with calls. I want them all recorded and assessed.' She pointed towards the still CCTV image of the masked man on Gemma Cooke's incident board. 'Now let's see if we can catch our killer and put this enquiry to bed.'

Senses on high alert he gently eased the door shut and tiptoed into the kitchen. He wasn't exactly sure the house was empty. He'd watched them both leave in their cars twenty minutes earlier, but he'd only discovered their whereabouts yesterday and he had not had time to get to know the lie of the land. This wasn't his usual method of working but he recalled his training. Sometimes you needed to adapt.

A sharp fizzing sound fractured the silence and made him jump. He stood stock-still and tensed. Suddenly, the smell of lavender assailed his nostrils; it was the air freshener. He checked himself, smiled and took a step forward. He made his way across the kitchen, into the hallway, where the staircase dog-legged up to the first floor. Careful not to grab the banister, even with gloved hands, he rested his foot on the bottom step and craned his head forward. Listening. He remained like that for the best part of a minute, and then confident he had the house to himself, for at least a couple of hours, he crept upwards.

Dawn Leggate sauntered into the kitchen. Michael was chopping vegetables next to the sink. She set down her bag on the kitchen table and let out a sigh.

Michael glanced over his shoulder. 'Do want to pour us a drink?' He dropped chunks of carrot into a dish and set it to one side. 'Dinner'll be another hour at least.'

Dawn took out a bottle of white wine from the fridge, poured two glasses and handed one to Michael.

He raised it in a salutatory gesture and took a sip. Licking his lips, he said, 'I didn't expect you to be home this early. How's it going?'

'Okay, I suppose. Nothing earth-shattering had come in when I left. A couple of the usual crank calls, like you normally get with these things.' She took a lingering drink of the chilled Chardonnay, and eyeing him over the rim of her glass said, 'How did I do?'

'You were good. Despite the handicap.'

'Handicap?'

Fighting back the urge to laugh he answered, 'The foreign language.'

She narrowed her eyes. 'Ooh, you Sassenach. You've some need to talk with that Yorkshire hill-farmer accent.'

He let out a hearty laugh. 'No, you did good. It was a good conference. You got everything across. The TV did you proud. As I say, I'm surprised you got home so early, I thought you would have been inundated with calls.'

'The phones weren't exactly red-hot when I left. Half a dozen of the team are staying on until midnight to see if anything comes in after the ten o'clock news.' She took another sip of her wine. The unexpected muffled ringtone of her work mobile grabbed her attention. She diverted her gaze towards her work bag. Setting down her glass she began guddling around in its side pockets. Fishing out her phone, she hurriedly gazed at the screen. She didn't recognise the number, but a call on her BlackBerry could only mean one thing.

She answered it.

A female, with a slightly gravelly voice, said, 'Superintendent Leggate. This is Detective Sergeant Macey, Metropolitan Police. I'm sorry to bother you at home. One of your officers gave me your number.'

'No need to apologise. How can I help you?'

'I saw you on the news. The Press Conference.'

'Oh yes, is this to do with the case?'

'I think so. I believe I may have something, which may be of interest to you.'

'What do you have for me, DS Macey?'

'It's about the locket. The locket with the initials JC. I think it's come from one of our jobs.'

- ooOoo -

CHAPTER FIFTEEN

Day Fourteen: 31st March.
Richmond upon Thames.

Hunter stopped beneath the canopy, at the entranceway of Richmond railway station, and took in his first glimpse of the town. Before him two lines of slow moving traffic, in opposite directions, jostled by. Blaring horns sounded everywhere. He checked his watch: 12.30 p.m. Only just gone lunchtime. And yet, the chaotic scene reminded him of rush hour back home.

He watched as two black cabs swung away from the main road and pulled into the station rank in front of him. He took a step back, set down his bag and avoided making eye contact with the cab drivers.

A young Japanese couple brushed past him and jumped into the back of the first cab. Within seconds the taxi was whipping away from the kerb and forcing its way into the nose-to-tail congestion.

He became suddenly conscious of Grace setting down her suitcase beside him. He heard her give off a long sigh and grab a lungful of air.

'Where's the race?' she exclaimed.

He glanced down at her footwear, black patent leather court shoes, and then met her gaze. 'Grace, don't blame me if you can't keep up. I can't help it if you need to make a fashion statement with non-sensible shoes for the occasion.'

She dropped her gaze. 'There's nothing wrong with these shoes. These are Vivienne Westwood. It's better than looking like a dog's dinner.' She fussed her coat around her. 'Who did you say would be meeting us?'

Inside his head, Hunter re-ran the previous night's phone call from Detective Superintendent Leggate. 'We've just had a breakthrough.' Her excited voice had opened. She'd told him that she had received a phone call from a Detective Sergeant in the Metropolitan Police who had informed her that the locket found on Gemma Cooke's body had come from one of their

165

jobs. 'I need you and Grace to go down to London tomorrow and meet up with someone from Richmond CID,' she'd said and finished by telling him to pack an overnight bag and given him the name of the officer he would be liaising with.

'DS Macey,' he said, turning to Grace. He cast his eyes back to the busy street. 'See if you can see anything that remotely looks like a police car.' Just as he'd finished speaking, a white Vauxhall Astra pulled into the kerb, taking up the space left by the departed taxi. The front passenger door sprang open. A slim built, long-legged, woman, wearing a dark blue trouser suit, jumped out. 'You two look like you're lost,' she said, with a throaty, broad, East End drawl. She held out a hand. 'It is DS Kerr and DC Marshall?'

Her gravelly voice reminded Hunter of the singer Bonnie Tyler. He took her hand and shook it. 'Hunter,' he responded, meeting her gaze. He was immediately drawn to her striking features – not just her pretty face, but also the colour of her shoulder-length bob of dyed hair. Copper red. And, as for make-up, she could give Grace a run for her money.

'DS Macey. Scarlett,' she said and nodded backwards into the car. 'My partner spotted you.' She smiled, revealing a perfect set of teeth. 'He thought you looked like cops. No offence.'

'None taken,' Hunter hoisted up his bag.

She shook Grace's hand and then opened the back door of the unmarked car for them. Then she went to the rear and popped the boot. 'Come on, let's have your bags. We're going to take you for some lunch. There's a nice pub just a couple of minutes away.' She checked their faces with an enquiring look. 'You are ready for some food, aren't you?'

Hunter met Grace's look. She nodded. He went to the boot and dropped in his bag. 'That sounds good,' he said, taking Grace's bag from her grasp and placing it beside his. He slammed down the hatchback.

As they climbed into the back seat, Scarlett said to Grace, 'Nice shoes.'

Grace targeted Hunter with a sarcastic smile as she closed the car door.

The Duke pub, was as DS Scarlett Macey had promised, only a few minutes' drive from the railway station. It had the outward appearance of being a traditional pub, but inside the decoration had an updated contemporary flair.

Making for a table, set in a far corner, Scarlett said, 'They serve nice food here.' She dragged out a chair and plonked herself down. 'Tarn will get the drinks.'

Hunter eyed Scarlett's colleague. The man, who looked to be early thirties, was slightly smaller than himself, and of bigger build – but in a broad muscular way. He had short fair hair and strong facial features.

With a questioning look Hunter said, 'Tarn?'

The man smiled. 'It happens every time. Long story, short. My mother and father were fond hillwalkers when they were young. They called me Tarn, and my sister Heather, because of their love of the countryside. He shook Hunter and Grace's hand. 'Tarn Scarr.'

'Tarn Scarr,' Grace repeated. 'You should be an actor with a name like that.'

'Just don't say porn star.' His eyes sparkled. 'Right, what can I get you? I know what you Yorkshire folk are like for your beer. They do hand-pulled real ale here.'

'I'll come to the bar with you,' Hunter offered. 'I'll see what they've got. My partner prefers wine.'

When Hunter and Tarn returned, Scarlett and Grace were busy in conversation. As Hunter set down the drinks, he'd couldn't help but think that the pair were chatting as if they were old friends, catching up.

Scarlett peeled her eyes away from Grace and looking up, met his. 'Don't worry we're not talking job without you. We're talking fashion. Exchanging tips.'

Hunter slid a glass of wine towards his partner. 'Now, why shouldn't I be surprised to hear that.' With his foot, he hooked out a chair and sat down.

Scarlett picked up a menu, and looking around the table said, 'Shall we order some food and then get down to business?'

They talked while they ate. Hunter told DS Macey and DC Scarr about the investigation they were running, especially how they were linking the 1988 murder of Polly Hayes, to the recent killing of Elisabeth Bertolutti, because of the T-shirt. He also told them of the CCTV image they had of the masked man in Sheffield, and how, from the witness, Linane Brazier, they had an exact visual comparison of the person who attacked Elisabeth. Finally, he told the two detectives about Dale and Scott. He watched the DS and DC exchange glances, but there was no recognition of the names in their looks. He said, 'We're certain they're brothers, but unfortunately we don't have any surnames. But we think they might be from around here, or at least they could live around the London area. Our witness met them in different bars around theatreland and got the impression, from talking with them, that they lived down here.'

Scarlett Macey downed the remains of her lager. She licked her bright red lips. 'That's interesting what you're saying about trophy exchanges, because as I told your boss we're certain that the locket – the one with the initials "JC" on it – belonged to a woman who was attacked here in Richmond in nineteen ninety-seven.' She put down her glass. 'How did you come across that? Was it found at one of your crime scenes or was it from someone you arrested?'

'It was found on one of our victims. She was wearing it.'

DS Macey swapped glances with her colleague again. 'The trophy exchange thing again. Although with our job, the woman wasn't killed.'

Hunter quickly pushed himself back in his seat. 'What, she's still alive.'

'Very much so. I spoke with her this morning on the phone. I've fixed up for you to meet her this afternoon. I've told her I'll be taking a photo of the locket for her to see – to confirm it's hers.'

Hunter gave Grace an excited flash of his eyes. 'That's brilliant news.' He returned his gaze to DS Macey. 'Did she get a good look of her attacker? Did she give a description at the time?'

She screwed up her face. 'Honest answer? Don't know. But, somehow I don't think so. I only got this information myself yesterday evening. An ex-colleague, who used to be on my team – he's retired now – rung me after your boss had been on the news. He was the one who recognised the locket. Apparently we had a series of break-ins and attacks on women during the nineteen nineties and he was a member of the team who worked on them. And you're going to find this next thing I tell you very interesting. Especially with what you've just told us. You see the person who attacked the witness, you're going to see this afternoon, wore a mask.'

After lunch, Hunter and Grace booked in at the small hotel they were staying in, left their bags in their rooms and then jumped straight back into the waiting CID car.

DC Scarr took the A316, Twickenham Road out of Richmond; DS Macey had told them the witness now lived in Teddington.

She checked her notes, and then talking back over her shoulder said, 'The person we're going to see is called Janice Crampton. She's a solicitor's clerk who deals with property conveyance. I've got written down here that she was attacked in her home in July nineteen ninety-seven. I don't know the full ins-and-outs of the job yet because the paperwork hasn't turned up. I've got this just from the initial crime report. It's recorded as an aggravated burglary. It says here that Mrs Crampton was confronted by a masked man in her bedroom, but we now know there was more to it than that.'

Quarter of an hour later they pulled up in front of a reasonably modern, three-bedroom, detached house. The four decamped and made their way up the tarmac driveway.

Janice Crampton had the front door open before they had time to ring the doorbell.

DS Macey flashed her warrant card.

'You said it was to do with my locket. Have you caught him?' Janice Crampton was a petite, thin-faced, dark-haired, woman, in her early forties. She wore a blue and white striped T-shirt and jeans.

Hunter stepped forward. 'I'm from South Yorkshire Police. It's to do with a murder investigation I'm involved in up there.'

Her face took on a shocked look. 'A murder. Goodness me.' She stepped to one side. 'Come in.'

They all traipsed down the hallway. Mrs Crampton led them into a lounge-cum-dining room, which was light and airy. She offered them an armchair and sofa. She chose an armchair with her back to the large bay front window.

'A murder to do with my locket?' she said, sitting down.

Hunter leaned forward, resting his forearms on his knees. 'I'm afraid I can't go into all the details, Mrs Crampton, but suffice to say, we think we've recovered the locket you reported stolen in nineteen ninety-seven. It was found on a female who's been murdered. Does the name Gemma Cooke mean anything to you?'

Her eyes drifted up to the ceiling. She pondered for a moment and then returned her gaze. 'No, should it?'

'That's the victim's name.'

'And she's the woman you found my necklace on?'

'We believe so. Would you take a look at this photo?' He slipped to the edge of the sofa, and held out the colour photograph of the locket found on Gemma Cooke's body.

Grace began taking notes.

Janice took the photo out of Hunter's grasp, scrutinised it for several seconds and then nodded. 'That's mine. See, those are my initials on it. My husband bought it for my twenty-first.'

Hunter took back the photograph. 'I want to ask you some questions about how you had this stolen, if you wouldn't mind?'

'Course not. Anything, if it'll help catch who did this. Do you think it's the same person who took my locket?'

'It's a possibility.'

Janice Crampton met Hunter's gaze. 'We had to move after it you know. We couldn't rest. Neither of us. Every little noise at night and we'd be up. We slept with a baseball bat beside the bed for months until we moved.'

Hunter kept eye contact. He gave her a reassuring look. 'I don't want to cause you any undue distress, but it would really help if you could go through what happened to you.'

'Do you want me to go back through that night?'

Hunter nodded. 'If you wouldn't mind.'

She crossed her legs. 'Well it happened on a Friday night. Me and Garry hadn't been married long. Just a couple of weeks, and we were still in the habit of going out every Friday to meet up with our friends. We always went into town and on that night we'd arranged to meet up with our best man and his girlfriend from our wedding. We went to a few pubs and then around midnight-ish we decided to call it a day.'

'So you came straight home?'

'Well, I did. Garry said he was hungry so he stopped by a kebab place. There was a queue, so he told me I needn't wait, and that he'd catch me up, so I left him. I actually got home before he managed to catch me up.' She took a deep breath. 'The house was in darkness, which surprised me, because I was sure I'd left the hall light on before we'd gone out. I remember letting myself in and trying the switch but the light didn't come on. I thought the bulb must have blown. Then I tried the upstairs light and that wouldn't work either, so I thought we'd had a fuse. I didn't know how to sort it, so I thought I'd leave it until Garry got home. I was busting for the toilet and went upstairs to the bathroom. That light wouldn't work either. Then I went into the bedroom.'

Hunter spotted the sudden face change.

She bit down on her bottom lip. 'The curtains were open and so there was enough light for me to see. I'd just taken off my locket and put it on the dressing table when I spotted the things laid out on the bed.'

'Things?'

'Yes, there was my black dress, I normally wore to "do's" and my black bra and knickers. I can remember thinking Garry must have done it for when we got in. You know what I mean. And then this man jumped out from the wardrobe.' Her look froze. 'This masked man. And not a ski mask. It was like out of a horror film. I just screamed. And as I did so, I heard the front door open. Garry had come in. He heard me straight away and came running up the stairs. The man just punched me. In the stomach. Knocked the wind out of me. And then he ran. He thumped Garry as well. In the face. Almost knocked him back down the stairs. I heard him go into the back bedroom. Garry went straight after him but the man had got

171

out through the window. He was so quick. He must have opened it beforehand.'

'And so he escaped?'

She nodded. 'We had a kitchen extension. It was a flat roof. He disappeared over the back fence. We rang the police straight away, and it seemed only like minutes before the first policeman arrived, but he'd long gone.' She pointed a finger towards the photograph Hunter still held. 'And that's when I discovered he'd taken my locket. A couple of detectives came and Forensics fingerprinted everything but they told us the burglar had been wearing gloves. And that's when one of the detectives told us how lucky we'd been.'

Hunter creased his brow and threw her a questioning look. 'What did he mean by that?'

'Well, what he did?'

'What he did?'

'Yes, with the lights. It wasn't the fuse. The man who broke into our house had taken out every bulb. And then, there was the rope.'

'Rope?' Hunter was suddenly conscious that he was beginning to sound like a parrot. He qualified his comment with, 'Where does rope come into it?'

'Beside my dress and underwear he'd left some lengths of rope. The CID man said it looked as though he'd left it there to tie us up.' The colour drained from her face. 'You can see now why I said neither of us could rest. We had a lucky escape. I just kept re-living it. We had to move. Even when we got in this house I couldn't settle. It took me the best part of two years to get over it. If you can call it that. I can still see that night now. Even after all this time.' She shuddered.

'I was going to say I can imagine it. But I can't. It must have been an awful experience.'

'You bet it was. I had nightmares about it.'

'If I can ask you another question?'

'Course. I find I can talk about it now, without breaking down.'

'You describe the man as wearing a mask and said it was like out of a horror film? Can you describe it?'

'Well, as I say, the only light I had was from outside, but it was fairly good light. It was still the middle of summer. As I say it wasn't a ski mask or anything like that. This was made of sacking or something similar. It was loose and baggy. And I recall these really dark eyes and this weird stitched up mouth. It looked like it had been sewn up to look like jagged teeth. It was pretty scary looking, I can tell you.'

Following the interview with Janice Crampton, DS Macey and DC Scarr dropped Hunter and Grace off at their hotel and arranged to meet up with them later for a social drink. DS Macey told them that she would bring along a couple of her team and they could make a night of it.

They met in The Red Cow, on Sheen Road. Hunter and Grace found it easily from the directions they had been given.

A plaque outside the two-storey, red-brick building, described it as the oldest pub in Richmond, and as Hunter stepped inside he noticed that it had retained most of its original character. Its most striking feature being the fine carved wood and gilded-glass central bar. Giving the place the quick once-over, he spotted DS Macey and DC Scarr against the far wall, seated at two tables. There were three other men with them. He caught Scarlett Macey's attention, and with a quick hand signal enquired if she wanted a drink.

She shook her head and pointed at the tables, which were laden with drink.

At the bar, Hunter saw that they had hand-pulled beer on draught. He bought himself a pint of beer, and a glass of white wine for Grace, and then they made their way across the crowded room to join DS Macey and her team.

Taking a seat, he took a generous swallow of his beer. It tasted good.

DS Macey said, 'What do you think about today then? The interview with Mrs Crampton?'

'The mask she describes the bloke wearing certainly fits with the description of what we've got. And the locket thing only makes me think we're probably looking at the same guy for both sets of jobs.'

Scarlett nodded and flashed a sideways look at her colleagues. 'I've briefed the guys about it. And I've also had another chat with the retired detective I told you about. He says he was part of a squad who worked on half-a-dozen similar jobs that happened in Richmond between ninety-one and ninety-seven. They didn't realise there was a link between them all until the incident involving Mr and Mrs Crampton. They worked on the investigation for over two-and-a-half years, but shelved the operation just before two thousand, after there were no further attacks.'

'Any forensics?' asked Hunter.

'None under the old tests. I've made a request for the samples and exhibits to be recovered from our archives to get them submitted for DNA testing. I've also requested the case file and reports. My gaffer has given the go ahead for us to carry out a fresh investigation. We're going to re-interview all the witnesses from the original enquiry, and now that we have the names Dale and Scott, we're going to see if they crop up anywhere. The paperwork should be on my desk tomorrow morning, so you and Grace can go through it with us and take back copies of what you need.'

'That'd be appreciated.'

Scarlett picked up her pint of lager and in a celebratory gesture said, 'Here's to success in our joint operation.'

They chinked glasses and drank.

- ooOoo –

CHAPTER SIXTEEN

Day Fifteen: 1st April.

Hunter woke up with a thumping head. He had a sickening hangover. One of the worst in years, he thought, as he tried to shock himself into some form of recovery under the cold shower. He found some Paracetamol in his toiletries bag and downed a couple with a cup of strong tea in his room. At breakfast, he could only stomach toast. He watched Grace devour a cooked full-English.

As she finished, she clattered down her knife and fork and exaggerated the licking of her lips.

'You're enjoying this, aren't you?' Hunter said, finishing another cup of tea.

'Now why would you think that, Sergeant?'

He speared a finger. 'Because I can see you are.'

'Some of us can take our drink and some of us can't.' She dabbed her mouth with her napkin and pushed back her chair. 'Shall we walk to the station just in case someone wants to be sick?'

He quickly glanced around the dining room, and happy no one was looking their way, gave her 'the finger'.

Richmond Police Station stood on a corner, beside a busy thoroughfare. The front of the building was two-storey, red bricked and of Victorian design. The rear, where the car park was, had a modern extension.

DC Scarr met Hunter and Grace at reception and took them up to the first floor.

They entered a CID office buzzing with activity.

Hunter saw that every desk had an occupant. Detectives were either on phones or tapping away on keyboards. He reflected how it mirrored his own department back in Barnwell when a job was running.

DS Macey greeted them. Hunter couldn't help but notice, that, like his partner, she was made-up and fresh looking. He hoped he didn't look as bad as he felt.

'Good night last night, eh?' she said.

At the periphery of his vision he caught Grace breaking into a grin. He aimed her a warning look, 'I'm afraid I'm paying for it this morning.'

Scarlett gave a hearty laugh. 'I don't know, I thought you Yorkshiremen were made of hardy stuff.'

'That one isn't,' muttered Grace.

He was about to reply when DS Macey said, 'As you can see we've made a start.' She pointed towards a large incident board fastened to the back wall. Over half of it had already been filled. The majority of it was taken up by times, dates, and a precis of each specific attack. Also displayed was a series of crime scene photographs – mainly bedroom settings. And they had the two e-fits of Dale and Scott pinned up. Beneath these, in red, were the words 'Suspects.' Emblazoned across the top of the incident board was the title 'OPERATION SCARECROW 2.'

As if following Hunter's eyes, DS Macey said, 'The original enquiry was called operation Scarecrow. You can guess why. I didn't know that, until I saw the paperwork this morning, so we're running with the same title, but with the number addition.' She chinned the room. 'I've separated each job that was part of the original investigation and delegated a couple of detectives to each of them. They're currently tracking down the victims and witnesses for re-interview.' She half-turned. 'And, I've organised a HOLMES team. They're going to have to convert the original data, but that shouldn't take long before they're up and running.' She flicked her head backwards. 'Come on I've had a photocopy done of the original file for you to go through. We can use my desk.'

DS Macey showed them to her desk. A set of filing trays at one end bore her rank and surname. She wheeled up two chairs, offered them a seat, and cleared a space, pushing aside the filing trays and a number of personal items. She plonked a thick bound file before them. 'I'll get us a drink while you make a start.'

Hunter eyed the chunky dossier. The front sheet had the typed paragraph, *'Operation Scarecrow'* – *Attempted murder, Rape, and Aggravated burglaries, in the London and Richmond upon Thames areas, 1991 – 1997*. He licked his forefinger, checked Grace was okay to progress and turned the page. He was faced with the summary of the incidents. He flicked his way through it and saw that it ran to eight sides. The rest of the file was made up of complainant statements and crime complaints. He returned to the first page and began reading slowly.

The first of the reported attacks occurred on Sunday 21st July 1991. The victim was thirty-six-year-old schoolteacher, Christina Hartley. She lived in her basement flat close to Waterloo Station. Hunter read that she had been out with friends, drinking in bars around Covent Garden, and had got back home at around 2.30 a.m. and gone straight to bed. Half an hour later she had been awakened by noises and found a masked man in her bedroom. He pounced on top of her, held a gloved hand over her mouth and started to fondle her breasts. She bit his hand and managed to scream, and he fled. When the police attended she discovered that the dress she had been wearing earlier that night had been taken. What stood out in her report was that she described the mask as being made of sackcloth with a sewn up mouth. What Hunter also registered was that Christina Hartley made three further reports to the police in the ensuing weeks after the attack. Two related to complaints of her being followed, or at least, she believed she was being followed, which was frightening enough, but a third account, and one which was even more disturbing, was a sighting by her of a similar masked man in the street opposite her home.

Hunter finished reading the first event and exchanged glances with Grace. 'Pretty scary, eh?'

'An understatement. Absolutely terrifying. That would have scared me witless and I'm a cop,' she replied.

They returned to the file.

The second reported attack happened, just over a year later, on Sunday the 16th August 1992. Jackie Slade, a thirty-one-year-old waitress returned home in the early hours to her rented flat in Richmond upon Thames, together with her new boyfriend. They had been out drinking in Westminster. When they entered the house it was in darkness and they found that the hallway light wouldn't come on. As they stepped into the lounge the pair were immediately confronted by someone wearing dark clothing and sacking type mask. The boyfriend challenged him and he fled into the adjoining kitchen and escaped through an open ground floor window. The police were called and they discovered that the telephone wires had been cut and there was rope lying on the bed in the master bedroom. Hunter saw that the disturbing factor about this event was that whoever had been in the flat, had removed a home-made video from Jackie Slade's collection, and had been watching it as she and her boyfriend had entered the house. He felt the hairs prickle at the back of his neck.

He read on.

The third attack was on Sunday the 19th June 1994. A two year gap. It was again in Richmond. Husband and wife, Russell and Kate Wheeler, awoke in the early hours to find a masked man at the bottom of their bed. He threatened them with a knife, ordered them out of their bed and tied them up. Then he went to their daughter's bedroom, nineteen-year-old Emily. There he tied her up and began indecently assaulting her. She managed to scream, and her twenty-year-old boyfriend, who had been sleeping in the guest bedroom, next to hers, came to her aid. There was struggle and the boyfriend was stabbed several times. The boyfriend was seriously injured but survived. The attacker escaped.

Hunter placed a finger by the last sentence and paused his reading. A pattern of similarity was emerging, but with it the level of violence was escalating, he reflected.

He pulled away his finger and continued. The next disturbing incident happened the following year, in the early hours of Sunday 18th June – once more, in Richmond upon Thames. Married couple, Dawn and Jamie Agar, were awoken by a masked man in their bedroom. He held a knife to Jamie's throat, and made his wife, Dawn, tie up her husband. Then, he asked where their twenty-year-old daughter was. They told their attacker that she wasn't at home. She had gone away for the weekend to a friend's house. He raped Dawn, while holding the knife at her husband's neck. Before he left, he tied up Mrs Agar beside her husband, and cut away a square from the bedding, to ensure semen-stained material would not be left as evidence. He took away Dawn's eternity ring from the bedside cabinet.

'The guy's also forensically aware,' Hunter said out loud.

Grace looked up from the report and exchanged glances. 'You can see he's growing in confidence with each attack, can't you?'

Hunter nodded and continued reading.

The next two reports happened in 1996 – Saturday the 11th May and Saturday 19th October. Single females occupied the properties which had been entered. One of the premises was a ground floor flat the other a second floor apartment. Both had been called in as burglaries, by neighbours. The police found that on both occasions many of the rooms' light bulbs had been removed from their sockets and several items of the complainants' underwear had been laid out on the bed.

Having read the previous account Hunter couldn't help but think that the women had been very lucky, by their not being home.

The last recorded episode, featured the incident at Garry and Janice Crampton's home.

And what did the police have to go on. Hunter saw that it was very little. Except for mention of the mask, all they had as a description for the attacker was male, around six foot tall and slim, yet athletic build. It matched any of thousands of men.

As Hunter finished the report he cast his gaze around the room. Each detective he focussed upon was engaged, either on the phone or on the computer, and he guessed that they all would be in the same mindset – determined to catch whoever perpetrated these terrible attacks.

As he mulled over what he had just read, he muttered beneath his breath. 'Their serial attacker is now our serial killer.'

Barnwell.

Hunter and Grace got off the train at Barnwell railway station at 8.35 p.m. Their journey from Richmond, via King's Cross, had taken a little over three-and-a-half hours. As they exited, a couple of taxis were parked up in the station rank. They decided to take one to save the time of arranging a lift.

Grace was dropped off first.

As the taxi drew up outside his home Hunter checked his watch. It was just coming up to 9.00 p.m.

After paying the fare he wearily tramped down the drive. Unlocking the front door, he kicked off his shoes and dropped his overnight bag down in the hallway. Then, he called out to Beth.

She appeared in the lounge doorway. She was in her dressing gown. 'Had a good journey?' she said. 'I thought you were going to give me a call when you got to the station.'

'There were some taxis so we grabbed one to save time.'

Hunter slipped off his coat and dropped it onto the stairs' bottom post. He pulled Beth towards him and kissed her.

'Missed you,' he said. He added, 'You smell good. Been in the bath?'

'Just got out ten minutes ago.' She turned towards the kitchen. 'Do you want something to eat?'

'I had a sandwich and a cuppa on the train.'

'Do you want me to get you a drink, while you jump in the shower? I'll pour myself a wine now I don't have to pick you up.'

'To be honest, I just fancy a cup of tea. I've had a hangover most of the day. We went out with Richmond CID last night. I was really bad this morning.'

Beth flashed him a grin. 'You're getting too old to be partying.'

'Tell me about it.' He gave a Beth a quick kiss, dragged his coat back off the banister, picked up his bag and climbed the stairs. He called back, 'Are the boys tucked up?'

'They're at your mum and dad's. They phoned up earlier and offered. And they said they'd take them to school in the morning.'

'We've got the house to ourselves then. Heaven,' he called back as started to undress.

Feeling refreshed, following his shower, Hunter returned downstairs. Beth was lounging on the sofa, sipping a glass of red wine. He spotted a mug of steaming tea on the coffee table. He also eyed the cardboard box he had retrieved from his parents' garage. The lid was off and some of its contents were spread out.

Flopping into his armchair he said, 'Who's been sneaking a look at my personal stuff? As if I didn't know.'

Beth grinned. 'Well, if someone will leave their personal stuff lying around they're asking for it to be looked at, aren't they.'

'I didn't leave it lying around. I put it with my painting things.'

'Well, the boys found it. I caught them this morning rummaging through the box.' She picked up an envelope and gently waved it. 'You were a sloppy sod in your younger days.' Turning it over she said, 'You never put "Sealed With A Loving Kiss" on the back of my letters.'

He took it off her and looked at it. 'If you want to know, I didn't send that letter. Polly sent that to me when she was on holiday.' In a scolding fashion he tapped her hand with the envelope. 'And come to think of it, young lady, you never send me letters like this.'

'Oh, Hunter Kerr, I'm always telling you I love you.'

He gave a short laugh and began picking up the items spread out over the coffee table. He gave each of them a quick look-over as he placed them back in their box. They evoked several flashbacks. The last things he picked up were four black and white photo booth photographs of Polly and himself in a lovers' clinch. He remembered those being taken in Woolworth's.

Beth sipped her wine. Then, angling her glass towards him said, 'What was she like?'

He dropped the photos into the box, picked up his mug of tea and settled back. 'What do you mean?'

'Well I can see she was pretty. But what was she like, personality-wise?'

He thought on the question for a few seconds, then said, 'She was nice, kind. It was such a long time ago though. We were teenagers. I thought I was in love.'

'Yeah, but since you met me you know what love is, don't you?'

With a cheeky grin he replied, 'Do I?'

'Ooh, Hunter Kerr. You wouldn't be without me for the world.'

He rested back his head. 'No I wouldn't.'

She took another drink. 'How did you feel when you found out about her being murdered?'

'It was surreal. Like a dream going on in my head. It didn't sink in at first. Not until the funeral. Then, it hit home. It affected me for ages. But, eventually you move on, don't you? You know it's why I joined the job all those years ago. Now it feels really weird, dealing with it, after all that time.' He glanced up to the ceiling, then re-met Beth's eyes. 'I'll tell you what was weird. And uncomfortable. Going to see Polly's parents and giving them the news.'

With a smile she said, 'I think you need something stronger than tea. You're going all maudlin on me.'

'Oh, go on then, you've twisted my arm. I'll have a small nightcap.'

- ooOoo -

CHAPTER SEVENTEEN

Day Sixteen: 2nd April.
Barnwell.

The BMW reversed out of the drive and braked in the middle of the road. The driver gave a quick glance towards the house, waved, and then, with a squeal of tyres, set off towards the end of the street.

From his hiding place he waited while it swung away from the junction. Into his head sprang the words 'Watching the detectives' – the line from Elvis Costello's song, and he couldn't help but smile conceitedly.

Detectives – I've shit 'em. He had already been inside the house once and they'd not even noticed. He looked at his watch. In another half an hour he knew she would be gone as well.

Perfect.

The plan was coming together. Like it always did. This time though, he wasn't going to jump in. He really wanted to freak her out.

He checked his watch again.

Now all he had to do was wait.

'The names Dale and Scott didn't ring any bells with the Richmond team, I'm afraid.' Hunter had just finished giving the MIT squad a rundown of his and Grace's visit to Richmond upon Thames.

Detective Superintendent Leggate's eyes left Hunter and scanned the room. 'Never mind, it's early doors. I think everyone will agree the visit was a success. We certainly have a bigger picture of what has emerged here. It certainly looks as though the Richmond jobs were a starting point for our killer. Though, given these attacks, unlike Elisabeth Bertolutti, who had a link to Richmond and London and met with our current suspects, I'm at pains to see where Polly Hughes and Gemma

Cooke fit into this. We don't have them linked to any events in London, do we?'

A couple of detectives returned shaking heads.

She settled her gaze upon Hunter.

He pursed his mouth. 'I don't recollect Polly ever going to Richmond or London, or mentioning it.'

Mike Sampson piped up, 'We know Gemma had an altercation with a man in the Frog & Parrot, which was followed by the masked man following her in Sheffield and possibly home. Do you think it could it be in both cases of unfortunately being in the wrong place at the wrong time?'

'That's something I want to explore. Hunter, I want you to speak with Polly's parents this morning. Check if they've ever been to these places, or if they've got relatives or friends down there.'

Hunter made a note of it.

'And I want twice daily contact with the Richmond team. Share what we've both got. Having them on board is going to be a big help, especially if our current suspects do live in their neck of the woods. Hunter and Grace, you've made the initial links with that team. I want you two to continue that contact.'

They both returned a nod.

'Have we got anywhere with the green cloak Polly Hughes was found wrapped in?'

Mike Sampson said, 'No one's come forward to identify it yet. I've chased up the Press Office to see if we can give it some more publicity. And it's on fast-track at Forensics. I spoke with them yesterday afternoon and they said they should begin DNA work on it in the next couple of days.'

'Okay, let's see if we can chivvy that along a bit quicker. It would be nice to find out where that came from, especially as it doesn't feature in the Richmond enquiry.' She clapped her hands, 'Okay, fresh day ahead everyone. Let's make every minute of it count.'

With a satisfied sigh, Hunter signed the last of the 'action reports,' scooped them up and tapping them together into a semblance of neatness he dropped them into his out tray. Relaxing his concentration he gazed out through the window.

The view wasn't great. He looked down over the rear car park. The only activity there was the dog man cleaning his van. He pulled back his gaze and scanned the room. Most of the team were still at their desks, handling calls or working at their computers. He spotted Isobel, from the HOLMES team, writing away on the incident boards. He could make out she was updating them with the information from 'Operation Scarecrow.'

Returning his eyes back to his cluttered desk he sucked in his breath. He hated being desk-bound. Though, looking at the material scattered across its surface, he knew he would be going nowhere today. He had a fair bit of Polly's exhibits to go through. He still hadn't finished reading her five-year diary and he'd brought in the contents of the cardboard box from home. He wanted to check if there was anything in there that made any reference to London or Richmond. An earlier phone call to her mother had failed to reveal any connection.

The first item he selected was the envelope with the acronym 'S.W.A.L.K.' written across its torn rear flap – the letter Beth had mocked him about last night. He slipped out the piece of folded paper. As he opened it up he smiled. At the top of the page an imprint of a pair of red lipstick lips smeared the opening line of 'Hi Hunter'. He imagined Polly's voice whispering his name, as she penned it, and remembered finding similar notes in his school blazer and text books. He began to read. It was the first of two letters she had sent him while holidaying in Cornwall, with her parents, and best friend Lucy, during July 1988. The opening paragraph was about how much she was missing him. She then proceeded to outline some of the things she and Lucy had been up to. As he got to the last paragraph, on the first page, he caught his breath. He read the paragraph again. Dropping the letter, he snatched up Polly's diary. Opening it, he flicked through pages speedily, quickly checking the calendar months and years, at the top corner of each page, until he found the dates he was looking for. Placing the diary flat down on his desk he began to read slowly through Polly's daily writings over a two-week time span.

As he finished he looked up and set his eyes on Polly's incident board.

That's it, he said to himself. *That's the link.*

He scooted back his chair and dashed out of the office.

Detective Superintendent Leggate's door was ajar.

Hunter tapped but didn't wait for an invite to enter.

'Boss, I've got something,' he said, pushing open the door and stepping into the office.

Dawn Leggate looked up from her desk. She extended a hand and offered Hunter the seat in front of her desk. He dropped Polly's letter on top of the paperwork the Detective Superintendent had been working on and plonked himself down in the chair.

Leaning forward he said, 'I've not mentioned this, but when Polly was murdered, I kept some of the things that were personal between us. I left them at my mum and dad's house when I left home and a couple of days ago I found them again. I've started to go through them to see if there was anything relevant, and a couple of those things were letters she sent me in 1988, when she was on holiday with her parents, and best friend, in Cornwall.'

He stabbed a finger towards the letter. 'Just read that last paragraph, boss.'

Hunter watched the SIO's eyes move along the letter. He gave her a few moments to read it, leaned in further, to get better sight of the writing, and said, 'As you can see, she's put down there, the sentence, "you've got competition Hunter. Me and Lucy have been chatted up by two good looking lads. But you've no need to worry I've told them I've got a gorgeous boyfriend back home."' He met her gaze. 'I'd forgotten, but now I can remember quizzing her about this when she came home and she ribbed me about me being jealous over it. Anyway, she wouldn't tell me who they were.' He produced Polly's diary, 'So, just now I decided to check the dates, when she was on holiday, to see if she'd put anything in there about them.' He opened the diary to the pages he had pre-selected and laid it over Polly's letter. He kept his fingers pressed firmly on the bottom of the facing pages to stop the book springing closed. He dipped his head. 'Just read these entries.'

Detective Superintendent lowered her eyes and silently read the entries Hunter was pointing out

Wednesday 13 July.
Met two lads today. Had a laugh with them, but not as nice as Hunter.

Friday 15 July.
Bumped into Dale and Scott again today. Could tell Scott fancied Lucy. Felt a bit of a gooseberry.

Monday 18 July.
Dale and Scott becoming a bit of a pain now. Everywhere we go they're there. Can't they take a hint.

Thursday 21 July.
Didn't go down to the beach today to avoid Dale and Scott. Going home tomorrow. Thank God. Looking forward to seeing Hunter.

Dawn Leggate's head jerked up. She met Hunter's eyes. 'Bloody hell. Get onto Devon and Cornwall straight away with this.'

He rolled out from beneath the bed and for a few seconds lay there, gently flexing his joints. He wasn't surprised as to how stiff he was. He had lain there for the best part of four hours, hardly daring to move, and controlling his breathing as he'd listened to the pair moving around the house. A couple of times he'd heard them pass by the door of the room he was hiding in. On those occasions he'd tightened his grip on the knife and not let go until they'd gone back downstairs. An hour ago they had come upstairs for the final time, and he'd listened to them bathing and preparing themselves for bed. He'd waited patiently until satisfied that they were asleep.

This is my time.

He eased himself up, rolled his neck, straightened his mask and tiptoed to the door. He grabbed the handle and listened at the panel.

The house was quiet.

Turning the handle, ever so slowly, he opened it.

He edged onto the landing and listened again. Adjusting to the gloom he could make out that their bedroom door was ajar. He inched his way forward.

Suddenly, a rushing noise invaded his hearing; the adrenaline had kicked in. He caught himself and steadied his breathing.

Regaining control, he stepped into their bedroom. He could just make out the outline of their forms beneath the duvet. From the sounds they gave off he could tell they were in a deep sleep.

He stood at the edge of their bed. The feeling of power surged through him. Right now he could do anything he wanted. But he'd already decided he wasn't going to do anything. Not tonight. Tonight, he was there for a purpose, and that purpose was to instil fear.

Scare the fucking living daylights out of her.

He slipped out his mobile phone and snapped off a photo. The flash lit up the room and for a split second he didn't stir.

When there was no movement from them, he slipped backwards out of the room.

That was the first part of the plan over.

- ooOoo -

CHAPTER EIGHTEEN

Day Seventeen: 3rd April.

He took a grip on his shuddering Despite the extra layers of clothing he had put on the cold was beginning to creep through. When he had slipped into position two hours ago he hadn't anticipated the temperature dropping so low.

Nevertheless, it had been worth it. For the last hour, hiding among bushes opposite the house, he had watched her flitting backwards and forwards across the lounge window. Now, however, he'd just lost that view. Her lover had closed the curtains.

He clenched his teeth and balled his hands into fists.

Suddenly, the front door opened making him jump. He tucked himself tighter into the bushes.

Back-lit by the hall light she appeared in the entranceway, carrying something.

Standing stock-still he strained his eyes to get a better look.

She stepped down onto the path and walked in front of the garage. The security light activated giving him a much clearer look. He saw that she was carrying out the rubbish.

Stopping by the wheelie bin, she opened it, deposited the rubbish and dropped down the lid. Then, instead of walking back into the house, she turned and looked in his direction.

His heart missed a beat. Holding his breath, he didn't move.

A few seconds later, she shook her head, shrugged her shoulders and then headed back indoors.

As she closed the front door, he let out the breath he had been holding and glanced up at the night sky. He smiled. Together with the camouflage clothing he had brought, the darkness had played its part.

As he emerged from the bushes he thought about his next move.

- ooOoo -

CHAPTER NINETEEN

Day Eighteen: 4th April.

Hunter was making his way across the station's rear yard when he heard his name being called. He looked up to the first floor and saw Barry Newstead half-leaning out of an open window.

Barry shouted, 'There's a DC on the phone from Devon and Cornwall wanting you. He says it's important.'

Hunter broke into a jog, quickly keyed in the door security code, took the back staircase two steps at a time and burst into the office.

He checked Barry's look, as he gestured towards his desk and Hunter spied the handset resting on his blotter.

Taking a deep breath, he picked up the phone. 'DS Kerr.'

The person on the other line announced he was DC Highton based at Wadebridge.

For ten minutes Hunter hung on to every word the detective said. He made copious notes on bits of scrap paper, and fired off the occasional question, but mostly, he listened. When he'd finished, before hanging up, he scouted the room. The person he wanted wasn't in.

He caught Barry's gaze as he replaced the handset.

Barry said, 'Looking at that face, the words cat and cream come to mind.'

'Just got a right result. Do you know where the gaffer is?'

Barry flicked his head towards the far wall. 'Last I saw, she was next door.'

Hunter could hardly contain himself as he breezed into the HOLMES team's office. He saw the Detective Superintendent checking through some house-to-house questionnaires. She had pulled up a chair and was sitting beside Isobel Stevens.

'Boss, have you got a couple of minutes. I did what you asked yesterday – sent down a photograph of the green hooded cape and some information about our murders, to Devon and

Cornwall, and a DC from Wadebridge has just got back to me. I think we've tracked down the origins of the cape found on Polly.'

Dawn Leggate lowered her papers. 'You have?'

'Yes, an unsolved murder in Cornwall going back to 1986. In a place called Harlyn Bay. And get this, that's the same place where Polly stayed on holiday.'

'Good God, Hunter, that's brilliant.'

'I know, great result, isn't it! Apparently, this DC's dad is a retired DI, and he happened to be talking to him about our job and showed him the photo. The ex-DI is almost certain it's from one of their unsolved murders. He worked on the case of a couple who were murdered while camping at Harlyn Bay. I've only got the sketchiest of details, so I've asked him to e-mail me or fax me something. He's going to get some more from his dad and then see what he can get from their archives.'

'Bugger that, Hunter. Get back onto him, and tell him you're going down to speak personally with his dad. Sort out some accommodation, book out a pool car and take Grace with you. And don't come back until you've detected our job.' She flashed him a huge grin. 'This is just what we've been waiting for.'

- ooOoo -

CHAPTER TWENTY

Day Nineteen: 5th April.
Harlyn Bay, Cornwall.

On a well-worn path down to Harlyn Bay beach Rodney Highton marched ahead of Hunter and Grace. A battering wind was meeting them headlong and making for an uncomfortable journey.

Head down, Hunter called ahead, 'Your son said on the phone that you're fairly confident this job is connected to ours.'

Above the sound of the wind Rodney shouted back. 'After seeing the photo he showed me the other day, I'm almost one hundred per cent certain that hooded cloak he showed me belonged to our female victim. You did say it was found on a murdered girl, back in your neck-of-the-woods, didn't you?'

'A sixteen-year-old girl, called Polly Hayes. She was stabbed, while out walking her dog, in nineteen eighty-eight.'

The former DI's pace was slackening. 'And our job was in nineteen eighty-six, two years earlier. That's too much of a coincidence wouldn't you say. I mean two females murdered. Ours was missing a green hooded cloak exactly like the one your girl was found wearing.'

'She was found wrapped in it,' corrected Hunter.

'And you've also said your victim had holidayed down here?'

'Two months before she was murdered.'

Highton stepped down off the path onto the beach. Hunter and Grace followed. The sand was damp and compacted.

Glancing back he continued, 'And you've also said you believed the killer you're hunting is swapping trophies between victims?'

'Not believe anymore. We know that as a definite fact.'

'Answers all the questions then! For me, this has to be the same killer.' He turned and rubbed his hands. 'I've been waiting years for this.'

And so have I, thought Hunter.

Heading off right, towards the jutting headland, Highton stopped after fifty yards of trudging through uneven wet sand. 'This is roughly where we found the murder weapon – a scythe.'

Hunter was only a couple of yards behind Rodney Highton, but he could only just make out what he was saying – the combination of crashing waves and the billowing wind, whipping in off the Atlantic Ocean, and the discordant cries of squawking seagulls, swooping and hovering around them, competed against his soft West Country accent. He leaned in and focussed on the wet patch of sand the retired DI was pointing to. He met his eyes and nodded. 'Any forensics?' Hunter asked.

Rodney shook his head, 'No. It had been in the sea for hours. It was only by sheer luck it was found. The tide was out.'

Hunter followed the line of the man's tilted-back head. He was looking up the sloping cliff face of the headland.

Pointing upwards, Highton said, 'We believe it was thrown from up there. There's a path leading from the campsite. It goes all the way around the headland.' He paused and added, 'The weapon used to kill the couple was stolen from the outbuilding of a farm, half a mile away from here.' The retired DI spun on his heels and faced Hunter and Grace. 'Come on I'll show you now where we found the bodies.' As he set off the wind caught his coat and whipped it around him like a cape. It seemed to catch him unawares for a second and he staggered. Then, catching himself, he leaned into the buffeting wind and put in a military style march back the way they had come.

Hunter watched his back and thought, *What a character.*

As he followed in his wake he found himself reflecting.

Yesterday, the laborious drive down to Cornwall had taken them seven-and-a-half hours. It had been 8.30 p.m., before he and Grace had booked into a small hotel in Wadebridge.

After grabbing a meal and a pint, Hunter had spoken briefly over the phone with retired Detective Inspector, Rodney

Highton and arranged to pick him up from his home that morning.

When they had pulled up outside his bungalow, he was waiting for them on the doorstep, wearing a pin-stripe suit, with collar and tie; dressed as if he was still on the job.

As he had climbed into the back of their car he had tapped the face of his watch and reminded them, 'You told me you'd pick me up at ten a.m. You're ten minutes late.'

Hunter had found himself apologising and had set off with a wheel-spin. Out of the corner of his eye he had caught Grace cracking a grin.

During the journey to Harlyn Bay, the former DI had told them he had been retired ten years and then moaned on about how the job wasn't like it used to be. 'Bureaucratic and soft' he had repeatedly said. At times, Hunter had found himself switching off. It had been like having an older version of Barry Newstead in the back of the car with them. He had been glad when they had finally pulled up at the campsite entrance.

They had been met by one of the site's joint owners, carrying out maintenance, who explained that they weren't open yet for visitors. Once they explained the purpose of their visit he was more than happy to give them unrestricted access and left them to it.

It had been Hunter's first view of the place where Polly had holidayed in 1988, two months prior to her brutal death.

Calling back over his shoulder Rodney shouted above the wind, 'This was my only undetected murder in thirty-five years. Good record that, eh?'

It dragged Hunter back from his thoughts. He agreed it was a pretty good record and asked, 'No suspects?'

Highton glanced back as he walked, 'None that you could put firmly in the frame for it. But I had my suspicions.'

After a couple more minutes of tramping across calf high, damp rye-grass, the retired DI stopped and turned. He drew a circle in front of him. 'This is where we found them. Roughly anyway. She was found inside the tent, and he was about ten yards away. Witnesses reported hearing shouting and screaming in the early hours but it was dark and so it wasn't until first light when they were found. A bloke going to the toilet block saw their tent collapsed and went to investigate. He found the husband first and called the police. He was in a hell of a mess. The blade had actually gone in under his chin and up through the roof of his mouth. It looked as though he'd been crawling around for a while before he died. There was blood everywhere. The wife was found by the police. She had been slashed and hacked repeatedly with the same scythe. The pathologist said she had literally bled to death.'

'Just remind me of their names again?' said Hunter.

'James and Helen Moore.' He pushed a hand through his thick, wavy, white hair. 'They lived not too far away from here – a little village out by Bodmin Moor. They were druids, the pair of them. Hence the cloak. They'd come here to meet up with others, to do whatever druids do. But they never actually got to meet up with any of them – their bodies were found the morning after they'd set up camp. They'd come here with their two fourteen-year-old sons – twins.' He darted a nod towards a small clump of bushes. 'The boys were found hiding in bushes over there – covered in their parents' blood.'

'Did they see who'd done it?'

'To be honest we didn't get anything from them. The pair were in a bit of a state when they were found. They weren't injured or anything, just kept giving us these weird blank looks.' He tapped his temple. 'We took them to hospital and a child psychologist had a look at them. She said that they were in a deep state of shock. We were told there was no point in interviewing them until they came out of it and so we tried to track down their relatives.' He shrugged his shoulders. 'We couldn't find one living relative – would you believe that – and so Social Services took them into care. And, that's when our problems started.

Hunter drove to the next village – Constantine Bay – and pulled into a pub car park for lunch. The pub was a traditional one made of Cornish granite with a dark slate roof. A sign next to the door said it served home-cooked food.

Hunter led the way inside. The interior maintained the traditional look with oak beams to the ceilings and light painted walls. It was laid out mainly for the serving of food as

195

opposed to drinking. Scanning the lounge he saw that most of the tables were occupied, but spotting an empty one next to a slate fireplace he pointed it out.

Grace shepherded Rodney Highton to the table while Hunter got the drinks.

He bought two pints of local hand-pulled beer and a glass of wine and made his way back. Grace and the retired DI were poring over a menu.

'The food looks nice,' said Grace, looking up as Hunter set down her glass.

He slipped off his coat, hung it over the back of a seat and sat down. Taking the top off his beer he said, 'Rodney, you were saying that you had your suspicions about who killed the couple?'

'Not at first we didn't. It looked like a frenzied attack by a madman, and initially we focussed our enquiries on known psychiatric patients and we also visited psychiatric wards at all the hospitals around here. But as we got into the job and the forensics came through, or should I say, lack of forensics, it just didn't feel right.'

'How do you mean?'

'Well, I'll start with the victims first.' He took a sip of his beer and licked his lips. 'These two were a couple with no known enemies. They lived a very quiet lifestyle and there wasn't anything untoward in their backgrounds. I mentioned to you earlier that we didn't find one living relative of theirs – well that's not strictly true. We did eventually find the pair's adoptive parents. In both cases they were abandoned babies and taken care of by Social Services. Helen Moore originated from Liverpool and James from Birmingham. When we spoke to their adoptive parents we learned that during their early lives the pair were quiet and introvert. Helen was bright and an avid reader but didn't want to stay on for further education. When she was seventeen she sat down with her adoptive parents one day and told them she wanted to find her own way in the world and then left. James was a creative young man, who fantasised a lot and who very much kept himself to himself. In fact at sixteen, he simply packed his bags, left a note telling his adoptive parents he was off to find work, and left home. That, in a nutshell was their early background.' He shook his head and took another drink. 'We have absolutely no idea how James and Helen came together. We just know that in nineteen seventy the pair married at Liskeard Register Office, rented a cottage on the edge of the moors and a year following their marriage Helen gave birth to twins.' Pausing for a few seconds he drifted his gaze around the pub. Then he turned to Hunter and Grace. 'I suppose the only thing that was slightly controversial was their practice of Paganism. They were involved with a group of druids around here.' He swung his gaze between Hunter and Grace. 'The press had a field day with that, I can tell you – rituals, dark arts and human sacrifices – that kind of stuff. You can imagine it, can't you?'

'But their murders had nothing to do with that?' asked Hunter.

'No. We're almost certain of that. We spoke to the circle of druids they mixed with – who were their only friends by the way – and all of them had alibis.'

'What were they doing camping?' asked Grace.

'It was a frequent thing apparently. They usually went off and camped near Bronze Age Monuments and the likes. Stone circles, that kind of thing.' He took another drink. 'You can see now what I said about the press having a field day!'

'And they hadn't upset anyone? And it wasn't a robbery?' questioned Hunter.

Rodney shook his head. 'We didn't have any motive whatsoever. On the face of it, it was a random killing.'

'But you said you had your suspicions?' asked Hunter.

'Only when we began to look closely at the twins. During our enquiries we discovered that they'd both been interviewed when they'd been eleven, following the death of a thirteen-year-old boy. The story went that a group of kids, including James and Helen's lads, went off playing hide-and-seek around a derelict farmhouse, and one of them – a thirteen-year-old lad – didn't come home. The local police organised a search that same evening, but they hadn't found the lad by nightfall and so had to abandon it. He was found the following morning in an old chest freezer in the cellar of the disused farmhouse. He'd suffocated. All the kids were interviewed, but on the surface it looked like a tragic accident – the kid had climbed into the freezer to hide and the heavy lid had fallen shut on him. The inquest recorded an accidental verdict.' He finished the remainder of his beer and set down his glass. 'There is an add-on to this. Once we heard this story we re-interviewed the people who'd been involved in this and discovered that one of the girls in the group had been fancied by one of James and Helen's boys, but the thirteen-year-old – the one who died – had got off with her and then repeatedly taken the mick out of them. Well once we'd heard this, we made arrangements to formally interview the boys, who by this time were in a care home just outside Wadebridge – but that never happened. We don't know how, but we guessed they must have got wind, because when we turned up the next day, they were nowhere to be found. Both of them had packed most of their things and disappeared overnight. We circulated them, and made loads of enquires at the time, but we never found them. They as good as dropped off the face of the earth.'

'And the names of the two boys?' asked Hunter.

'Dale and Scott – Dale and Scott Moore.'

After dropping Rodney Highton back at home Hunter and Grace returned to their hotel in Wadebridge. Hunter rang Detective Superintendent Leggate and gave her the news.

'That's brilliant, Hunter,' she said down the line. 'Are you liaising with anyone down there about this?'

'Yeah. I've filled in Rodney Highton's son with what his dad's told us. He's in Wadebridge CID. He got back to me ten minutes ago. He's spoken with his DCI and they're setting up an incident room down here. They want me and Grace in tomorrow morning to give them the heads up on what we've got from our jobs. They're setting up HOLMES as we speak, and currently pulling together the paperwork and exhibits from the original job. I've passed on your name so you should be getting a phone call shortly from the SIO who'll be running it.'

'Good. What about Dale and Scott Moore? Are you on to anything down there? Do we have an address, or anything for them?'

'Not as yet. That's one of the priorities. They're trawling their systems, and going back over the original file to see if any friends or contacts were listed at the time. However, that's not looking too good. Rodney Highton is of the opinion that the pair were loners, who relied on each other for company.'

'And what about the Met? Have you informed them about this?'

'Not yet. DS Macey was my next call.'

'I'll make sure that's done. Do you need any more resources, Hunter? Do you want anyone else to join you?'

'Not at the moment. DC Highton tells me that they're currently pulling together a team. I'll get back to you tomorrow morning straight after the briefing and update you on that.'

'Okay, Hunter, and once again well done – it looks as though things are knitting together nicely.'

- ooOoo -

CHAPTER TWENTY-ONE

Day Twenty: 6th April.
Wadebridge, Cornwall.

The incident room had been set up in the CID office at Wadebridge police station. Hunter and Grace rose early at the hotel, and gave breakfast a miss to get to the station well before morning briefing. They were met in reception by DC Stuart Highton. As he led them upstairs he told them that extra resources had been drafted in from other parts of the county, and so they weren't surprised when they entered an office bursting at the seams and bustling with activity.

Two large wipe boards had been set up at the front and Hunter scrutinised the display. One of the boards was full of photographs – mainly black and white, together with an aerial photo of Harlyn Bay and a large scale ordnance map of the area. He stepped closer to the boards and focused on the crime scene shots. Even in black and white, the sight of James and Helen Moore's mutilated bodies was horrific. On the adjoining board were details of their killings and a list of priorities. He noted that they had acquired copies of the suspect e-fits which Linane Brazier had helped construct. Besides those were two head and shoulders colour shots of two teenage boys. They looked alike, and were dressed similarly, in white shirts, with blue and black striped ties. Below these, in red ink, had been written, 'Dale & Scott Moore – 14 years,' and he guessed these were old school photographs from the original case file. Even given the fact that these images were twenty three years old, he knew that with computer technology they would soon be able to pull together something which would closely resemble what Dale and Scott looked like now. This was a good start, he thought.

Hunter and Grace had no sooner sat down with Stuart Highton to discuss things, when a tall, slim, flaxen haired man, in a dark blue suit strolled into the room. Chattering faded away as he made his way to the front.

Stopping beside the incident boards he cleared his throat and glanced in Hunter and Grace's direction. 'For our guests here this morning, I am DCI Stainthorpe and I am running this investigation.'

Hunter gave him a courteous nod.

'Okay, let's remind ourselves of why we are here.' He shot a sideways look at the boards and then returned his gaze. 'On the twenty-fifth July, nineteen eighty-six, James, a primary school teacher, and Helen Moore, a social worker, both thirty-six, were murdered at Harlyn Bay...'

Hunter listened intently as the DCI outlined the circumstances of the slayings, which translated in not too dissimilar detail what retired DI Rodney Highton had already imparted the previous day.

Ten minutes into his speech DCI Stainthorpe said, 'I am told that the original enquiry got bogged down with rumour and innuendo from quite a number of sources. The fact that these two were part of a circle of druids created all manner of suspicion. The original team had to deal with dramatic headlines, witnesses who'd heard rumours that the children were involved in animal sacrifices and that they'd been made to dance naked. The fact of the matter is that none of that was true. The circle of Druids James and Helen belonged to were respectable, law-abiding, professional people and the only thing they practised was Paganism – and only in respect of worship. That was it. I have no doubt once the media get wind of our re-investigation of these murders those issues will crop up again. However, we have already prepared press statements to refute all those rumours. With regards the investigation itself, despite the fact that a large number of people were interviewed no firm suspects were identified. That was until these two came into the frame...' he paused and slapped a hand over Dale and Scott's school photographs '...following the accidental death of a thirteen-year-old boy.'

Again, Hunter listened on as the DCI revealed details of the incident Rodney had already mentioned.

Continuing, Stainthorpe said, 'After running away from the care home Dale and Scott Moore effectively dropped off the radar. And with no one else in the frame the investigation into their parents' murder was wound up in nineteen eighty-nine.' The DCI dropped his gaze upon Hunter. 'Now, following the murder of three women in South Yorkshire, these two have arisen as suspects again.' He extended an open hand toward Hunter. 'I'd like to bring you in here, DS Kerr. Can you tell us about your killings and how Dale and Scott Moore fit into your enquiry?'

For the next half-hour Hunter had the floor, explaining in detail the 1988 murder of his girlfriend, Polly Hayes, and the recent slaughter of Gemma Cooke and Elisabeth Bertolutti. He also outlined the evidence they had gathered during their enquiries, and then, he disclosed the links to the attacks in Richmond upon Thames during the 1990s.

As he finished DCI Stainthorpe picked up the lead again. 'It would be fair to say that Dale and Scott Moore have a lot of questions to answer and are our chief TIEs. I therefore want all the stops pulling out to Trace, Interview and Eliminate these two as soon as.' He stabbed a finger over the two suspects' e-fits. 'We must consider these men as a real threat, as well as a danger to women out there, and with that in mind I have arranged a press conference for two p.m. this afternoon. I have already cleared it with the Met and South Yorks. By this evening their names and faces will be slapped across every TV in the country.'

By four o'clock Hunter had had enough. He'd spent the day rooted at DC Stuart Highton's desk, reading through a copy of the original file into the murders of James and Helen Moore, and listening to updates coming in – though unable to get involved – and he was frustrated.

He'd caught up with DS Macey on the phone, who'd told him she was on her way to join them and anticipated her arrival to be around 5.00 p.m. He'd given her the name of the hotel where he and Grace were staying and then arranged to meet them in a recommended pub-cum-diner in Wadebridge.

From the police station he went to the hotel and following a quick shower and change of clothing, Hunter contacted Detective Superintendent Leggate and gave her an update. Then, he called on Grace in her room and shared his frustration. She'd told him that what he needed was a pint. He hadn't argued and they'd set off early into Wadebridge town centre.

It hadn't taken them long to find the place DC Highton had recommended – it was a large Victorian pub on a corner by the High Street.

As soon as they entered they spotted the copper red hair of DS Scarlett Macey, who along with her partner Tarn Scarr, were already at a table with drinks in front of them. Hunter acknowledged them with a raised hand and went to the bar while Grace made her way across the lounge to join them.

'This is a surprise. I wasn't expecting you two for another hour or so,' said Hunter, returning from the bar and setting down his pint of local ale. He handed Grace a glass of chilled white wine and pulled up a chair.

Tapping her colleague's shoulder Scarlett replied, 'The roads weren't that bad so Tarn was able to put his foot down. We got here half an hour ago. We've managed to get booked in at the same hotel as you. We thought you'd still be at the incident room so we dumped our bags and came straight down here. I'm famished – I could eat a horse. We've just ordered some food.' She pointed out a menu at the end of the table. Picking up her pint of lager she continued, 'How's the investigation going?'

Hunter relayed the discussions from morning briefing. 'I hope you don't mind, but as you weren't around I told them about the Richmond attacks.'

Scarlett shook her head, 'Not at all.' She took a long drink of her lager and then putting down her glass added, 'I couldn't believe it when your boss told me about this latest job. Talk about serial killers. Do we know if it's one or both of them involved?'

Hunter shrugged his shoulders. 'We don't know if they're working together, or independently, or what. There's no doubt they were together when the thirteen-year-old mysteriously ended up dead in the freezer, and they were together when their parents were murdered, and as we know they've been in each other's company when they've been talking with one of our witnesses in London. But, as to our murders, only one person has been seen.' Hunter picked up his beer. 'How've you got on with your enquiries?'

'Really good. Some positive results,' answered Scarlett. 'You know we've been re-visiting victims and witnesses from the Richmond attacks?'

Hunter and Grace nodded.

'Well, initially we had a bit of difficulty tracking down some of them, because they've moved, but we've so far traced the victims and witnesses from two of the jobs and we've had a result.'

Hunter's eyes widened.

'I don't know if you can remember all our jobs – but one of them was where a couple woke up to find a masked man at the bottom of the bed. He tied them up, but then the boyfriend of the daughter, who had been staying there, disturbed the attacker. There was a fight between the boyfriend and the masked man and the boyfriend was stabbed.' She engaged Hunter and Grace's eyes and looked for acknowledgment.

Hunter nodded. He remembered.

'That couple are called Russell and Kate Wheeler, and their daughter, who was nineteen at the time of the job, is Emily. Well we tracked them down to Brighton a few days ago. Emily's now married to the boyfriend who was stabbed. When we dropped out Dale and Scott's names, you ought to have seen Emily's face. She almost freaked out. It would appear that nine months before the attack she'd met somebody called Scott in a pub in London, but after a couple of dates with him she'd called it a day. She said the guy was getting a bit intense with her – wanted to know what she was doing all the time. And he'd dropped it out that he'd spotted her a few times when she'd left her workplace to go for lunch. She got the impression he was following her around, so she told him to back off or she'd call the police.'

'Wow,' said Grace. 'And that's the first time she's mentioned this?'

'Until we mentioned Dale and Scott's names she'd not given it a thought. It had been so long between her finishing with him and the attack.'

'You've said you'd had a result with two jobs?' said Hunter.

'Yeah, the other one involved a couple called Jamie and Dawn Agar. Do you remember that one?'

Hunter screwed up his face. 'To be honest, Scarlett, there's that many jobs floating around in my head now, I'm losing track.'

'No problem. Well, Dawn was raped in front of her husband by her masked attacker, and then he cut away a section of the bedding she'd been lain on and took it away with him.'

Hunter could recall it now. He acknowledged with a nod.

'Well, I don't know if you also remember, but before he raped her he asked the couple where their daughter was – she was away for the weekend. It appears that the detectives, who initially interviewed them, didn't put any great significance upon this at the time, but we managed to trace that daughter – Claire – she was twenty at the time of the attack, and we asked her if the names Dale and Scott meant anything to her. And guess what?'

'It did!' Hunter responded.

'Certainly did. They'd bumped into the brothers in a pub in Richmond when she'd been out celebrating her nineteenth birthday. She was out with a crowd of friends, but ended up chatting with them. She left them in one of the pubs because a party had been arranged back at her home. It would appear these two gatecrashed it in the early hours and she ended up arguing with them, because she wanted them to leave. There was a bit of a scuffle between them and some of her mates and she called the police, but they left before they arrived.'

Hunter took a mouthful of his ale. Over the rim of his glass he said, 'There's a theme re-occurring here, isn't there? From what you've just told us, and from what we've found out during our enquires, it seems that everyone who's been attacked, or murdered, have had some sort of run in with either one or both of these two, at some stage before the event. On the face of it, these murders appear to be have been carried out for no other reason than that someone had the audacity to say no to them. That is pure evil.'

Around the table everyone nodded.

Hundreds of phone calls poured in following the TV and radio appeal by DCI Stainthorpe. Many of the calls related to past sightings, or past knowledge of the pair and were of very little help. However, just before midnight, information from two different sources gave the Incident Team the breakthrough they had been praying for.

- ooOoo -

CHAPTER TWENTY-TWO

Day Twenty-one: 7th April.

The beaming smile on DCI Stainthorpe's face was so firmly fixed that not even a wrecker's ball could demolish it, as, with a spring in his step, he marched to the front of the incident room. He stood next to one of the wipe boards and faced the room. With an outstretched arm he banged a fist over Dale and Scott's e-fits.

'Bingo,' he shouted. Still smiling he announced, 'We've got a lead on the pair.' He pulled away his arm from the board. 'Last night we got a call from the man who runs the post office-cum-general store in a little village called Minions, which is on the eastern flank of Bodmin Moor – he's known the pair since they were young, and he says they've both been in his shop in the last week buying bits of food. Rember we learned that they used to live with their parents in a cottage on the edge of that village.' The DCI picked up a red felt pen and drew a circle around an isolated shaded area on the large scale ordnance survey map. He tapped the pen over the drawn area. 'The cottage doesn't show up on the map but I'm told it's about quarter of a mile from Minions. Apparently after their parents were killed, and Dale and Scott were put in the children's home, the council boarded the place up, and it's remained empty ever since – or at least, we thought it's been empty. Given the info from our post office owner it's my guess that Dale and Scott have been using this place as their bolt-hole – most probably, ever since they ran away from the home. I've arranged for a couple of officers from the Intelligence Unit to do a recce around the place this morning. They're going dressed as hikers so as not to spook them, and see if there are any signs of activity around the building. If the feedback is positive, I want an operational plan putting together and a warrant getting immediately.' He rested the pen on the ledge of the wipe board and rubbed his hands together. 'The good news doesn't end there.' He broke into a smile again. 'Another of the calls we got, following the appeal, was from an army sergeant who is currently based at Winchester – training new recruits.' He paused and scanned the room. 'Dale and Scott were both in the navy – Royal Marines. Joined up in nineteen ninety-eight.' Pursing his lips he continued, 'Which explains why, until recently, we've not had any attacks since the last one in nineteen ninety-seven. Both of them were released from the navy in May last year. And this is where it is also interesting. After they were released from military prison – they were serving time there.' He paused again and surveyed the faces of his team. 'The sergeant, who gave us the information, was a corporal in their unit, and he says that while they were serving in Afghanistan the brothers were given the job of guarding captured Taliban. One of the prisoners was found hanged in his cell and it was found that he'd been tortured beforehand – and quite badly as well it would appear. The hanging was hushed up, but Dale and Scott were court-martialled over it and found guilty of assault, but not of murder. They were given a five-year jail term and then dishonourably discharged.' He took in a deep breath. 'Released onto the streets to begin their deadly attacks again.' The DCI stared into the centre of the room. 'Well hopefully, we can bring their reign of terror to an end this time. And soon.'

It was mid-afternoon when the call came in that the Incident Team had been hoping for.

The plain clothes detectives from the Intelligence Unit had found the cottage, but had not been able to hang around because they were so exposed out on the moors. They reported that the place was still boarded up, and had security fencing around it, but they had found recent tyre tracks leading to the rear, and they had found a vehicle. Attempts had been made to secrete a transit van beneath tarpaulin. They had been unable to get close enough to check it out, but confirmed it looked new enough to not be one that had been abandoned.

Upon receiving the news DCI Stainthorpe called every detective back to station and to a packed Incident Room he regaled the good news. As he brought the briefing to an end he said, 'Right, I've got some phone calls to make to bring in some extra resources. I want someone to go down to the magistrates' court pronto and swear out a warrant and I want an operational order knocked out.' He clapped his hands, 'It's a sixty thirty start tomorrow morning everyone.'

- ooOoo -

CHAPTER TWENTY-THREE
Day Twenty-two: 8th April.

Despite the early start the atmosphere in the Incident Room was electrically charged. The office was bursting at the seams with uniformed and plain clothes officers. For some it was standing room only.

At the front a new ordnance survey map had appeared. It was a large scale one of Bodmin Moor and the surrounding area. Pinned to that were several A4 colour photographs.

DCI Stainthorpe took the briefing. 'Operation Scarecrow three,' he announced. 'This morning's focus is on the arrests of Dale and Scott Moore and the preservation of evidence in relation to the murders of their parents, James and Helen, in nineteen eighty-six, the murder of Polly Hayes, in nineteen eighty-eight, and most recently, the murders of Gemma Cooke and Elisabeth Bertolutti. Plus, we also believe they were responsible for a series of rapes and aggravated burglaries, in the Richmond upon Thames area during the nineteen nineties.' He paused, then continued, 'We believe the pair are currently living in a cottage, which is their old home.' He slapped a hand over one of the photographs. It was an aerial shot of a small square cottage with a rear extension leading to a group of outbuildings. 'The Force helicopter took this yesterday afternoon on a fly-past.' He prodded at a section of the photo. His forefinger was targeted over a small grey oblong shape. 'There is a possibility that they have access to a van, which is currently hidden beneath tarpaulin. When we raid the premises I want this securing and immobilising immediately.' He scanned the room. 'In a minute I am going to hand over to Inspector Forbes, from Task Force. He is Bronze Commander who will be orchestrating this operation on the ground. He will be issuing you with your instructions. But first I want to just point out these to you.' He tapped three other colour photos pinned to the map. 'Not far away from the cottage are these landmarks. They are Bronze Age burial chambers. These are all avenues of escape or hiding for the pair, so I want you to bear these in mind when you are securing the perimeter.' He took a deep breath and tight-lipped added, 'These two are ex-military. They are used to this terrain and as we know they are no strangers to violence. They have a lot to lose, so we must ensure we give them no quarter and certainly no room for escape.'

A twenty-strong team travelled to Minions. Ten heavily armoured Task Force Officers in their personnel carrier led the way, closely followed by a dog man. Hunter and Grace brought up the rear – they were sharing a car with DS Macey and DC Scarr. In between were local CID Officers. If there was a likelihood that Dale and Scott would resist, there were certainly enough of them.

As the convoy passed through Liskeard, and began its long climb up to the highest village in Cornwall, they found themselves confronted by a swirling mist and dropping temperatures. By the time they entered the village it had become a pea-souper, and all of them had been forced to drop their speed to a crawl while making their way along the main street.

Hunter was surprised by how small the place was. Within a couple of minutes they had passed two rows of whitewashed buildings and had reached the end of the village. Thirty seconds later they were passing an old mining engine house, which Hunter saw had been transformed into a heritage museum, and were turning onto a dirt track, which took them directly onto the moors. They were on the final stage of their journey.

After five minutes of bouncing along an undulating boggy lane Hunter spotted brake lights ahead. The fog gave a halo effect around them. He slowed the car and drew to a halt. Seconds later dark clad figures emerged from the Task Force Personnel Carrier. He put on the handbrake and turned off the engine.

Hardly a sound was made by anyone as uniformed officers kitted themselves out with body armour and detectives donned stab vests. Then they went into a huddle and listened to the

Inspector issue his final instructions in a hushed voice. After confirming that everyone understood their role he led the way on foot.

Within a couple of minutes of tramping across the damp ground Hunter was at sorts with his bearings, especially faced with an impenetrable blanket of grey. The fog was dragging itself across the moor in clumps and layers and it reminded Hunter of a scene from the Sherlock Holmes movie, *The Hound of the Baskervilles*. Thankfully, he could still make out the inspector at pole position.

Within five minutes the pace of the yomp had slackened. A hundred yards further on Inspector Forbes came to a halt. He put on his reinforced crash helmet.

His team copied.

Then, ushering everyone together, in a low voice he checked in with, 'Okay, does everyone know what they are doing?' Wisps of cold air drifted from his mouth.

There was a round of nods.

'Right this is it. Strike, Strike, Strike!'

Everyone set off at a jog.

Hunter watched the Task Force officers fan out. Some disappeared into the mist. Seconds later, the silhouette of the cottage came into view. He could make out the security fencing barring their way. It was the heavy mesh panel type set in concrete posts. Hanging from one of the panels was a large yellow sign, bearing the logo of a security firm, warning away trespassers. It was heavily weatherworn. In front of him two officers were bolt-cropping a chain. Two of their armed colleagues backed them up. It only took a matter of seconds, and then they were pulling apart the panels and dashing inside the compound. Hot on their heels was the dog man and the squad of detectives.

Hunter wasn't far behind, and although he couldn't see what was going on, because of the shroud of fog, from the sound of pounding feet and cries and calls going on all around he knew that the team were surrounding the cottage like a school of sharks.

It took three blows before the front door splintered and crashed inwards.

Hunter followed three Task Force Officers in, backed up by detectives from Wadebridge, who starburst into the inner reaches of the building. He entered a long room with a stone-slab floor. He quickly took in his surroundings. A bare electric bulb burned from the ceiling – that told him that someone was living here. Wallpaper, the pattern of which was ancient, peeled in places from damp walls. In the middle of the room was a table covered in dirty crockery. Many of the plates had remnants of food – again, confirmation that recently someone had made this their home. Ahead, and to the right was a steep stairway. From the stomping sounds above him he knew that officers were already searching bedrooms.

Suddenly above, he heard a banging and crashing noise, quickly followed by the sound of scrambling feet. At the back of the house a call went up that made him realise someone was doing a runner. Hunter spun on his heels and made for the door. Training his ears he picked up the sound of someone scrabbling up and over the chain-link fencing. He bolted down the short path and hared out through the way they had come. Taking a sharp right and leaping across a narrow ditch he landed heavily onto the boggy moorland tufts. His ankles jarred and it made him wince. Recovering quickly, he set off towards where he had last heard the clambering. He couldn't see a thing but he could hear. Someone was panting heavily not too far ahead. He picked up his pace, at the same time increasing his breathing, dragging in lungfuls of cold air. Within a few seconds he knew he was making ground when a wispy dark silhouette appeared before him. He was about to shout ahead when a call went up behind him – it was as if someone had read his mind.

'Police – stand still.'

It was a warning cry – Hunter knew what was coming. He remembered his training and skidded to a halt, slamming his arms down by his side and fixing himself statue-like.

Seconds later he caught what sounded like the echoing, thumping sound of a horse bearing down on him. Hunter held his breath. He flinched as a monster of a dog shot past him, and then just as quickly disappeared into the swirling grey shroud. A few seconds later he heard a growl and a piercing cry come out of the mist. He couldn't help but smirk – the dog had done its job.

He felt a tap on his shoulder as the dog man sprinted past. Hunter followed him.

Ahead the screams of physical pain were getting louder.

Less than ten seconds later Hunter was watching over a man yelling and rolling around, trying to dislodge his lower arm from the mouth of a snarling German Shepherd. The man was in a great deal of pain.

The dog man shouted, 'Leave Prince,' and a split second later the police dog had released its grip and was slavering over its capture. The dog man pulled back his dog and slung on a lead.

It gave Hunter a better view of their prisoner. He was a slim man, with broad flattened boxer-type nose. His eyes met Hunter's and they glistened with hate. He realised how good the likeness was to the e-fits.

Was this Polly's killer?

Hunter eyed him up – he could feel his emotions rising and balled his hands into fists. Then, catching himself, he took in a sharp breath. The air was thick and cold and caught the back of his throat. He coughed, let it out and relaxed his hands. As he bent down to make the arrest, out of nowhere, four detectives appeared and Hunter found himself being pushed aside.

The man kicked out wildly, but it was a futile attempt. He was pounced upon and quickly overwhelmed by a swarm of hands. Yanked upwards, he gave off another squeal of pain.

'You're nicked,' shouted one of the detectives.

'Get fucked,' the man yelled.

One of the detectives grabbed at his hair and demanded, 'Where's your brother?'

'Fuck off.'

It didn't take long to handcuff him – the man offered no resistance. As he was dragged away, Hunter could see from the bowed shoulders that the prisoner's fighting spirit had been sapped.

They trooped back over the moor, to the cottage, their captive's feet hardly touching the ground. When they got back to the perimeter fencing Hunter could see that the man's arm was bleeding profusely. He pointed it out to Inspector Forbes, who, after a quick check, determined he required hospital treatment before being taken into custody.

He was driven away with a police escort to Liskeard Hospital.

With a degree of frustration Hunter picked up where he had left off and tramped back up the path to the cottage. Stepping inside the front door he heard noises coming from the floor above and made his way to the stairs. The steep stairway was in semi-darkness. He tried the light switch at the bottom but there was no bulb in the holder. He carefully negotiated the steps. On the top landing Hunter halted and looked around – wondering how on earth someone could live in these conditions. The place was squalid and exuded damp and coldness – the conditions seemed rawer inside than outside.

The door immediately in front was ajar. He heard the sounds of a cupboard being opened from within. He called out 'Grace?'

'In here, Hunter.'

Pushing open the door he stepped into a room that smelt stale and sweaty. A patch of light streamed in through a gap in the boards covering the window allowing him to pick out objects within the sparsely furnished room. Against one wall was an old fashioned brass bed covered in stained sheets. Grace was standing in front of a set of drawers. She was peering inside the top one.

'I've found some women's underwear,' she called out. 'And what looks like Gemma Cooke's watch from the description.' She pointed backwards, 'And just check out what's on the bed.'

Hunter followed the line of her arrowed finger. In the centre of the messy bed he saw a laptop computer. The lid was up and the screen was on.

Grace glanced over her shoulder. 'I've had a quick look – its Elisabeth's. He's right in the doo-dah.' She turned around. 'By the way which of the Moore brothers is he?'

'He's refusing to talk.'

'And no sign of the other one?'

Hunter shook his head, 'Not yet. They're still searching the outbuildings – and the dog's having a nose around.'

'Well, at least we've got one of them – and a load of evidence. That's a start.'

Following debrief Hunter telephoned Detective Superintendent Leggate and gave her an update. 'It's Scott Moore we've got. We've identified him by his mobile phone, and he's got Dale's number stored. The techies are going through it at the moment to see if we can get a location.'

'But you've no idea where he is at present?' she asked.

'None, boss. We've been ringing the number stored on Scott's phone all afternoon but he's not picked up. He's completely gone to ground.'

'What about Scott – is he saying anything?'

'Not a dicky bird. Won't even confirm his name. To be fair they've only done one interview with him. He was at the hospital four hours getting treated for the dog bites' – he started to smirk and fought it back – 'ten stitches he's got.'

'Serves him right. Did no one tell him our gang's bigger than his.' She paused then continued, 'You said you've recovered evidence?'

'Yeah, Elisabeth's laptop and Gemma's watch. Definitely theirs. And DS Macey has identified some ladies underwear from two of their jobs. It's certainly stacking up against them.'

'Are they happy down there that it's both brothers involved?'

'Well we've finished searching the cottage where they've been living – it's a right shit-hole of a place – there's very little in it and we've not found any mask, so it looks as though Dale has it.'

'So what's the plan of action now?'

'They're gonna bed Scott down for the night and start interviewing him again tomorrow morning. The technicians are going to work on his phone overnight and see if we can get a location for Dale. There's nothing else me and Grace can do until tomorrow so we're calling it a day.'

'Okay, well done, Hunter. And pass on my thanks to Grace. Keep up the good work you two and let me know how you get on tomorrow. As they say, tomorrow's another day.'

Barnwell.

It was beginning to rain. He fastened up his hood and cursed. He couldn't do this much longer – hiding away like this. Soon will be her time, he told himself. *That bitch would soon know she couldn't do this to him.*

He shook off the droplets of rain from his waterproof jacket and focussed on the house across the street.

If he leaves the house tonight, she's history.

Cornwall.

Hunter was enjoying the final mouthful of his Cornish pasty when the pub door opened with a clatter and in stepped DC Stuart Highton. Hunter watched his head dart from side to side and then they locked eyes. He strode towards him.

Out of breath he said, 'I've just come from your hotel – your partner said you were here.'

Hunter swallowed the food. 'Has something happened?'

'I think it's about to,' Stuart replied. He thrust a mobile towards Hunter's face. 'Scott's mobile,' he announced, 'And look what he received half an hour ago. The techies opened it.' Highton pressed the enter button and a picture and text message appeared on the screen.

Hunter viewed it. The image was dark and grainy. He dismissed the picture for a few seconds as he read the text: 'The bitch has it comin ha ha.' He looked at the image again, screwing up his eyes as he tried to make sense of it. Suddenly, he realised what he was looking at. Urgently, he delved into his jacket for his phone. 'Fuck me – I need to get hold of her!'

Barnwell.

In the darkness of the bedroom Dawn Leggate slipped off her jacket and started undoing her blouse – she needed a shower, after the frustrating day she'd had. Pulling the cotton blouse away from the waistband of her skirt she stepped towards the curtains. Taking a hold of the right hand drape she began tugging it across the window. Outside it was raining. The wetness was making halo effects around the streetlamps. She glanced across the street, to where a path wended its way towards woodland. A car passed below her, making sloshing noises, and as the headlights picked out the hedgerow she jumped. She saw movement – just a will-o'-the-wisp movement – but it was enough for her to realise there was someone hiding among the bushes by the path's entrance.

Quickly composing herself she continued closing the curtains, but as she brought them together she created a gap – just small enough to peak through. She searched for a few seconds and then she caught a glimpse of the figure lurking among the shadows. She studied the shape carefully, but could only make out that whoever it was had on dark clothing and had covered their face. A knot formed in her stomach. She let go of the curtains and ran to the top of the stairs.

'Michael, there's someone hiding in the bushes opposite the house.'

Michael Robshaw appeared at the bottom. 'What?'

'Honest, Michael. I've just been watching them for the past couple of minutes. They're just stood there watching the house.' She could feel herself starting to shake. She felt sick.

Her words spurred him into action. Picking up a pair of trainers by the hall radiator, he slipped one of them on. Then picking up the other he shouted back, 'Get on to the station. I'm going round the back to sneak up on them.'

Dawn hurried downstairs for the phone.

Michael Robshaw clambered over the garden fence and landed heavily on the other side on his knees. He felt the wetness on the grass instantly soak through his trousers and he cursed. Pulling himself up he listened. All he could hear was the sound of the rain hammering upon the roofs of nearby parked cars. He poked his head around the corner of the house. He couldn't see a soul. On tiptoes he sprinted across the street, only stopping when he collided with a line of conifer trees, which bordered a garden. He slunk against them and again listened. No sound of life. The path to the woods was only twenty yards away. He knew that in the last five of those he would be exposed, but hopefully, he thought, pressing his back against the shrubbery, he would have the element of surprise on his side. Edging crab-like he kept to the line of the trees, only stopping when he came to the end. Then, he craned out his neck and focussed on the path ahead. He could just make out the shadow of someone hiding in the bushes by the entrance – exactly as Dawn had described.

Quickly adjusting his posture, Michael took in a huge gulp of air and sprang forward, like a sprinter coming out of the blocks. He saw the figure turn – Michael realised he had been spotted, but he knew it would be too late for this adversary. He hit the individual sideways with a rugby tackle – forearm and elbow smashing into the sternum. He heard the breath explode from the shadow's chest and saw them clatter head-over-heels, only stopping when they banged headlong into a thorny hedge. A squeal of pain issued. Michael lurched forward, grabbing hold of the person's coat, and dragged them back through the bush a second time. Then, he manhandled the stranger to the ground. Pinning one arm high up the person's back he heard a man's voice blurt.

'You're breaking my fucking arm.'

Michael reached up and whipped back the hood to reveal his face. As he did so, Dawn appeared by his side.

She cried, 'My God – Jack.'

Michael glanced up and was faced by her shocked look. He said, 'Jack?'

'Jack', she repeated again. 'My husband – Jack.'

From his prostrate position the man yelled. 'This is your fucking fault, bitch!'

In the distance came the sound of police sirens.

Juggling the painting she was carrying, Linane Brazier finally unlocked the front door and let herself in. Switching on the hall light, she back-heeled the door shut and made her way into the kitchen. Quickly unwrapping the bubble-wrap she spun the picture around and propped it up against a wall cupboard. She stood back and admired it.

The oil work was the one Elisabeth had purchased. She had finally cleaned it up. For a good couple of minutes she scrutinised the seascape. The Lamorna Cove scene looked as fresh as the day it had been painted. Running herself a glass of water she leaned against the sink and viewed the painting again. She was pleased with it. She only wished Elisabeth could be here to see it. A tear erupted from the corner of an eye. She dabbed it away.

With a sigh she drained the last of her water and set down her empty glass. Then, with one eye still on her painting she toe-heeled off her shoes, undid her coat, took out her mobile and speed-dialled her boyfriend's number. Clamping the handset between ear and shoulder she finished removing her coat and dropped it over the back of a chair.

Tony's phone went straight to voicemail. She huffed, and then left him a message – telling him she was home early and would be fixing up a meal for when he came home. Ending the call, she set her mobile down on the work surface, went back into the hallway and jogged up the stairs – she was in need of a shower.

She showered quickly and while drying decided she needed a glass of wine to celebrate. She wrapped her hair in a towel, put on her dressing gown and returned downstairs. As she passed the dining room she caught the gentle whiff of scented flowers. She poked her head in through the half-open doorway. She saw that the table had been laid and that a perfumed candle was burning in the centre.

She hadn't heard Tony come in. Puzzled by what she saw, she called out his name.

Silence.

She called his name again and stepped into the dining room. And, that was when she got the shock of her life.

Standing in the middle of the room was the same masked man whom she had seen kill her best friend.

Her heart leapt into her mouth.

She knew what she should have done, but her legs wouldn't let her. Fear enveloped her and froze her to the spot. She couldn't even scream.

The murderer was upon her in an instant, grabbing her and pushing her back against the table. Wrapping his hands around her throat, he started to squeeze and a thousand stars flashed before her eyes. Her hands scrambled around as she fought to support herself – it felt as if her spine was going to snap. Suddenly, her fingers found metal – it was a fork. She snatched it up and with a wide arcing swing delivered a blow to his head. The fork pierced the side of the mask and a painful yell went up. He instantly released his grip. It gave her enough time to right herself and kick out. She caught his knee, but her efforts weren't that strong, and he recovered quickly, pouncing forward and grabbing hold of her dressing gown.

This time she let out a scream.

He took her by the throat again and squeezed even harder. Pushing his masked face closer to her face he began counting backwards, starting from ten.

The count was slow. Deliberate. The voice menacing. At four, it was as if her legs were melting beneath her. She knew that the life was being forced out of her but she couldn't do anything about it. Her vision became clouded.

As she began to drift away, in the depths of her semi-consciousness she thought she could hear Tony's voice and in that same instance she felt a sharp blow to her side and then a searing hot pain invaded her body. She hit the floor with a thump throwing open her eyes. Above her, dark shapes thrashed wildly, and many shouts and cries intermingled with one another. She could still make out Tony's among them but none of it was making sense.

And then it all stopped.

'Linane!'

Tony was calling her name.

'Linane! It's me. Are you okay?'

She blinked open her eyes. Tony was leaning above her. He leaned in, said 'Thank God,' and then he eased up her head and cradled her face to his chest.

When she came to for the second time she was in the lounge, lying on the sofa. The room was full with people. Many of them were officers in uniform. She spotted Tony talking to a paramedic.

She called his name and he came to her.

'Linane,' he said.

She tried to get up and a sharp pain shot down her left side. He stopped her rising any further.

'Don't move. Just lie there.'

She moved a hand to her side.

Tony took a hold of it. 'Try not to move. Don't touch it.'

'What's happened?'

'Don't you remember?'

'Vaguely. It was the man who killed Elisabeth.'

Tony nodded. 'Yes it was.'

She felt the pain again in her side. 'Am I hurt?'

'You've been cut, Linane. But, it's not bad. The paramedics have strapped you up. They're taking you to hospital in a few minutes. Everything's going to be okay.'

Her mouth was dry. 'Honest?'

'Honest.' He met her eyes. They smiled to her and she knew he was telling her the truth.

'What about Elisabeth's killer.'

'We got him, Linane! We got him. He's not going to hurt anyone else.'

Harlyn Bay, Cornwall.

As Hunter stepped down onto the beach a spray peppered his face and a strong pungent smell hit him. The odour was a mixture of seaweed and salt that caught the back of his throat. Breaking his stride he roamed his eyes around the bay. A full moon gave everything around him a silky sheen top light and he began to pick out the landmarks he remembered from his visit two days earlier. He stopped his gaze out to sea. As far as his eyesight took him bands of bright light played on the choppy surface of the Atlantic. It was mesmerising. Twenty yards ahead he watched the nearest wave climbing and rising into a wall of translucent blue/green. Then, almost in slow motion, its top edge fractured, and a mass of tumbling water exploded forward, creating a foaming cauldron of white. He watched the action again, trying to store the sequence and colours inside his head for later, when he next got the opportunity to paint, but his thoughts were continually

222

disturbed. All he could think about was that this was where Polly had met her killers.

He had come here at this late hour because he couldn't settle. He'd left Grace and the others celebrating in Wadebridge. He'd had a couple of beers with them, but as he'd finished the second pint he'd realised he wasn't in the mood to celebrate.

For years he had dreamed that this day would be different – that he'd be ecstatic – knowing that someone was finally going to answer for Polly's murder, but now that day had arrived he felt nothing like that.

He began to watch the waves again. Suddenly his mobile went, making him jump. He pulled it out of his jacket pocket and looked at the screen. It was Detective Superintendent Leggate.

He'd been trying half the night to get hold of her but her phone had been switched off.

He answered, 'Evening, boss.'

'Apologies, Hunter. I can see you've been trying to get hold of me. You wouldn't believe the night I've had. Anyway, enough of my problems. You've heard we've arrested Dale Moore?'

'Yeah, Bully rang me a couple of hours ago from the hospital. His girlfriend was just going into theatre. How is she?'

'Fine – thanks to you, Hunter. The knife missed her vital organs. She's had quite a few stitches, and she's going to have a nasty scar, but she's going to be fine.' She paused and then said, 'It's a good job you recognised who was in the photo Dale sent Scott, otherwise Linane might not be here now. Your phone call saved her life, Hunter.'

He smiled.

Dawn Leggate continued, 'How have you got on with Scott? Has he talked?'

'No, not said a thing. Three interviews they've had with him. But to be honest, boss, it doesn't really matter. We've recovered enough evidence down here to link him to most of the murders and a couple of the Richmond attacks. What about Dale?'

'He's saying bugger all as well. But like Scott it doesn't matter. We've got him with the mask and we've got him for the attempt murder on Linane. I'm guessing it's the same knife as the one he used on Elisabeth Bertolutti so he's not going anywhere other than jail. We've got them both bang to rights and they're going away for the rest of their natural.' Pausing, she added, 'What have you got left to do down there?'

'There's not much else me and Grace can do. We're going to give our statements to the team down here and then set off back tomorrow. The Wadebridge lot are going to sort out the charges and the remand file for Scott.'

'Okay, good. Well done again, Hunter. I'll see you two when you get back tomorrow. And now, I've got a not too happy husband to sort out who's locked up in our cells.'

'Your husband's locked up?'

'Long story, Hunter. I'll tell you about it when you get back.'

She ended the call.

Hunter stared at the phone's screen for a few seconds. Then he shrugged his shoulders and slotted it back in his trouser pocket.

Dropping his gaze he spied a flat pebble at his feet. He bent down, picked it up and weighed it in his hand. Then glancing up he skimmed it into the incoming tide. It bounced once and then disappeared beneath the surf.

Shifting his gaze out to sea he hoped that Polly's haunting memory would disappear as quick.

- ooOoo -

224